D1743099

MAP OF ISSEHAI

Saransa

Chor

Elikdale

Hushat Urga

Birkith

Perq Cyndor

Varhep

Italau

Kullako

Alliket

Daruik

Veshul

Hunter's Forest

Sialstone

Hesthil

Marah

Sashak Island

Lenthar Rundait

Eastern Watchtower

Narra

Blakereath

Western Watchtower GALDAMESH

Okonia

The Western Point

Southern Watchtower

Barren Islands

Gulderneck

Qu'rok

Gillia

Yassie

Ekar

Feldon

N

Merrywood

Wekin

Blakmarsh

Thunle

W E

Shorq

Cranwell

Igrat

S

To my friends for always supporting,

To my girlfriend for always inspiring me,

To my parents for always telling me I could be whoever I wanted to be,

And finally to all of my readers, without who I would be nothing;

This book could not have happened if not for you.

Thank you.

Prologue

'**I**'m afraid I can't stay,' Horus stammered, finishing his pint with great haste and placing the glass back on the bar with a shaky hand.

His eyes flashed around the same seven people in the tavern over and over.

'Slow down,' said Kyln. 'You look like you've seen a ghost.'

Despite his friend's words Horus was already tying the cord on his coat, his arm tensing as his hand brushed against the pommel of the sword. Even now he could feel its power.

'I'm sorry, but I just know somebody is coming for me.'

'What are you talking about?' Kyln asked, his eyes wide with concern.

Horus shook his head and turned to the door. Kyln stopped him.

'Let me go,' the smaller man demanded. 'I have to get out of here!'

All eyes were on them.

'Calm down my friend.'

'If I disappear after tonight, tell Shael I love her.'

He barged past his friend and fled the tavern.

'Tell her yourself!' the voice of his companion called after him, 'After all, *I'm* not her father!'

Horus delved into the chilled night air, the streets dark and damp. Buildings with lightless windows faced one another, separated by a path of cobblestone. He wondered why he had even gone to Crow's Tavern, perhaps he had hoped somebody would listen to him. He could not bear to tell the story though, nor could he explain the churning in the pit of his stomach.

It's not your fault, it's not your fault, it's not your fault, he reassured himself, truly believing he had been a victim of chance. After all, what was he supposed to do when that old beggar jumped out at him three days before? Horus did what he believed any sane person would do, he cut the man's throat with his knife. *It was in self-defence.*

He sped to a jog.

He had wanted to get away, to leave the body untouched, and tried not to wonder where such a clearly un-wealthy man got such a beautiful sword. The blade called to him though, in a way which he could not describe. He had not gotten half a block away before feeling compelled to turn back and take the sword for himself. The rush had left him jittery, and even now he shook from more than the cold. He knew somebody would come for it eventually. He had felt eyes on him at the market that morning, sensed a presence following him.

'I'm not crazy!' he cried to a street sign, birds flying away hastily.

He had seen him – the red-haired man. Not ginger nor auburn, but red. On every corner, in every store, at every turn Horus took. He was certain he was being followed, even now when he had not seen the man since sundown. Perhaps he had gotten away, he thought, and he fed on that gradually deteriorating hope.

The moon shone bright over the open sea. Horus knew it was the only way. He unsheathed the blade which gleamed like a million tiny crystals. So beautiful, so powerful. With it he could rule the world.

'Maybe I can keep it,' he whispered to himself. 'I won't do anything bad with it...unless I have to.'

He shook his head frantically, crying out as he fought the call of the blade. With two hands, he swung it around and launched it – far over the edge of the pier and into the water. He basked in freedom, sighing deeply as he turned away. *It's over.* But it was far from over. Three steps were as far as Horus got before the draw of power grasped at him again.

'No!' he grunted aloud.

Another step. Everything in his head told him to keep moving, to go home to his daughter and to forget all of this business. His gut however had a different plan, and his gut was winning.

He turned back to the water, staring into the cold abyss. In that moment he knew he could not leave the weapon there, and before his head had a chance to kick back in he was leaping towards it. Water engulfed him, pulling at his clothes and trying to push him back to the surface. He opened his eyes, the saltwater stinging them with no remorse. But he saw it. Even in the blackness it glowed, bright and unyielding. It was magical. He swam against the waves, diving deeper until it was once more in his grasp.

When Horus surfaced he cried out, realising what had happened. He sheathed the sword and walked, headed for his home.

'If it wants me, then I guess I'll have it,' he muttered, though he did not expect a response.

'Somehow I doubt it.'

The voice was high and shrill.

The woman before Horus wore robes, her skin pale and sickly.

'Don't come near me!' Horus cried, holding the shining sword aloft.

5

His opponent laughed.

'Foolish man,' she spat. 'You would do well to realise who you are talking to.'

With a click of her fingers Horus's blood froze, his body stiffened and despite all of his might he could not move a muscle. The coldness around his joints intensified, and he would have cried out in pain if not for his lips being frozen together.

'That's enough, Greskel,' another spoke, and the man from before came into Horus's view.

The woman tutted. With a wave of her hand Horus collapsed to his knees, panting and coughing.

'Please,' he begged, looking up at the figure before him.

His hair was crimson and spiked, his grin firm and cheek-splitting. He laughed, low and hearty, leaning over to make eye contact with the weakened man. Horus was filled with hope for a moment, the face of this stranger seemed genuine and caring.

'Please,' Horus sighed. 'You can have the sword. Take it for all I care, just please don't hurt me.' He held the blade out, still breathing heavily. His opponent took it, marvelling at its beauty.

Greskel stayed back, but watched on with admiration.

'Master,' she said, 'Is it the one?'

'Indeed it is,' he declared, standing and giving it a light swing. 'Finally, after all of this time. An Elder Blade.'

'Take it,' Horus repeated. 'But please let me go.'

The red-haired man chuckled, not warm and hearty this time but high and manic.

'I'm afraid it doesn't work like that my friend!' he cried with glee, in one fell swoop slicing the blade through Horus's neck. The body collapsed to the ground, the head rolling into the water.

'Finally!' the killer cried out. 'I can feel it, the power – it's surging through me!'

'What now, my lord?' Greskel asked.

'Now, my dear sorceress,' he cackled, 'We begin the ritual. But first, I think it's time to pay a visit to an old friend.'

He sheathed the sword and the two fled into the night – leaving the body of Horus to rot on the side of the pier until morning.

Chapter 1

Yodrick Alton

Water flew from me as I sprinted through the stormy weather, my feet destroying puddles in my hurried attempt at escape. Voices called after me, though their shouts fell upon deaf ears as the sound of heavy rain drowned them out. Around corners I swerved, and over walls I clambered, all the while the guards pursued me. I must have run for hours, the powerful wind blowing in from sea and swooping through my coat as my fist clutched the coin purse. *Why had I been so sloppy? Why had I not scouted the area first?* Luckily for me the guards could not hope to know Cranwell as well as I – or so I thought.

Rushing into a back alley I breathed a sigh of relief, thinking I had finally lost them. But there he was in front of me – a large figure blocking the light of my exit. He stood at over six foot tall and was almost as wide. It was impressive that he had managed to catch up to me with how fat he was. Even in the dingy weather his crimson waistcoat was visible, hanging open atop his chainmail; that and the black hat marked him as a town guard. Neither items fit him particularly well, and the coat was especially small on his hulking body.

'I've got ya now ya li'l rat!' he spat at me.

I spun around, only to be met with the face of another guard stopping me from escaping the way I had come. The second was shorter, but slimmer and nimbler. He held a rapier, outstretched and ready for use if need be. I assessed my options and it appeared clear to me.

'Sorry lads, not today!' I chimed, charging straight for the fatter man.

His eyes widened as I rushed at him, his arms reaching out to grab me as I came closer, but he was far too slow as I ducked and slid past him. I leapt up and continued the dash, following the alley out into the street where the fog obscured my vision. Before I knew what was happening I was falling, icy water engulfing me.

I tried to gasp but choked on the cold liquid, thrashing about as I felt the hand of death clenching harder and harder around my breathless lungs. I felt something foreign and clung to it, realising it was a rope and I was being pulled to the surface, coughing and spluttering as the air hit me. I looked up with dread to the guards who had saved me.

'Looks like it's not your lucky day after all,' the slimmer one cackled.

I allowed them to help me back to the pier and reluctantly handed over the purse as they bound my wrists. Oh how stupid I felt for charging right into the sea – not my proudest moment. Of course I tried another time to make my escape, though they expected it and the second pursuit was short-lived. They were less forgiving after that, and handled me roughly as they dragged me towards the cells.

'So what group do ya belong to?' the larger man interrogated me as the other stuck the point of his rapier into my back, forcing me to keep walking.

I stayed silent.

'Not so cocky now are ya?' the voice from behind sneered. 'But go ahead, answer 'is question. The crows? The blades? Or are ya just a lone scallywag goin' around stealin' off of the nice folk 'round 'ere?'

'I'm no thief,' I grunted.

'Well could've fooled me,' the fatter man chuckled. 'I definitely peg 'im as a crow.'

'But what about the knife we found on 'im? Nah, I'd say for certain he's an apprentice for the blades.'

'I'm no mercenary neither,' I protested.

The sword in my back stopped pressing and the slimmer guard's face appeared in front of mine. His breath smelled foul – of booze and vomit. He grinned at me deviously, showing his whole six teeth, all a sickly yellow.

'Then tell us lad,' he sneered, 'What are ya?'

'I'm a pirate.'

I chuckled to myself as I said it. The last time I told a guard that little fib his jaw dropped, but these two were smarter than they appeared. When they heard the nonsense they laughed, hollered even.

'Well Mr. Pirate,' the other guard said, 'Perhaps you'd be so kind as to tell us which crew you sail with. Who's ya captain? Orig Slim Bones Harker? Brendan Raven Jones?'

'Daxon,' I stated.

At this their laughter stopped and they faltered. They knew I was lying, but still the idea I could be even acquainted with the vicious killer had them shaking in their boots.

'So aye, you might want to unhand me in case my boss finds out about...'

Before I had finished, my back was against a wall and a hand was around my throat.

'Now you listen here ya little cunt!' my toothless attacker growled. 'I won't be hearing any crap about Daxon from you again unless ya want two empty holes where ya eyes used to be. Understand?'

I could not help but grin, and a fist came my way.

When the blackness faded and I awoke, my head and arms were suspended. It took some time adjusting to the daylight to figure out I was in the stocks. I had been here plenty of times before, being the pickpocket that I was, and I knew I would be here again. It was not the worst thing; the stocks were positioned on the pier so I could gaze out into the harbour. Boats and ships of all types were coming and going, and the luxurious blue waves beyond them stretched off into the horizon.

Cranwell, the town of passers-by and dirty lowlifes. Even as I watched on, somebody was robbed for their purse. Towards the harbour two men bickered loudly. The argument was ended when one pushed the other into the water, spitting curses all the while.

A good place for traders since you encountered people from all across the world – a better place for thieves since those people often carried gold. You could come here empty handed and leave set for life, provided you had the skill. And if you did not fancy the criminal life or wanted to change yours entirely, you could jump on a boat and start anew.

The faces around here were mainly pale, but there were a few darker ones. Cranwell did not discriminate – yeah you would get a few thugs who went around abusing people for being black, but it was hardly an epidemic.

Not many people stayed here long due to the crime rates, it was not a place to settle down and have a family. For me it was home however – I knew the streets better than anyone and could navigate them like the back of my hand. Admittedly last night did not go entirely according to plan, but it presented me with a new handful of opportunities. It was incredible how much you heard from passers-by – how many little details they gave away so easily when you were no threat to them. I was already picking out my next targets, a middle-aged pair far too well dressed for the likes of this place.

'...and you'll escort me to my boat without any problems?' the woman was saying to who I could only presume to be her lover. It was in hushed tone, but within my earshot.

'Of course darling, nobody will dare come near you with me around, your jewels are safe.'

Perfect. Now all I needed was a date and time. But as I tried to listen in to their preparations an incoming ship's horn blew from the water. I drowned it out as much as I could, but the moment was over – they continued walking and it seemed I had missed what sounded like a perfect score. I was listening out for another potential target when the slim guard from yesterday appeared before me.

'Comfy there sunshine?' he smirked.

'Very much so,' I parried, watching his expression drop.

Past him the ship docked, closer to us than the others. A fist smashed into my face and I felt my nose burst.

'You keep bein' cheeky like that and you'll be in the stocks 'til ya look older than your own balls.'

Pain swelled in my face, but my attention was drawn by the oncoming sailors who were now on the pier walking towards us. Dark leather coats adorned each of them, as well as a black bandana atop each man's head.

'Look at me when I'm talkin' to ya!' the guard demanded, moving around the stocks to kick me in the stomach.

I grunted, tears forming in my eyes.

'What's going on here?' the frontrunner of the men enquired as they closed the gap.

His face was scrawny, with sunken cheeks and a wisp of hair below his chin. He was the palest of the group, all of the others with a noticeable tan and one darker than the rest.

The guard had been going for a second kick when they interrupted him.

'None of ya business!' he spat, disregarding the men as he struck me again.

There were half a dozen of them, all with weapons at their hips but not for holding rapiers like the town guards carried; these were thicker, all different shapes and sizes – one of the men had a blade at each hip.

'At least tell us what he's here for,' the duel wielder asked – he was the most built of the men, half a head taller than the rest with rippling muscles visible despite the thick coat.

'Kid stole a purse in the town square, claimed to be a pirate too.'

'Surely that's not reason enough for this behaviour. Put him in the stocks sure, but is there any need to beat him?'

Finally, in aggravation the guard spun around to face them properly.

'Now listen 'ere,' he growled; it almost covered the tremble in his voice –

almost. 'Move along or I'll have the rest of Cranwell town guard here to put ya all in

the stock as well.'

The frontrunner smirked. His hand moved to the hilt of his blade and gripped

firmly. 'So, the lad is a pirate ay?' he chuckled, ignoring the idle threat.

'Of course not!' the guard tutted. 'He says he's a part of Daxon's crew by the

maker's sake!'

I did not know these men before me, nor had I ever encountered them, but I

could read faces well enough. At the sound of Daxon's name their faces turned to

stone, but there was no fear in their eyes. A man at the back of their group stepped

forward, his eyes bright. Long hair dangled out of his bandana past his stern face –

dyed green to look like seaweed.

'The boy isn't lying,' he told the guard. 'So how about you release him to us

and we'll make sure he gets back to Daxon.'

'This is nonsense!' the guard protested stepping forward and into my view,

but as he spoke the green haired man unsheathed his monstrous blade. I had not

gotten a good view at the size of the weapon until now, and I was blown away. It

was a square bladed machete – the hilt was simple and wooden with no hand guard,

but the blade was longer and broader than its wielder's arms. He pointed it at the

guard, the weapon alone closing the gap between them and its un-tapered edge

hovering inches from his face. To me it looked like an enormous butcher's knife,

easily able to hack a man's head clean off provided the wielder was strong enough.

The guard retreated slightly, turning and walking away, calling, 'I'll be back!

And next time the numbers will be more even!'

Bring it on.

'Thanks for that,' I grunted. 'I would've taken on that slimy bastard myself, but him and his buddy...'

'Shut up.' It was the frontrunner who had cut me off, as his green hair friend spun his mighty blade. 'Why did you tell the guard you worked for Daxon?'

'Oh that, well I suppose it was just to scare him.'

'So you think Daxon is frightening?'

'Not particularly, but everyone else seems to think so. Even after a decade the folk here in Cranwell still shiver at the sound of his name.'

'So if I told you Daxon was a close personal friend of mine, what would you say then?'

The way his eyes bore into me urged me to be afraid, but I remained calm and collected. He was just trying to scare me the way I liked to scare the guards.

'I'd ask you to thank him for me – I've been using his name to shake up the guards for years and I've never expressed my gratitude.'

The scrawny man waved a hand and turned. His green haired friend approached grinning and hefted his mighty katana. I closed my eyes as I mentally kicked myself, but instead of sudden nothingness I felt something crack above me. I moved and the top of the stocks fell from my shoulders, split in two by the strike.

'Hang on,' I muttered, stretching out my back. 'You're not gonna kill me?'

'Not yet,' the dual wielder grinned. 'We're taking you to your good friend Daxon!'

A hand gripped me on either side and I was hauled off through the streets of Cranwell, *how much of this was a joke?* I had no doubt in my mind that these were pirates, villainous plunderers and brothers in arms. Wolves of the sea and everything else you wanted to call them. Piracy was technically illegal, though those in charge of the law often let it slip – after all there were no rules on the ocean. Around these parts the title of pirate warranted a certain degree of respect, after all Cranwell was a town of particularly nasty criminals, and pirates were the worst of the worst. Each crew stuck to its own code of arms, but those ranged from actual honour to merciless killing for pleasure.

There were several hidden streets in Cranwell which housed secret taverns and low profile organisations. I was certain they would take me to one of these, and was surprised when instead they hauled me through the doors of a renowned pirates' tavern near the town square. While it was known to house the sea dwelling brigands primarily, it was not an illegal establishment. Guards would often drink there in fact as it offered one of the finest selections of ale brought through from all across the world.

Accordion music swept over me, typical pirate shanties; however, it was almost entirely drowned out by the roar of conversation. With doubts in my mind that one would ever encounter Daxon here of all places, I was shoved towards the bar where a one-eyed innkeeper glanced over us sceptically.

'What'll it be lads?' he grunted in a low, gruff voice.

The scrawny pirate turned to me. 'You old enough to drink boy?'

'I'm fifteen,' I replied.

'Close enough!' he hollered, turning back to the barkeep. 'Give us seven pints of your finest ale.'

The server's one eye bore into each of us before he laid an upturned hand firmly on the counter.

'Coin first!'

Within a second my captor's blade was out – a long jagged sword stained with what appeared to be fresh blood.

'I think you'll find it's on the house!' he retorted.

I expected the old barman to back down, but he instead slammed both hands angrily on the bar.

'You know the drill!' he yelled. 'Pay or get the fuck out! Nobody drinks for free!'

The pirate clenched his fist around the blade, his lips pulling back into a snarl.

'I'll pay their cost,' a low voice sounded from behind us.

With a firm hand on either side still holding me in place, I was unable to turn towards the speaker. Everything seemed to go quiet – voices died down and even the music stopped. All that could be heard was the footsteps of the man coming closer.

'Lower your weapon Wes, you impulsive imbecile.'

The voice was smooth, educated, full of authority.

Wes grinned and sheathed his blade. 'What took you so long boss?'

Silently the man came to the bar and threw down a purse of coins. A long black beard covered most of his lower face. His eyes were a dark brown, his gaze severe and unwavering. Like the half dozen pirates standing with me, he wore a long black coat – however atop his head he wore not a bandana but a black captain's hat.

Golden rings covered most of his fingers, and a black pendant necklace hung below his throat.

'Sorry about my men,' he apologised to the barkeep, ignoring Wes. 'They tend to get a bit over their heads when I'm not around to keep them in check. Make that eight pints, and keep the change as a token of my apologies.'

The one-eyed man seemed nervous as he picked up the purse and began to pour the pints. Could my captors have been telling the truth? Could this be...him?

'Who's the lad?' he asked his men, not bothering to look my way.

'We were hoping *you* could tell us,' the green haired pirate replied, chuckling to himself. 'Apparently he's one of our crew – you been hiring recruits without us?'

For the second time the man ignored a question. Instead he simply grabbed the first pint the server laid on the counter and took a long, hefty swig. When he put the glass down, it was half empty – his eyes found mine.

I had heard tales of how the mighty Daxon could make an entire army retreat with a single stare – I never believed it until that moment. He had no facial scars, nor an eyepatch, he was not the tallest man in the room nor the broadest, though he was still without a doubt the most intimidating person I had ever seen.

'What's your name boy?' he demanded.

If a guard (or anyone else for that matter) ever asked me, I would always provide a fake one. In fact, I doubted I had even said my real name for over five years. Yet for some reason I was compelled not to lie to this man.

'Yodrick...Yodrick Alton.'

Mouthing the name, he averted his gaze, picking his glass back up and finished the pint in another long swig. 'So, he was claiming to be friends with me ay?' he asked his crew.

'Aye sir,' the duel wielder confirmed. 'That's what the guard told us at least.'

'And what do you say in your defence boy?' he directed towards me.

I paused, positive I would have to be careful about what I said to this man. I could lie, maybe add a bit of flattery, but he would see right through that. 'Using your name shakes up the guards more often than not, some even let me go with a warning if they're gullible enough to think I'm one of your crew.'

'Seems as good a reason as any I suppose,' the fierce man said, passing the rest of the pints around to his crew before laying mine in front of me. 'But I hope you understand I can't have lads like you going around and hurting my image. Drink.'

He seemed serious. I hesitated before picking up my drink and taking a swig. I was accustomed to ale, but it usually tasted like piss water. This stuff was strong, but the flavour was not half bad. I drank some more, already feeling the warmth spread through me.

'So what are you going to do to me?' I dared ask.

'I could cut something off boss,' Wes offered with a sly grin. 'Teach him a lesson so he won't be using your name again.'

'Pipe down!' he barked to his associate, dulling the devious sparkle in his eyes, 'You're beginning to get on my nerves, I swear if I had more sense I would've thrown you into the ocean years ago.'

I tried my best to stay out of the argument about what they should do to me, and instead focused on drinking my ale. My eyes glanced to the door, but even as ideas were tossed around a hand stayed firm on my sleeve.

The man in question had been silent so far, even back at the stocks. A bandana lay atop his head and his eyes were a sunken grey. From the way his gaze never shifted, I imagined he was blind. He was the oldest of the group without a doubt, though still at his hip was a sheath, seemingly longer than most. Eventually the group seemed to come to some kind of agreement, though I had missed the vast majority of their conversation.

'Well, it's settled lad!' the green haired pirate told me with a grin, I gazed up at the group questioningly. 'Welcome to the crew of The Iron Stallion!'

'Huh?'

Chapter 2

The Iron Stallion

Everything was a rush of confusion, loudness and alcohol. Daxon had cleared up some of my questions, explaining that the easiest way to stop me lying about being a part of his crew was for me to join them. This unfortunately led to more questions which I was promised would all be answered the next morning.

In Wes's words, 'For tonight, don't worry about a thing. Tomorrow the hard work starts!'

I was officially introduced to all of the men. The green haired man was Korhal, the large duel wielder was Mamorhah, Varen was the blind man, and I had already gathered that the sunken-faced man was Wes. Additionally, there was Wargal (a short, stocky man with several knives around his belt) and Brongrim, an archer in practice but with a short dagger as a sidearm – he was built like a twig, with dark skin and had several scars over his face with an eyepatch to boot.

The mead, beer and rum came by the tonne. Within only a few minutes of us being there, most of the other customers disappeared – the ones who stayed either brave or foolish. Old sea shanties were played by the musician and the crew sang along with cheer and merriment. Daxon however stayed solemn, his cold gaze staring off into the distance. He drank, but did not join in with the celebrations.

The door to the tavern flew open and in filed a dozen guards. In amongst them were the two who had captured me. The musician and what remained of the other customers were ordered out, the door closing behind them.

'Sirs, lay down your weapons. You are all under arrest,' one man said, stepping forward.

He wore the gold coat of a guard captain.

'What for, *sir*?' Wes countered cockily, his hand wandering towards the hilt of his jagged blade.

'You have interfered with the law of Cranwell by breaking that boy free. And more so, I hear rumours the villain Daxon is amongst you.'

Daxon stood abruptly from his seat, the wooden stool falling over behind him. He strode fiercely towards the captain. Stepped forward swiftly, the other guards drew their rapiers to block his path. The captain lifted a hand to dismiss them, allowing the pirate to close the gap. Inches from one another, Daxon's dark eyes bore into the older man.

'I am no villain,' he spat. 'And you would be wise to kindly remove yourself and your lackeys from this place. We shall be on the seas by morning.'

He turned his back to the guards and moved towards us.

'I'm afraid that won't suffice,' the captain scoffed. 'If you refuse my demands, my men will take you all by force.'

Behind him the scrawny guard was grinning, brandishing the few teeth he had. None of the guards looked much better than he – each likely recruited from Cranwell's slums by their appearance. Rather than acknowledging the man Daxon went straight to the bar, whispered a word of apology to the barkeep so only I and a few others could hear. He picked up his pint glass and began to drink.

'Seize them!' the guard captain ordered.

Finishing the last of the beer from his glass, Daxon spun around and hurled it into a charging guard. It shattered against the man's head, knocking him into a heap on the floor.

Dead.

Seeing their comrade fall, the others soon charged. Within seconds blades were out and a brawl was upon us.

Varen's sword was out finally, the blade was thin but as long as any I had seen. Despite being blind, he quickly cut down two of their men without as much as a second thought. Wargal's knives went soaring, picking off targets. Within a minute the original guards were all but defeated, however dozens more pi ed in through the open tavern door. The innkeeper hid behind the counter as the battle went into full swing.

I stayed back as Mamorhah unleashed his duel swords. One was jet black, both blade and hilt – trimmed in crimson with a demon depicted on the pommel. The other was a bright white, trimmed in gold with an angel whose wings made up the hilt. The humongous man barked for me to stay behind him while he cut down anyone who would dare take him on. From my protected position, I watched Daxon as he kicked a man to the ground, giving the guard no hope as Korhal's monstrous katana sliced through his neck.

Brongrim and Wes stayed near the door, sword and dagger stopping more guards from joining the fight as they sliced them down without remorse. Without my knife which had been confiscated by the guards, I knew if anyone rushed at me I was defenceless. Mamorhah over-extended, moving a few feet forward with every enemy he put down. Before long there was enough of a gap, and a particularly fierce looking guard rolled through and came face to face with me. His rapier flashed, slicing my cheek as I dodged a potentially fatal blow. I sidestepped his next lunge and kicked my foe hard in the knee. It collapsed inwards and he staggered.

'Lad! Over here!' the barkeep cried as he threw me a sword.

I caught it by the hilt and sliced the guard down without delay. As I watched the lifeless man tumble to the floor and saw his blood dripping from my steel, my body tensed up.

The screams, the blood. Strangers pointing towards the roof as they saw me. 'Scoundrel!' 'Killer!' 'Murderer!' His body was still intact, but he was face down in the dirt. Crimson liquid slowly spread from his body. I ran.

'Watch out!'

I snapped out of it as another guard rushed me. I went to lift my sword, but he kicked it from my grip. My heart stopped as he readied his blade. Daxon appeared out of nowhere and tackled him to the ground, saving me at the last moment.

The pirate captain hurled his fists into the guard's face over and over until his body went limp. Daxon untangled himself from the corpse and handed me back my fallen blade. I took it as his cold eyes met with mine.

'Stay focused!' he commanded, turning away to slay yet another enemy.

I tried to keep my concentration as I downed another two men, my arm already tiring under the weight of the sword. Everyone was laden with blood and corpses littered the floor. It became harder to distinguish between friends and enemies, but eventually the ringing of steel on steel stopped. I was amongst the nine men left standing.

Somehow the captain of the guard had stayed alive, his gold coat now stained red like those of his dead inferiors. All of Daxon's crew had survived – the barkeep however must have joined the fighting, for he lay dead in the middle of the floor. Daxon kneeled and slowly closed the man's single eyelid.

'Apologies my friend, know your sacrifice will not be in vain.'

Out of everyone, Daxon had the least blood on him. As some of the others wiped off their blades I noticed our captain had never even drawn his sword, though his fists were stained a dark crimson. The guard captain rushed for the door, only to be blocked by Wes whose jagged blade moved closer to his throat. The once proud man turned and fell to his knees, tears in his eyes.

'Please sir, do not kill me!' he begged.

The dark pirate moved to him, straightening out the hat atop his head as footsteps echoed on the bloody floor.

'How many have you killed in your time old man?' Daxon growled. 'How many men do you see here? Dead because of your stubbornness and pride, sacrificed by your order.'

He sobbed, blubbering illegible pleas for mercy. Korhal moved towards them and laid a hand on Daxon's shoulder.

'We take no prisoners,' he muttered, 'Nor do we slaughter a man on his knees. Despite his pathetic state, he was once a captain – a respectable man. He deserves a good death, by your blade.'

I dropped my sword and moved forward, watching as Daxon's features hardened.

'So be it.' He scooped up a sword from one of the fallen and threw it before the grovelling man. 'Stand and fight, like the man you once were.'

Reluctantly the guard captain grabbed the blade and got to his feet. Daxon unsheathed an exquisite weapon. It shone bright, as if it were made of diamonds. I could not have imagined the glow which emanated from it, nor the feeling of my energy draining from me as I laid eyes on the beautiful sword. The guard lunged, thrusting his rapier at Daxon's chest; he stepped back, easily avoiding the fragile stab.

'Fight!' the pirate commanded.

Again the guard charged, this time Daxon parrying his blow with the flick of his wrist.

'Fight!'

Finally, the guard attacked with vigour, swinging his rapier like the trained captain he was. Daxon parried each blow, hitting hard with the last and knocking the thin blade from the guard's hand. As swiftly as he had disarmed him, Daxon lunged and stabbed his opponent through the stomach and the man's eyes went wide. As he pulled the sword from its victim, blood poured – though none seemed to stain the blade. Instead it even appeared to glow brighter as the man fell. Daxon kneeled over the dying man.

'Today you die a good death, it will not be in vain.'

He stood and sheathed his blade once more.

'Come on lad,' Varen whispered to me as he came up behind me. 'We best be going.'

We were all cautious while leaving the tavern, worried more guards would show up. I had not realised how much time had passed until we exited into the cold air of night. They told me to grab anything I needed in Cranwell, for that night we would set sail. Daxon sent Mamorhah with me, partially for my protection and also to make sure I would not escape. In all honesty I knew even if I wanted to get away, it would make no difference. My contacts and connections, the entirety of my life, all were in Cranwell. And surely I could not stay here after that massacre tonight – somebody would recognise me. If the remaining guards of the town did not recognise me, one of the customers from earlier surely would. I had no life here, not any more.

Mamorhah grumbled as again and again the large man was made to climb and clamber over walls and across rooftops in order to get to my destination.

'Twice today I've had to protect you,' he sighed. 'Don't expect it regularly, I'm no babysitter.'

'Understood.'

'From what I saw, you were quite capable of handling yourself in a fight. Who taught you to swing a sword?'

I paused, remembering a much simpler time.

'Not like that Yodrick,' he had told me, showing me not to drop my guard. He smiled as he corrected me. Even when criticising, he could always make me feel good about myself. I could not have been particularly old back then, only four years at most. Still, the image lingered in my mind so vividly – everything about him. His eyes, his hair, and especially that laugh. So hearty and deep. The way he held me, the way he held mother too. We were happy.

27

'My father.' I told the bulking pirate.

'Well he didn't teach you correct stance; you were sufficient at slicing but your form was all wrong.'

I grunted a half-arsed acknowledgement and led us into the alley. The good part of where I lived was it was practically unreachable to any who did not know Cranwell like the back of their hand. The architecture of the town dated back to centuries ago, however several decades back they modernised it with new buildings. Because of this, some design flaws meant houses did not back onto one another perfectly, causing hidden alleys such as this, which one could not reach simply by walking.

This meant dropping into alleys from rooftops, but that was a skill in its own. Only some buildings provided sufficient leverage to get to these places, and even at night only some buildings could be scaled without attracting attention. For this alley it meant cutting across the back end of main street, vaulting over the seven-foot wall, climbing up the side of the baker's, creeping along the slope of the roof to the next street over, dropping into a secluded square behind the florist's store to get to a hole in the fence which led to the back of the maker's temple. From there it was a risky climb up to the bell tower which was high enough to access the tops of two-storey buildings, which led in a straight line to an alley which we climbed into.

'By the maker this place is a lot of hassle to get to!' Mamorhah grunted as he shook his legs out after the drop.

The huge overhang of a bricked up window formed a sturdy roof to my home – wood and nails renovated more and more over the years formed my walls and door. I moved inside, reaching under my pillow to grab my back-up knife, a ring and necklace. I adorned the jewellery and stashed the knife in my boot, taking a final glance around the tiny home and saying a silent goodbye.

'That didn't look like much,' Mamorhah complained.

'Well, I'm assuming you'll provide me with everything I need,' I retorted, drawing a grumble out of him.

By the time we got back to the main street he seemed fed up with all of the climbing. We strode to the harbour where I could finally admire their ship properly. It was almost indistinguishable in the dim moonlight, but true to its name the mast was a large sculpture of a stallion's head, masked with rustic paint to give it the appearance of iron. Its mane flowed almost all of the way down the bow to the deck.

Varen and Wes were there waiting for our arrival and helped us aboard the vessel. As soon as my feet touched the wood, Wes waved a hand towards the shadowed figure of Daxon up on the bow manning the wheel. He called an order and in seconds the anchor was drawn. The ship gave a large shudder and jolted into motion. Cranwell slowly began to disappear from view as we sailed towards the sea, my home gone for the foreseeable future.

'Varen will show you to your quarters,' Wes said. 'You'll be woken up early tomorrow so get as much sleep as you can lad.'

Varen simply gestured for me to follow. We followed a hatch down below deck and into a corridor of wooden doors, stopping at the furthest one of the right.

'This is it,' he stated. 'Good night.'

He spun and walked back wordlessly. I had never seen a blind man navigate his way around (and much less fight) as well as Varen did. When he turned away from the hallway I opened the unlocked door. Lit lanterns illuminated almost everything below deck, and I was not surprised to find one in my room. Though its flame was dim, I made out a simple wardrobe, a bedside table, and a nice bed. A round window allowed me to look out at the dark sea. It was the type of room you would get at a well-managed inn, so I was not complaining.

A second door led to a smaller room which housed a sewage hole, an empty tin bathtub, and a water pump. I shed my clothes, wetting my shirt to extinguish the lantern. In the blackness I climbed beneath the soft sheets of my new bed. Tiredness struck me as my head hit the pillow – it had been a long and eventful day. I allowed my body to relax as I faded into a well-deserved sleep.

Strange dreams beseeched me that night, a mixture of images from my past and present. Again I was on that rooftop looking down on the dead boy. But instead of locals pointing and accusing me, everything was still. The only figure was Daxon who stood beside me.

'Why did you do it?' he asked. I I glanced at my shaking hands as I had that day.

'I...I didn't mean to,' I stammered. He tutted and shook his head.

'Your father would not be happy.'

'What would he care?' I countered angrily. 'He's dead.'

I was on a boat, but not the Iron Stallion. It was my father's fishing boat, the one I had never gotten to sail on – he had promised me that I could when I was older. He was not there however, and I was sailing by myself. My hands appeared different, as did everything else now that I was looking. There was a sword at my hip; I unsheathed it and found Daxon's beautiful blade. The crystal-like metal shone bright. I sheathed it and looked down at the rippling water below me. As it cleared it showed my reflection, but it was Daxon's face staring back. Suddenly the boat lurched forward and I was thrown overboard, the reflection rushed up to meet me and suddenly I was engulfed in water; then I awoke.

It took me a moment to figure out where I was. Daylight streamed in through the cabin's window, making the room brighter than before. My door was open and a stranger stood in the doorway holding an empty bucket of water, its former contents all over me. It was a woman, long black hair flowing from her bandana. I panicked for a moment but soon noticed her attire. Like the others she wore a black coat, though beneath it her blouse was white and unbuttoned enough for me to see the top of the lacy red bra.

In place of trousers she wore leggings beneath a long skirt which came past her knees and had a rip up the side for manoeuvrability. She was stunning – tanned skin, darker than most of the others, and piercing green eyes which fixed on me. Acutely aware of my bare boyish chest on display, I pulled up the blanket to cover myself. She smirked.

'Don't worry, no need for such modesty on this ship,' she laughed, her voice smooth and slightly exotic. 'I was sent to wake you, Daxon wants you on the main deck, and I wouldn't keep him waiting if I were you.' She held a bundle in her hands which she threw on my bed. 'Wear these.'

With those words she left and closed my door behind her. Slightly rattled, I threw my covers off and grabbed the bundle.

I made my way up to the main deck in my new attire. While not as fancy as the crew's outfit, it was an improvement on my old clothes. Black breeches which fell to below my knees, and a white cotton shirt – both baggy and comfortable.

Simple sandals covered my feet and while I had no bandana nor hat to keep my unkempt hair in check, I did wear my ring and necklace.

Wes was up in the crow's next keeping lookout, and Korhal seemed to be at the wheel. Daxon, Wargal and Brongrim awaited me on the main deck, alongside the woman who had awoken me and a man who I had not met. The man was as dark-skinned as Brongrim and held a hatchet in each hand with more tucked into his belt, and Brongrim had his bow and quiver over his back this time.

'I expect you to be here each morning at sunrise,' was the first thing Daxon said to me as I closed the gap. 'You won't receive a wakeup call after today, and if you're late you'll be lashed. Understood?'

'Understood!' I answered firmly, fearing the lashes as a phantom pain spread across my back.

Despite being a loner in my recent past, I knew how order and routine worked.

'Before you are two new faces – Gurdgrin and Akaya are the two members of this crew who you have not yet been acquainted with.'

Akaya grinned slyly and Gurdgrin raised one of his weapons in salute – he was a robust man though appeared capable of slaughtering me if he wished.

'The four of us will supervise your weapons training for today,' Wargal told me cheerily. 'If you're up to it you and I can start our session right now.'

Weapons training sounded interesting, though with such a diverse and dangerous group of trainers it would most likely be incredibly dangerous. Still, here in front of half of the most revered pirate crew in the world I refused to lose face.

'I'm ready when you are!' I responded, loudly and clearly.

'I know you have a lot of unanswered questions,' Daxon stated. 'And later today I shall answer some of them. As for now however I have other business to attend to, so I leave you in Wargal's hands. Farewell.'

He turned and strode away. The others soon followed his lead, each scheduling to return at a specific time to train me. I bowed slightly to each as they departed, leaving only Wargal and I on the main deck.

'You ready?' the short man grunted at me.

'Let's do it.'

Chapter 3

A Pirate's Life

'**A** pirate, no matter what weapon he chooses to wield, must be able to use a knife or dagger.'

I had wanted to use my own blade, however Wargal had insisted I use one of his. We came face to face, each with a single blade in our right hand, circling one another.

'While I choose to use my knives as projectiles, I always keep hold of one or two for close combat – as all good fighters should.'

'Agreed!' I grinned, watching the short man's stance for a gap in his opening. I barely blinked and my knife went flying out of my grasp, pain seizing my hand as Wargal moved his steel to my throat.

'Focus is key,' he instructed. 'Especially when so close to your enemy that a single lunge can close the gap.'

He retreated from me, blood dripping from an open wound below my knuckles. I held my left hand to it and gasped at the sting.

'Well, what are you waiting for? Retrieve your blade.' I turned to where my weapon had landed, silently cursing the pirate. 'And by the way, your stance is horrendous.'

'I've been told,' I grunted through clenched teeth.

The man had seemed nice enough at first, but I soon came to realise he was a harsh instructor. Again and again he slashed at my hand to disarm me, each time cutting deeper and deeper into the flesh. He had no mercy – every time criticising my form or my grip or my movement. The repeated insults and the building pain soon drew my temper. As we started a new bout I lunged at him with blade in hand. He sidestepped quickly, his leg darting out as he tripped me and I fell face first into the deck.

'Too impulsive!' he scoffed. 'Now stand up and do it the way I told you!'

I wanted nothing more than to punch the man, but I reserved myself. With each defeat I wanted to beat him more, but every time he sent my blade flying and gave me a new cut. It continued until the hour had passed and he finally allowed me to tend to my hand. The wound was thick with dried blood which was already scabbing over, but simply moving it now sent agony up my arm. Wargal threw me a soaked cloth and I draped it over the wounds.

'Bastard!' I cursed as the sting seeped into my hand.

'Aye lad,' the pirate grinned sadistically. 'Water feels nicer, but rum makes sure the wound doesn't fester.'

'How thoughtful of you,' I groaned sarcastically.

'Tie the cloth tightly around that, you'll probably need use of that hand for training with Gurdgrin.'

I gave Wargal a scowl, though he smiled back and helped me bandage the injury.

'Thanks,' I grunted, and he gave me a pat on the back.

'You did well for your first session lad, but know your training here will be painful. If I had it my way I'd go easy on you until you got the hang of it, but Daxon calls the shots.'

I watched the short pirate thoughtfully as he took a swig from his rum and offered me a drink. Gulping it down I noticed it was strong; I must have visibly grimaced because he laughed. Wargal told me he would see me at dinner that night and sauntered off, whistling a shanty as he disappeared. I was only left alone for a few minutes before Gurdgrin showed up, still proudly holding his hatchets. He came and handed one to me which I took with my left hand.

'You see those targets over there?' he asked in a low, thick voice.

I gestured my affirmation, seeing a line of about a dozen wooden target stands, riddled with gapes and holes from heavy use. When he was sure I was watching, the pirate pulled his wielding arm back and stepped up to hurl the weapon. It soared through the air before burying itself into the centre of a target. I could not help but grin at the impressive feat.

'Now you,' he grunted simply.

My elation dropped. I was reluctant to use my right hand, but even with it I had not a hope in hell of landing a hatchet anywhere near my target. Still, I gave it heave with my left arm. The weapon spun off to the right, hitting the floor prematurely and spinning down the deck.

'This may take a while,' he sighed, 'Again!'

After a dozen attempts at hitting the target, I honestly thought I may be getting worse. Gurdgrin seemed to agree as, after a severely bad shot where the hatchet spun into the air and towards the bow of the ship, he took the weapon from me. I was instructed to walk towards the targets. I obeyed, disappointed to be failing at this seemingly simple task. I turned just in time to jump out of the way of the weapon flying towards me, the metal axe-head practically skimming my face as it passed me, landing once again into the centre of a target I had been standing in front of. I held my arms out frantically.

'Are you crazy?' I cried, but was met with a low chuckle.

'My friend, *you* are the one standing in front of a target range!' he laughed, throwing another hatchet.

I barely got out of the way the second time.

'You told me to stand here!' I countered.

'Well,' Gurdgrin said, 'Perhaps avoiding my hatchets will help you pick up a lesson on how to not throw them like a small child having a tantrum.'

A third one came racing past my head, and I turned to move. Wherever I went however, Gurdgrin did not cease with his throwing. He had half a dozen hatchets on him, and each one came within an inch of killing me on the spot. When he ran out of projectiles I shakily stormed up to him, practically frothing at the mouth.

'You tried to kill me!' I screamed at him.

He faced me with wide eyes, his palm resting on my shoulder. 'Trust me boy, if I had been trying to kill you, you'd have been dead after only one hatchet.'

He retrieved his weapons and tucked them into his belt, grinning and wandering off like Wargal had. So far in this training I had temporarily lost the use of my dominant hand and had been used as target practice for a crazed hatchet thrower – this was not going well. The next instructor of mine to show up was Brongrim who carried a practice bow as he approached me. He greeted me and handed over the weapon.

'I'm hoping this means I'm not being used as a moving target,' I joked.

Brongrim frowned and raised a patchy eyebrow. 'Gurdgrin?'

'Yeah...' I sighed.

'Pay him no attention,' the archer told me. 'He's been like that for years. He enjoys frightening people, but he would never go against the captain's orders by killing you.'

'His orders?' I enquired.

He nodded.

'Daxon has given strict instruction you are not to die during this training process – I don't understand why exactly, but he seems to have a stake in you staying alive. Like all good things in life, I advise you don't question it.'

That seemed strange, the legendary pirate villain Daxon had an interest in a boy from Cranwell. Peculiar.

Archery practice was much more enjoyable than the other training. I was not particularly good at it, though I did manage to hit the targets on several occasions. My hand still throbbed but the injury did not impact my fingers and so I was able to draw the bow. Brongrim seemed much calmer than the others. He made me focus on my breathing as I pulled back the bowstring, instructing me to breathe out as I released the arrow. When our hour ended I was disappointed, out of the crew he seemed the most laid back.

Finally, my fourth teacher of the day approached me – the beautiful Akaya. She bore no visible weapon so I was confused what the lesson was in, but I soon learned. Without a word of conversation, she struck me in the chest and knocked me off of my feet.

'I've been instructed to train you in hand-to-hand combat.'

Many would not imagine a slim, attractive woman such as Akaya would be such a word class brawler; I imagined those who held that belief often died by her hands. She was clearly not pulling her punches as she struck me a dozen times in a few seconds, audibly cracking bones in the process. Any notions of it being wrong to hit a woman which I had previously held were quickly lost as I put my guard up and tried my best to fend her off. I had been in scraps on the streets of Cranwell, though never anything like this.

Again and again she punched hard and kicked harder. Her strikes were lightning, and no matter how quickly I moved I could not stop them. After less than ten minutes of this rushed action I was panting for breath, but glancing at Akaya she seemed to be biting her lip – almost as if she was getting pleasure from fighting me. I had met my fair share of fierce women in Cranwell, some of whom used their sexual appeal to gain control over weaker men. I was not entirely sure it was what Akaya was doing, not yet at least. I began to pick up on her patterns, and even blocked a few of her strikes. After that I began to retaliate, getting a few short punches in here and there.

But as I was becoming more confident, she stepped back and slowly loosed another button on her blouse, showing off more of the lacy red bra beneath. She stared into my eyes as she did it. I knew to her there was nothing sexual about it, it was her way of psyching me out, although I still felt the involuntary bulge rising in my breeches. Before I could figure out what to do, her fists came flying again, one hitting me square in the face. I fell backwards to the floor with a bloody nose, Akaya standing above me as she re-buttoned her blouse with a sly grin.

'You men are all alike,' she scoffed. 'Small minded and easy to manipulate.'

We still had a good twenty minutes of our hour left to go, but she strode away without a single regard for the schedule. I lay there for a moment, recovering from the fight, ashamed in myself for how easily she had gotten the best of me.

I struggled to my feet, my entire body now in shambles from my day of training, and by my guess it was not even nine yet. I hobbled across the deck in the hope of finding Daxon somewhere.

'Where ya off to little birdie?' the cocky voice of Wes called from the Crow's nest.

'Do you know where Daxon is?'

'In his quarters most likely, but I wouldn't disturb him if I were you.'

I groaned, aggravated. 'Tell me where!' I demanded with false confidence.

'Don't ya know anything about ships?' Wes scoffed. 'Captains' cabins are always at the stern.'

I did not bother to respond to the pirate, instead turning and walking towards the back of the boat. Like on the main deck, there was a hatch leading down. I followed the staircase and was met with a single door at the end of it. I took in a deep breath, prepared to speak to the most notorious and supposedly villainous pirate in the world. I knocked.

'What is it?' the voice called almost the second my knuckles hit the wood, the tone more irritated than angry.

'It's me, sir...Yodrick...sir.'

A moment of silence, followed by another. Each second felt like a lifetime, stretching out as my heart pounded faster.

'Come in.'

The words were well welcomed, though as I entered the room a larger concern hit me – Daxon did not appear happy.

His quarters were larger than mine, the foremost part of it acting more like an office. He sat behind a splendid mahogany desk, carved with a great degree of time and care. For some reason it struck me as off, a man of his calibre owning something so elegant and beautiful. I knew even as the thought crossed my mind it was a truly ridiculous thing to be contemplating. My eyes elevated to the stern bearded man before me, sat on a stool with his eyes now clearly fixed on me.

'I did not expect you yet,' he grunted.

'Umm...my training with Akaya, well...it was cut short...sir.'

His eyes rolled and he gestured to the stool on my side of the desk. 'Take a seat,' he ordered.

'Aye sir.'

'And stop calling me sir!' he spat. 'It's bad enough the others do it.'

'Sorry, captain,' I said, hurriedly sitting.

On his desk was a large book, bound in black leather – its pages old and worn. As soon as he noticed my eyes on it the captain slammed it shut.

'You look run down,' he acknowledged, his gaze shifting from my hand to my bloody nose. 'With more training that won't happen as much.'

I nodded, expecting more words which never came. Daxon slumped on his stool, his fingers interlacing above the rim of the desk as the seconds ticked by.

'Well?' he questioned abruptly.

I was taken aback. 'Uh...well what? ...captain.'

'I told you I would answer your questions,' he reminded me. 'So go ahead and ask – I will answer what I can.'

'Why did you let me join your crew?' I asked out of instinct, the question coming out more abrasively than I would have liked. 'I mean if you wanted to stop me using your name, why not just kill me and be done with it.'

'You were honest,' he replied. 'You gave a valid reason, and you were truthful with me. Also, I knew from the second I looked at you that you'd be loyal. I need loyal and honest men in my crew – unfortunately I don't find many these days.'

'And that was your only reason?'

'Is it not reason enough?' He had stumped me, and his gaze was bearing into me again, 'What do you know of me Yodrick?'

'Only what I've heard in stories about you,' I told him. 'The stories of ten years ago – what you did.'

'And what are those stories exactly?'

I gulped, my heart racing once more.

'That a decade ago you and your crew sailed up to Cranwell, clearly pirates but virtually unknown. Some say you went into the first building you saw and burned it to the ground, others say you went through the streets slaughtering people – regardless, they all say a lot of people died that day by your hands. From then on you became a legend, plundering ships, killing other pirates, never meeting an enemy you couldn't defeat.'

'So what do you think happened, on that day?'

'Honestly, I'm not sure,' I admitted. 'But I know there are two sides to every story.'

'Is that why you're not afraid of me?' I shook my head, 'Why then?'

'Because if you were going to kill me you would've done it already.'

'And that's the only reason?' he asked.

'Is it not reason enough?' I dared.

His eyes widened, the faintest of grins passing his lips. 'Well played, but know I will not reveal the details of that day to you, at least not yet.'

'Understood, I expected as much.'

'And don't get the wrong idea boy,' he warned. 'I may have let you join my crew for the time being, but you are still – in essence – a prisoner here. You can't just leave whenever you want.'

'I expected that too.'

The atmosphere felt much more settled and relaxed now, my heart no longer raced looking at this man.

'So is there anything else you want to know?' Daxon asked me.

'What happens to me now?'

He stood, gesturing for me to do the same. 'Walk with me.'

We moved back to the main deck, and Daxon rested his hand on my shoulder as he walked beside me. Wes was still up in the crow's nest, and it seemed Mamorhah had taken over from Korhal up at the wheel. Akaya was hanging on ropes, opening the main sail as a strong wind caught us. The captain called out an order for her to *get the bucket*.

'You will live on this ship and pull your wait,' the captain instructed. 'This means chores and occasionally more important duties. Each morning you will train your combat skills with various crewmates, and hopefully in time you will be confident enough with a weapon to be of use to us in a combat situation. Tell me, can you read and write?'

'Only a little,' I admitted. 'I learned the basics from my parents, but have hardly used it since I was six.'

'In that case you will spend many of your evenings with Varen so he may teach you.'

'But he's blind.'

At once I was upon my knees, holding my right cheek in pain. Daxon lowered the hand which he had used to strike me, and offered it out to me. I took it bitterly as he pulled me back to my feet.

'I do not wish you to think of me as a cruel man,' the pirate said mournfully, 'But I will not have the abilities of my crew be doubted, especially not Varen's. He will teach you.'

'Aye captain.'

'You will also have some time to yourself, I suggest you use this wisely. With time you will become one of us, hopefully a fully-fledged member of this crew and no longer a prisoner, although if you step out of line at any point I will not hesitate to throw you overboard.'

Akaya returned a moment later with a bucket full of soapy water and a sponge. She laid it down, winked at me seductively, and disappeared again.

'Now for your first chore!' Daxon hollered. 'Swab the deck. I want the entire main deck done by nightfall. I'll have someone sent up every hour with a fresh bucket.'

I thought he was joking, but when he walked away doubt began to creep into my mind. I glanced around, feeling lost and confused.

'It's simple birdie,' Wes called. 'You have to use the sponge.'

I cursed him under my breath as I got to my knees and began scrubbing. Instantly my training from earlier began to take a toll on me as I leant over with both hands on the sponge, moving back and forth. It was exhausting, and after an hour it became tedious. No sound came aside the crash of the waves and the occasionally mocking comment from Wes up in his basket. My hands were beginning to wrinkle, and after another hour hunger struck me. Akaya appeared for the second time since I had started to give me fresh water, though said nothing. I had cleaned a significant portion of the deck when Wes climbed down from his tower, sniggering as he purposely walked across the area I had cleaned – mud still thick on his boots from the streets of Cranwell.

'Do you mind?' I called out.

'Not at all.'

He smirked, making his way to the lower decks as Brongrim appeared and took his place up in the nest. I had to go back over the area where Wes had walked, and was starting back on the rest of the deck when he reappeared.

'Oh, not this again,' I sighed before noticing the bucket in his hand.

'Don't worry lad, it's just your fresh water. And I snagged you some bread from the dinner hall.'

He passed me the bucket and what appeared to be stale bread, grinned, and disappeared again. I begrudgingly bit into the food as I continued working. After that Akaya continued to bring my water, and I measured how long I had been doing this by how often she appeared. She looked as radiant as ever, and as the only woman on the ship she definitely drew more eyes than just mine. My muscles ached and my sleeves were wet from the water, though true to Daxon's instruction I cleaned the entirety of the top deck by the time he returned and the sun began to disappear beyond the horizon.

'You did good lad,' he commended. 'Now come on inside and get something to eat.'

I followed him below deck and through some passageways to a dining hall. One long bench was stretched out with plates covering it. It was clear from the crumbs an abundance of food was once there, although all that remained was scraps. Wes was the only one still eating as he licked dry a chicken bone. Throwing the carcass onto the table, he stood and passed us as he grinned at me.

'Eat up birdie.'

I sat, gathering the remains of the meal and shoving them into my mouth. Daxon stayed until I was done, sitting in silence all the while. When I was finished (though still hungry) he stood.

'Get to bed Yodrick, you have an early morning ahead of you.'

He left, leaving me with only my thoughts and an unsatisfied hunger. I staggered back to my quarters and collapsed on the bed. Within moments my eyes were drooping closed without my consent and the only feeling was exhaustion.

They flew back open in an instant as a monstrous noise washed over the room – like thunder but louder. Everything shook, and commanding cries sounded from the hallway; all incomprehensible except one.

'We're under attack!'

What had I gotten myself into?

Chapter 4

Dramiculo

Rushing out of my quarters I was met with more darkness; the lanterns all shattered and extinguished. I kept my hands to the wall for support, though even as I did so I felt my sense of balance was off. The yelling had abandoned the corridor and was now on the upper deck, but as I tried to make my way to the hatch I was thrown back. I went flying to the ground as the entire ship tilted, my head smashing against a wall and glass coming down on top of me. I groaned, gritted my teeth, and cried as I pulled a shard from my arm, my hand, and a smaller one from my cheek. The hatch had flown open letting in some moonlight, though it was now on a steep incline.

I got to my feet and dashed up the slope. Each time the ship showed some sign of leveling, another shudder sent it off balance. I fell twice more but made it out of there in the end. The main deck seemed steeper still, Varen and Gurdgrin at the wheel desperately trying to get the ship back upright. They caught my attention for only a moment before my eyes flashed to the flames. The bow was ablaze, another ship close by. Its mast and flag were illuminated by the fire, both portraying the head of a dragon.

A dozen figures were silhouetted before the flames. Without even a weapon in hand I dashed towards the fire. Wes was holding off two men adorned in crimson, and grinned as I approached them from behind. I wrapped my arm around the neck of one, hoisting his head back while Wes's jagged blade slit his throat. *Five people.*

R. B. S. SNAITH

The other adversary turned to me, giving my ally an opening to cut him down at the knees.

'Who are these people?'

'Pirates for certain, but never seen their flag before,' he told me.

'Bastard!' our enemy grunted as Wes kicked away his blade and grabbed him by the throat.

'You chose the *wrong* crew to ambush.'

His grip tightened, choking him, but I grabbed Wes's arm before he could finish the job.

'Wait!' I cried. 'He could be useful to us.'

His face now deadly, the pirate glared at me; his ratty features sharp in the firelight. 'We take no prisoners.'

'Wouldn't it help to find out *who* exactly is attacking us?'

Wes's face softened as he turned back to our captive. The crimson pirate spat a mouthful of blood before Wes could even pose the question.

'I'm not telling you anything!' he grunted.

'Well then we have no use for you,' my ally gleamed, hoisting the man to his feet and dragging him to the edge of the ship.

'Wait!' our enemy cried. 'We're not pirates! We're mercenaries.'

'Who hired you?' I cut in.

'Some pirate captain, we don't know his name, I swear! He just paid us to ambush your ship, extra to not ask questions. Please! I can't swim!'

'You're mercenaries?' Wes pressed, the man affirmed. 'Well, you're clearly not very good ones.'

One push and the man was falling from the ship, Wes turning to me with wide eyes and a grin. *Six.* It seemed we had been victorious is fighting off those who had gotten onto the ship. Brongrim came down from the crow's nest, smiling to himself as he admired the arrows imbedded in our enemies. What was more, Varen and Gurdgrin had stabilized the ship and the others had extinguished the flames.

'Where's Daxon?' the hatchet wielder asked as we reconvened.

Everyone was present aside from him.

'When the pirates boarded our ship, he boarded *theirs,* he cut down a bunch of their men and ran off somewhere,' Akaya informed us.

'No doubt to look for their captain,' Wes chimed. 'Cocky bastard! And they're not pirates, they're mercenaries.'

'What do mercenaries want with us?'

'I'll explain later, right now we need to get our captain back.'

We were all in agreement; Varen, Wargal, Brongrim and Akaya would stay on the ship while Gurdgrin, Mamorhah, Korhal, Wes and I would board their ship and find Daxon. I was almost left on the ship before Wes vouched for me.

'Let the boy come, see if he has it in him,' he had said, and there were no objections.

We walked over bloodstained wood and past dozens of corpses as we followed Daxon's trail.

'I wonder how much of this blood is his,' Korhal muttered grimly.

'Nonsense,' Brongrim decreed, 'Nobody can touch the captain.'

From behind Wes whispered something under his breath, so quiet nobody else could hear it.

'*Darkskull could...*'

I doubted he even meant to say it, let alone for me to hear it. *But who was Darkskull?* The crimson trail came to a crossroads in the lower deck, bodies leading one way but ripped fabric and blood leading another.

'Did he double back on himself?' Mamorhah suggested.

'I don't know,' Wes said. 'But we should split up. Mamorhah, you and the boy come with me; you other two, see where that trail of bodies leads.'

Korhal agreed and led Gurdgrin down the hallway while we followed the trail of blood to a locked door. Mamorhah sniffed softly and grinned.

'Over half a dozen inside, none of them Daxon though.'

'Alive?' Wes enquired.

The large man sniffed again and confirmed it. Colour me impressed. Without warning, Mamorhah unsheathed his duel blades and caved the door in with a hefty kick. I drew the sword I had scavenged back on the Stallion as the first two enemies caught glimpse of us and gathered their weapons. Still, neither were match for Mamorhah nor Wes who sliced them down before they had a chance. The others had more time and charged in, one slipping past the two pirates and singling in on me. I parried his first blow, though the backhand from his rapier caught my cheek. I thrust at his chest but he leapt back out of my reach and threw a knife straight into my calf. I stifled a groan.

My vision blurred slightly as pain washed over me. Still, I was conscious enough to dodge his next two attacks. He threw another knife and I caught it on the flat of my blade. He began to reach for more and instinct took over. Raising the broadsword above my head with both hands, I hurled it with all of my strength. It spun in the air once and struck my opponent hard in the chest, its edge cutting into him. I leapt forward, grabbing the weapon back from his now toppled body and slicing his throat before he could get back up. Wes and Mamorhah had already finished off the rest.

'While broadswords don't typically get used as projectiles, I think Gurdgrin would be proud.'

I smiled at Wes's comment, but before we could move on my eyes glazed over and I felt myself falling.

He was there again, but this time I was older; older than he had ever seen me. We stood close, his greyish-blue eyes bearing into me like a mirror image of my own.

'Such a handsome lad!' he chuckled.

'And brave too,' her voice chimed. 'So much like his father.'

'He certainly didn't get his looks from me though.'

I smiled, like I had every time he talked that way. She mockingly scolded him, joking that I was as much a reflection of him as I was of her. Oh how beautiful she looked back then; back when he was with us. Such dark features, wasted on her she claimed. Eyes like polished obsidian.

'Yodrick!' came the voice. 'Are you alright lad?'

The speaker was the captain, hunched over me with his hand firm on my shoulder.

'Wh...wha...?'

'You were wounded,' Mamorhah clarified. 'We had to pull a knife from your leg, you lost a fair bit of blood.'

All of the others aside from Wes were around me. They assessed the scene passively, seemingly aside from Daxon whose deep brow gave way to wide eyes and an ever-so-slightly unhinged mouth.

'You feelin' okay?'

'Like I've just been stabbed,' I groaned, lifting myself up.

'Where's Wes?' Korhal voiced.

'I left that slimy bastard in the captain's quarters, I found something interesting there which you all should see.'

Back through a trail of dead bodies, we came to a room lavished unlike the rest of the ship. Ornaments and trinkets covered the cabin, most either silver or gold. The fabrics were unlike anything I had ever seen, silks hanging from the ceiling in all different colours like a rainbow of royalty. My nostrils, though still soiled with a metallic scent, became awash with perfumes from across the globe. Over a beautiful desk – not unlike Daxon's – the fresh corpse of a lavishly dressed man lay. Wes paced the room, his brows furrowed and nostrils flaring.

'The man certainly liked things fancy,' Gurdgrin scoffed as he ripped away a strip of silk.

'Think of the riches though, this bastard's loot will cover our drinking costs for a month!' Korhal chimed.

'We're not keeping it,' Daxon stated blankly.

The others' eyes widened.

'Captain, with respect...'

A booming fist smashed against the desk. 'I said no!' Daxon cried, cutting Mamorhah off. 'I refuse to profit off of anything given as payment by that snake!'

53

More than one of the crew closed their eyes and nodded, though I was clueless.

'Who's the snake?' I dared.

'Farrow Bloodneck,' Wes said stalely, finally adding his voice into the mix.

'Hold your tongue scoundrel!'

'The boy asked a question Daxon,' Wes retorted.

The captain's hand clasped to his hilt, although as the moment passed he released it again. 'Speak.'

'He's another captain. Not as known amongst common folk such as yourself, but for other pirates...'

'He's legendary,' Gurdgrin finished. 'The pirate of all pirates, or so they say.'

'It's true,' Daxon spat. 'I had the displeasure of meeting him once or twice. And now it seems he's trying to finish what he started.'

Even as the captain spoke I sensed an anger there – something he was trying to hide.

'What do you mean?' I asked.

'He sent these mercenaries,' Wes answered instead. 'They call themselves the Dramiculo – some of the fiercest killers on the sea. Daxon found a letter in this lovely gentleman's pocket, it told him this life of luxury was only a fraction of what he would have if his crew succeeded in killing us. Or more specifically, *him*.'

'Don't point that finger at me or I'll break it,' Daxon growled. 'Everyone back to the ship!'

I was told to abandon the morning schedule and get some sleep while the others filled the rest of the crew in, accepting the invitation happily. The light of dawn was already streaming in through my window when I reached my chambers. Resting was a relief, but I could not help from waking every half hour in pain. I opted to try again with some mead in my system, making my way down the second hatch towards the dining hall.

I stopped shy of the door when I heard voices inside.

'…never seen anything like it. He was like a different person,' the first said, though muffled through the crack of the doorframe.

'He definitely has a soft spot for the lad.'

'But why?' a third questioned. 'Who's this kid to him?'

'No clue, but not just anyone could make him scream at me like that.'

'Oh please Wes, the captain puts you in line every sodding day,' yet another person voiced.

'This time was different; he *makes* him different,' Wes answered.

Could they be talking about me?

'Different how?'

'Well I see the kid collapse and I run straight for help. He's coming the other way and I tell him what happened. Suddenly he starts barking at me, "Why did you bring him here? This is all your fault! He's going to die because of you!" as if the boy is the most…'

The voices began to die down and I leaned closer to hear, but was met with a loud creak beneath my feet. The voices stopped altogether and before I could think of anything else I was running, scampering back up through the hatch and towards the safety of my cabin. I slammed the door closed and leapt between the sheets.

What was that all about?

Chapter 5

Merrywood

I lugged myself up to the main deck around midday, still exhausted and in pain, not having slept a wink after what I had heard. Wes passed me, whistling a sea shanty. He grinned; nothing out of the ordinary. Several others also crossed my path and they seemed to be doing the same, almost as if they were trying too hard to act normal. Looking for a distraction to keep my mind off of the strange behaviour, I reported to Daxon's quarters for instruction. Only, he was not there. I wandered aimlessly around the ship until someone directed me to the food hall. When I got there Daxon was drinking alone. Several empty tankards lined the bench around him.

'Captain?'

He faced me, his eyes bloodshot. It seemed to take him a second to recognise me. 'Y...Yodrick I...lad,' he slurred. 'Come sit- come sit by me boy.'

I did as he asked, mounting the seat across from him. From closer up I noticed the spillages, both on the table and his clothes. The smell was pungent, overwhelming almost.

'How long have you been here captain?' I enquired.

'What day is it?' he grinned, swigging the rest of his drink before pouring another. He set it aside and narrowed in on me. 'We drop anchor in Merrywood today,' he mumbled. 'We'll get some supplies and find any information we can on Farrow.'

He said the name awkwardly, almost as if it pained him.

'Captain, can I ask something?'

'Ask away lad!'

It may have not been the best time to talk, his pupils kept expanding and receding and his whole demeanour seemed off, but perhaps with him drunk I would get some answers.

'You seem to have a history with this Farrow Bloodneck…'

'That's a statement boy, I thought you were asking a question.'

'Excuse me, captain,' I stumbled. 'What I'm asking is *who* exactly is he?'

He closed his eyes for a moment, and when they opened he appeared serious, grim. His face was stern, reminding me of the first time I laid eyes upon him – *strange to think it had only been two days.*

'I thought we went over this,' he grumbled. 'He's a pirate captain.'

'Like you?'

I jumped out of my seat as he smashed an empty tankard on the bench – fragments of glass flying everywhere. He held his head in his hands, shaking.

'No!' he spat, 'Not like me. Nothing like me.' A moment of silence. 'Or…at least I hope not.'

'What do you mean?'

He stood, swung himself over to my side of the bench and approached me. My body tensed. My heart pounded. His eyes met mine.

'Tell me Yodrick, do you think I'm a bad person?'

'I think you have a bad reputation,' I answered safely.

'That's not what I asked dammit!' he cursed. 'Do *you personally* think I'm a bad person.'

'Honestly captain, I haven't made my mind up.'

He rolled his eyes and turned away.

'I've killed people. I've slaughtered them. Not once or twice but hundreds of times. I lose track of the amount of people I've killed. Some of those mercenaries – the Dramiculo – they begged for mercy. A dozen men shitting themselves and crying for their lives. I still killed them, I cut them down.'

'They attacked us,' I reasoned. 'They started it.'

'Aye, and I finished it,' he scoffed. 'All fear Daxon, the dreaded pirate.'

Akaya entered. 'Captain, we're approaching the city.'

'You lot get started, Varen knows what supplies we need.'

'What about gathering information?' she asked.

'I'll be with you before sundown. Go, take the boy with you.'

'But captain...' I began to protest.

'Go!'

His face was a plum red, his hand shaking as he pointed to the door.

'As you say, captain.'

Back on the deck I witnessed Merrywood gradually come into view. I had never seen a city other than Cranwell, and this put it to shame. A thick wall surrounded most of the city, ten-foot-high white stone marble; thick enough for guards to walk two abreast atop it. The harbour housed dozens of ships, security extra strong on the water. Buildings seemed to cover almost every inch of the city, although as we drew closer I realised most of it was out of sight, stretching off into the distance. Akaya rested her hand on my shoulder. My heartbeat quickened, though it was clearly more of a reassuring touch.

'Take no heed of the captain,' she said. 'He's unpredictable when he drinks.'

I recalled the fearsome look in his eyes as he told me to leave.

'Why don't you stop him?'

'It's not our place,' Brongrim answered, moving closer along with Gurdgrin and Wargal. 'He's the captain, and we are his crew. That's just how it is.'

'He needs it,' Wargal added. 'To soothe the pain.'

All seemed grim.

'What pain?' I enquired.

'Oh poor lad,' Gurdgrin grimaced. 'You have not felt it yet then? The guilt.'

'What guilt?'

'The guilt of killing of course,' Akaya spat. 'Don't you think of the men you took down in Cranwell, or the mercenaries from yesterday? About their families, or their lives outside of the combat?'

Seven, I've killed or helped kill seven.

'Not particularly,' I answered honestly for the most part but with a hint of doubt. 'In both situations they came at me. I was keeping myself alive.'

I believed what I said but the fact that I kept count meant that I was not entirely okay with it.

'Perhaps the lad is a better pirate than us all,' Gurdgrin chuckled, however his voice was level and stale.

I was given a new bundle of clothes and instructed to change, though did not know why. I came back to the deck to find everyone dressed differently. Akaya wore a long maiden's dress and a headscarf, while I and the men each adorned a collared shirt with dark trousers. They gave me sword in the sheath, simple steel, nothing fancy. Everyone also discarded their normal weapons in place of the less conspicuous steel.

The city came clearly into view, though as we approached dozens of guards readied arrows at us. They allowed us to drop anchor and dock, although as the nine of us strode onto the pier we were surrounded. Archers closed in from our left and right, and a line of guards with unsheathed blades blocked our path. These were not the guards from Cranwell, that was for certain. All wore plate mail with chainmail trimmings (rich purple and jet black) and in place of flimsy rapiers they wielded hefty broadswords.

One stepped forward, his armour a shining azure which contrasted with his followers. 'I am Captain Harzenkar, commander of the ocean guard of Merrywood – please state your business.'

'Follow our lead,' Korhal whispered to me before moving to meet him. 'Greetings righteous captain, we are humble travellers on our way to Galdamesh to seek our fortune. We simply wish to stop here to gather supplies and drop in on some old friends. We would be most grateful for your passage, and we promise to be gone by the morrow.'

'And why I pray do you carry weapons, if you are but humble travellers as you say?' Harzenkar countered.

Akaya bowed her head low. 'My lord, the seas are rough and awash with ruffians. Hear, only last night our ship was damaged. See the port bow there? A pirate ship nonetheless – they came out of the black of night and crashed into us. A second more and they might have boarded.'

Her eyes teared as if the illusion were real. She made a decent damsel-in-distress, though I much preferred her aggressive charm.

'Calm your woman,' the captain called. 'You can pass, but I must demand you leave your swords here. Merrywood is not as violent as the open sea, and I doubt you will have a need to shed blood during your stay.'

'Thank you my lord,' Korhal said as Wes dramatically put his hands on Akaya's shoulders to calm her.

The guards stripped us of our swords, archers still at the ready until we were all unarmed.

'Enjoy your stay,' the captain said, and within minutes we were deep into the city.

Everything here seemed cleaner; the pavements were white and near stainless. The people looked better too, less scrawny and more finely dressed. All outfits appeared to be hand-tailored to the individual, and a few even wore silk. They smelled better too, perfume wafting through the streets as they passed by. Despite being so close to Cranwell, it seemed warmer here, and it reflected on the tanned faces of the locals.

'What about when Daxon decides to join us?' Mamorhah asked. 'Won't he be surprised by the level of armed guards?'

'Let him be surprised,' Wes scoffed. 'Let's just hope he sobers up by then.'

As we descended through some backstreets I saw the ugly s de of Merrywood – dozens of men and women lying on the un-pathed roads; dressed in rags, smeared in dirt and calling out weakly to us to ask for money. The crew walked on by and I followed their lead, trying not to pay attention to the abundant poverty.

We had some places like this in Cranwell, but it was nowhere near as bad. Another side street exposed a group of white citizens – half a dozen of them – kicking a black man and yelling out racial slurs like *'mongrel'* and *'black demon'*. I wanted to interfere, and I clenched my fist. Wargal's hand grasped at my arm.

'Not a good idea lad,' he told me. 'It's not our fight.'

He was speaking softly enough that the others could not hear.

'It's wrong,' I told him, 'And we can do something about it.'

His sympathetic eyes found mine.

'I know lad, but it'll attract too much attention. The mission comes first.'

I begrudgingly nodded and allowed him to lead me away with the others.

We moved back onto the main streets as we approached the town square. There were fewer stalls than in Cranwell and more actual shops. More guards patrolled the streets, all much more well-built and kept than back home.

'I can't believe that man,' Akaya was saying. '*"Calm your woman"* by the maker, if I've ever wanted to punch someone so badly.'

'Security has definitely gone up in this place,' Gurdgrin muttered. 'Shame.'

I pushed the earlier incident from my mind to marvel at the beauty of the square, from the fabulous stone structures to the bustle of trade. In comparison Cranwell's was utter dirt.

'Right,' Wes said as we reached the main square, where all of the main shops faced in towards a statue of an unknown man. 'We should split up to gather supplies.'

'I'll get some food.' Akaya offered. 'Though I'll need some help carrying it.'

Mamorhah volunteered his services, already sniffing out where the best food was.

'And I'll get the mead!' Gurdgrin hollered.

'Okay,' Wes agreed. 'But take Brongrim with you, otherwise we'll be out of coin by the afternoon. We need someone to talk to a ship maker about getting the port fixed up.'

'I'm a good negotiator,' Varen chimed in. 'But I'd have someone come with me to make sure they don't rip me off.'

Wargal offered to go with him. That left me with Korhal and Wes, though they failed to explain what we would do. Everyone agreed to reconvene back at the square in an hour, and with that all but the three of us went off.

'What's our job?' I asked.

'Walk with us Yodrick,' Korhal instructed. 'We need to chat.'

As I complied I felt my stomach churning. We took a route down a narrow alleyway, away from the prying eyes of the locals.

'We know you heard us last night birdie,' Wes said outright.

'I...I don't know...'

'Cut the crap!' Korhal interjected. 'We heard you outside the door.

'What we don't know is how much you heard, which is why we're here. So, you better answer honestly.'

Do I lie? Do I tell the truth? Lord, I wonder what they'll do to me.

'Everyone thinks Daxon is losing his touch, at least I think that was the point of it.'

'Aye,' Wes said gruffly. 'What else did you hear?'

'The captain is angry at you,' I murmured. 'For taking me onto the mercenary ship. Because I got hurt.'

'It seems that way,' Korhal sighed. 'So how about you tell us why that is? Why does the great pirate captain Daxon care about a runt like you from a washed up place like Cranwell?'

'I don't know.' I admitted.

Within a moment Korhal unsheathed a hidden knife and had it directed at me. I raised my hands in defence.

'I don't know anything, I swear.'

'I think he's telling the truth,' Wes interjected, lowering his ally's arm.

'I don't know why Daxon took an interest in me,' I continued. 'I was surprised when the lot of you took me on board rather than killing me. By the maker, like any kid growing up in Cranwell I was terrified of Daxon most of my life. We used to tell ghost stories about how he came in the dead of night to kill us children.'

'And yet you seem exceptionally un-frightened by him now,' Wes called out.

I shrugged. 'Like all childhood fears, you get over it. After all he's just a man – a dangerous man no doubt, but still a man. I figured out when I was young the worst thing anyone could do to me was kill me, and even the guards tried that a fair few times. I have no reason to be afraid.'

Both men turned away and muttered to one another before nodding, Korhal taking me by the shoulder – his green unkempt hair practically in my face.

'We'll take your word for all of this,' he said, lifting his knife towards me once more. 'But speak a word of this to the captain and we'll make sure it's your last. Understand?'

I nodded.

After our *lovely* chat the three of us still had plenty of time. The two talked about the next step in the day's plans (all of it going over my head) and Korhal ran off to *set things up* as he said. Wes kept me close, his gaze flicking to me every second as I shadowed him.

He led me into a blacksmith's shop of some kind, where finely made weapons covered the walls and stands – all proudly on display. The collection ranged from longbows to war-hammers to stilettos and everything in between. Out back behind the counter was as an empty doorway, from which a fierce red glow shone and illuminated half of the building. Noise rang out from the room as steel clashed against steel, always for a few chimes at a time followed by a muffed hissing sound.

'Anything take your fancy?' Wes enquired. 'I know you've only had one morning of training and haven't tried out all fighting styles, but you don't seem entirely useless with a sword.'

'I'm not sure,' I told him, my gaze quickly shifting from his face. 'I didn't mind the archery training, but I'm nowhere near good enough to fight that way.'

'I like the modesty,' Wes chuckled. 'It takes years of training to become a good archer, and Brongrim is one of the best. If you've noticed, we all try to use different fighting styles – that's no accident. We want to have all of our bases covered.'

I nodded along, looking over the fine craftsmanship of the deadly tools. *Where exactly would I fit in? I'm better with a sword than anything else, but half of the crew already use swords so much better than I.* The chiming stopped and a man came to the counter. He was shirtless, with rippling muscles spanning his entire body and sweaty from the heat of forging.

'Oh, sorry,' he hollered. 'I didn't hear you come in. What can I do for you fine folk?' Wes strode forward, pulling out a purse of coins and throwing them on the counter. 'My young friend here would like to purchase a weapon,' he chimed.

Was he truly buying me one? The smith glanced over me sceptically.

'Well, as you see I have plenty of daggers for self-defence, and if...'

'No,' Wes cut him off. 'I was thinking something a little...bigger.'

The large man groaned and shook his head in disappointment. 'I'm afraid I can't. New laws say I can only sell my more combat-based stuff to the guards, and they all get their swords from the Jarl anyway. Business is tough these days.'

Despite this, Wes's smirk remained. 'Would you be willing to perhaps bend the rules just this once?' he sneered, tossing another handful of coins onto the counter. The smith's eyes widened at the sight of gold.

'What kind of weapon were you thinking?' the shop owner asked me.

I glanced around, not seeing too much of interest. Wes said a few things to him, and he disappeared back into the back. When he came out again it was with a selection of weapons. He urged me to try them all out, and I glanced over them. The first was a war-hammer which I could barely lift for the weight, let alone swing. Next was a mace, though it felt too bulky and did not have much reach. The hatchet I disregarded, remembering my terrible aim back on the ship, though next to it was a larger axe.

The wooden handle was about four feet and thin enough for me to comfortably wrap my hands around it. The wood itself was dark – perhaps mahogany – glossed to a perfect shine, and coiled with a thin layer of steel. The blade was wide and curved which made me think it would be heavy, but as I lifted it I realised I held it with no more difficulty than a sword. I tried it in cne hand which was tricky due to the extra metal on the haft and my still-throbbing hand but it was wieldable and easily so with two.

'What do you think?' Wes tried me, seemingly noticing the glint in my eye.

'It's much lighter than I thought,' I commented.

'Indeed,' the smith agreed. 'I added the iron for stability, but it's light enough. And the steel is thin but sharp. You might not fell any trees with that thing – and to be honest you'd be a fool to try – but it'll cut through any armour, even plate-mail.'

I gave it a light swing. It rushed through the air easily enough, and while it had no spike on its other side as I had seen in some cases, I could turn it quickly by simply adjusting my grip. Additionally, the long handle would make for a decent defence.

'You like it?' Wes pressed, something sinister in his expression which I disregarded.

'I do,' I told them both.

'In that case we'll take it,' my ally chirped.

The smith grinned and snatched up the coin, beginning to wrap the head in a thick cloth. As he handed it over he warned to be wary around the guards, and if we got caught not to rat him out. Wes promised for both of us and we bade farewell to the smith, with him calling out to remind me to be careful handling it – I could understand why.

With the blade exposed, it would be a hazard if I were anything but vigilant at all times. Additionally, there was no easy way to carry it aside from carefully holding it at the top and using it like a large cane. In my common garbs the guards turned a blind eye to me, never giving as much as a second glance – that meant I was safe, for now at least.

We all met up again at the square. Several of the crew eyed me curiously, their gaze shifting between Wes, Korhal and I. *So they were all in on it.* Everyone recounted their success, with Wes telling the others of my new weapon of choice. Both Korhal and Akaya turned to me curiously, or perhaps simply examining the weapon. What came across strangest of all was the widening of Varen's unseeing eyes at the news. Luckily we swiftly moved on from the topic of myself, and Korhal lead the conversation.

'I managed to secure a meeting with our contact,' he said, more to the others than to me. 'He says he has news on Farrow.'

'We should go right away,' Wargal said.

'Not without Daxon,' Akaya debated.

'Leave him,' Wes encouraged. 'He's completely content staying on the ship and drinking himself into a stupor.'

'He'd want to be here for this!' she growled. 'You should understand more than anyone.'

Their eyes locked intensely, Akaya cracking her knuckles and Wes's hand drifting towards a dagger at his hip.

'Stop!' a voice cried.

It was not until everyone was looking at me that I realised it was mine. Their gazes all bore into me expectantly. 'I don't completely understand this whole thing about Daxon, but it's irrelevant,' I reminded them. 'No matter your problems with him, he's our captain, but regardless you shouldn't be at each other's throats over this.'

Silence ensued and I thought all would turn on me, until Varen stepped forward. 'The boy speaks wisely,' he said to everyone. 'The Iron Stallion is not a crew of villains and thugs; we have a code. We do not shed the blood of our own, so both of you step down!'

Akaya's fists unclenched, though Wes remained unmoving.

'With respect Varen, I think we both know that us speaking of codes and honour is hypocritical.'

My expression was reflected in the faces of some of the crew – confusion. Varen was taken aback, while Akaya and Korhal simply stood there stiffly with faces of stone.

'If you want him here, the two of you can go and get him.'

With that Wes turned away from the others and paced rapidly. Korhal murmured a few things to Akaya and Varen and they disappeared into the city streets.

'Well, what are we waiting for?' Korhal said flatly. 'Let's get going.'

Tension was high, though we all followed Korhal to the apparent meeting spot. It was an old, abandoned temple, detached from the rest of the city. He knocked twice, once, then three more times. Nothing. He repeated the knock. Nothing again. Mamorhah sniffed at the air like I had seen him do before.

'Something isn't…'

But before Mamorhah could even finish his thought, the ring of steel being unsheathed made its way into the air. We spun around, only to be met with at least twenty Merrywood guards.

'Well, looks like ol' Yakal's information was spot on,' one laughed.

'We've been tricked, it's an ambush!' Korhal cried.

Fuck!

Chapter 6

Eadoin

The swords were drawn, the few archers amongst their ranks aimed their arrows at us, and an overwhelming sense of doom descended over the group – or at least over me.

'You're outnumbered three to one,' a guard called. 'Surrender now and my men will grant you a quick death.'

'No chance!' Wargal spat.

'Please little man,' the same guard berated. 'You don't even have weapons, what can you…'

The man dropped dead with a knife in his throat before he could finish, I had not even seen Wargal grab for it but already he had another blade in each hand. Where he was hiding them I had no idea. The others drew their side arms as the archers released their arrows. One struck the shorter pirate, piercing into his leg. He clenched his teeth but still loosed another knife into an archer's eye.

My allies charged forward and I remembered I had an actual weapon with me. I threw off the cloth, revealing the wide curved blade of my axe and taking up its hilt with both hands. I charged alongside my allies, the warm flush of adrenaline taking hold of me.

I swung the mighty weapon at the neck of the nearest guarc, the blade cutting through the chainmail and sinking into the flesh enough to pierce something vital. Blood sprayed and the man began to choke, though managed a weak thrust of his sword which pierced my side before he toppled to the ground. The weapon's balance was still new to me – I should have been able to take his head clean off.

Another pain erupted in my shoulder and I turned to an archer who was already knocking another arrow to his bow. I clumsily threw the blade of the axe in the way and by some miracle deflected it. His eyes widened as I began my stride towards him, but seconds later was slain by a savage slice to the throat from Gurdgrin. Wargal was down, hit by two more arrows – one to his other leg and one to his chest. The others were deep in the heat of battle, having managed to take down their four archers first and narrowing in for close combat.

Knives and daggers clashed with broadswords in a fight which should have been over before it started, but the crew were fearless. I stood away from the main bulk of the fighting to avoid being flanked, giving me plenty of space to wave around the lengthy battle-axe and stopping any further threat to the groaning Wargal. With clumsy blows I managed to fend off the next two guards who came at me, spinning my axe around with little direction or strategy. I managed a strong downwards thrust into the shoulder plate of my next attacked; as I pulled the weapon back it sliced through his flesh as easily as a sword would. My arms ached and the shock damage to my hands with each blow was intense, though the haft stayed sturdy with the iron reinforcement.

Amongst the mess of bodies, Brongrim was on his knees. I felt my grip tighten, though my legs stayed fixed in place. I glanced back to Wargal. His eyes were on me. He said nothing, but gave me a firm nod. I nodded in return and charged into the mass. One hefty side swing staggered two guards enough to let me into the midst of the fight. I heard their armoured bodies clatter to the ground behind me, not bothering to look back. I went straight for Brongrim who still had dagger in hand, slashing aimlessly at the legs of our foes. I grabbed his shoulder with one hand, hefting up my axe with the other as I pulled him to his feet. He staggered, a gaping wound in his left thigh.

I threw his arm over my shoulder, using the weapon to support myself under the weight as I struggled out of the pit.

I threw him down next to a fallen archer where he picked up the discarded weapon and went to work, stopping to give me a smile and a quick, 'Thank you.'

I stepped back into the onslaught, cutting down another two guards who Gurdgrin finished off. He was bloody. We all were. I soon realised I had over-extended as enemies closed in around me. I tried to turn, but could not keep my eyes on all. As I blocked an attack from the front I felt a sword sliding into my back. Wooziness overtook me and I staggered, my surroundings becoming only shapes and sounds. I collapsed, my gaze unable to shift from the approaching newcomers who I could not make out.

Shouting. The clash of steel on steel. A glowing light. *Was it over?* I never fully passed out, or at least I do not think I did. Which meant that after the noise stopped, I felt every second of somebody stitching up my back. It was utter agony, but I could not do so much as cry out. It kept going, lasting seemingly forever. I felt someone lifting me, then nothing.

When I fully came to, I was indoors. I did not know where, and my neck refused to respond to my command. Opposite me, Mamorhah's hulking figure sat, his attention distracted. I was sitting also, but as I tried to renew contact with my body a mind-shattering pain erupted and I cried out.

'So you're alive,' Mamorhah muttered. 'Didn't think you had it in you.'

He stood and closed the distance between us.

'Wh…where are we?' I groaned.

'We took refuge inside the temple,' he said. 'Daxon says I'm supposed to make you take it easy.'

'Daxon?'

'He showed up with Varen and Akaya just as we were on the edge of defeat – they won the battle for us.' I tried my hardest to move despite the pain, but all I accomplished was a shuffle in my seat. 'Don't!' the pirate scolded, 'You're lucky you weren't paralysed – in time all of your wounds will heal but for now you need to build your strength.'

Some of the crew were around us. Akaya was sharpening a knife, Wes was hunched over with head in hands.

'Did anyone else get hurt.'

'Yup,' he said bluntly, pausing for a second as his eyes rolled. 'Wargal is dead.'

My strained fist clenched, sending a shooting pain up my arm. 'I should've stayed to protect him,' I muttered, a small tear coming to my eye.

'Don't beat yourself up kid, we might have lost more if you hadn't charged in – Brongrim for example.'

'How is he?' I questioned.

'Well he's living out the pirate stereotype, soon he'll have both an eyepatch *and* a peg leg.'

'He lost it?'

The large man nodded. 'We saw the wound, knew it wouldn't heal. We had to cut it off.'

Korhal appeared before us.

'How is he?' the green-haired pirate enquired.

'Better than most,' Mamorhah answered.

I noticed his empty hanging sleeve.

'Your arm?' I said, more as a statement than an actual question.

Korhal nodded and rolled up the sleeve to where there was a newly-stitched stump above where the elbow had been. 'It's not too bad,' he told me. 'I only need one arm to wield my machete – saying that, I'll have to get used to fighting with my left.'

'Who else got hurt?'

'Daxon has a lovely new scar on his back, Wes and I are each missing a few fingers, and Gurdgrin got some pretty bad cuts practically everywhere on his body,' Mamorhah said.

'Akaya and Varen got away fine,' Korhal added. 'Lucky bastards.'

Despite their protests I pushed myself to my feet, my legs shaking violently under the weight. My hand traced around the new cut on my back still fresh and bloody. Everyone aside Daxon was here. In the corner of the great temple hall Varen kneeled over a figure.

'Sit down lad!' Mamorhah demanded.

'I want to see him.'

His face reddened, but a deep sigh reassured me. He stooped down so I could swing my arm over him for support, and he helped me towards Wargal. Varen was cleaning him, several broken arrowheads on the floor beside them. His eyes were closed, and his once tough face now seemed solemn. His arms were crossed over his chest, a knife in each hand. I wiped away another tear.

'I...I don't know why I'm so upset,' I whispered.

Varen rested a hand on my shoulder as I kneeled down painfully. 'It is one thing to look upon a dead enemy,' he spoke. 'But it is something very different to look upon a dead friend. It is times like these that I don't envy your sight, for I doubt I could bare to see what you see now.'

'I hardly knew him,' I admitted. 'But he seemed like a good man.'

'He was.'

Daxon burst in through the entrance, a rope in his hand. As he pulled it, another figure was thrust into view. The rope was around his neck and a sack was over his head. I heard crying. The captain kicked his captive to the ground.

'This him?' Wes called from across the room.

Daxon nodded. We all approached. Daxon ripped the sack off, a crying old man beneath it. He was scruffy, his hair and beard both wispy and knotted, black with grease.

'Yakal!' Korhal grunted. 'Fancy seeing you twice in one day.'

'Please don't kill me,' Yakal pleaded. 'I didn't mean to...'

'Our faithful contact,' Wes cut in. 'Selling us out to the guards like we're a gang or ruffian miscreants or simple thugs.'

'I had to!' he cried. 'They would've thrown me in prison if I didn't.'

Varen stepped forward and hoisted him up by the throat. I staggered back, as did most of the others. 'My friend is lying in the corner dead,' the older pirate grunted. 'All because of you, and what you did!'

His grip tightened and Yakal began to choke, gasping for air.

'Enough Varen,' Daxon muttered. 'We still need him.'

The blind man obliged and threw him to the floor, giving him a swift kick to the rips before he backed away. Daxon knelt down.

'Farrow Bloodneck – what's he up to?'

'I don't know,' the filthy man sobbed.

'Well then you are of no use to me.'

Daxon reached for his blade.

'No, wait,' the scoundrel cried. 'There is something I *do* know!'

'Out with it.'

'The word is he's using mercenaries to take down all other pirate crews.'

'Why?' Daxon demanded.

'Something about finding the other weapons. What's the word he used? Umm... that's right – Elder Blades.'

Daxon's eyes widened, his arm shaking and twitching as it rested on his hilt.

'You're sure?'

'That's what I heard,' he said. 'Not sure what one is, I've never heard of them before. But apparently he has one and wants the others.'

'That makes no sense,' Daxon stammered.

'It's what I heard. That's everything. So how about we forget this ever happened?'

'Not likely.'

Daxon drew his blade as Yakal cowered, but Wes stepped forward.

'I think you should let the boy handle this one,' the rat-like man said.

All eyes were on me.

'Why?' the captain asked, the earlier fire gone from his eyes.

He seemed sober, standing upright with an expression of stone.

'He cut down a quarter of the guards himself, and grounded at least three more. Plus, he's the only reason Brongrim is still alive.'

'Wes tells the truth,' the crippled archer agreed.

'So be it,' the captain said, turning away.

Wes fetched my weapon for me. I could still hardly move, and even holding the axe was a burden. I crossed eyes with Daxon who was staring intently – not at the scene before him but at me. Somebody pulled Yakal to his feet and handed him a sword.

'We take no prisoners,' Korhal recited, echoing the words he had given to Daxon the first night we met. 'Nor do we slaughter a man on his knees. This is our way.'

My opponent timidly strode towards me. I stayed my ground, knowing it was a bad idea to move too much. He leapt into a sprint, closing the gap in less than a second. I turned the handle of the axe and deflected the steel of his sword with iron. He staggered back, and I took my chance to step up and swing down the curved blade into his shoulder. I pulled it back and, in a fluid sideward motion, hacked into his neck. His lifeless body fell to the ground.

'He died how he lived,' Daxon grumbled. 'Pathetic.'

'What now?' I asked, keeping myself upright by leaning heavily on the axe, but feeling as if I would topple any second.

'We have what we needed here. We bury Wargal and we head back to the ship.'

Out around the back of the temple was a small field, a few graves already there – clearly long abandoned by any outsiders. We found a nice patch, away from the others. Wes got a shovel from…somewhere, and we all took turns digging up the ground. Brongrim hobbled around supported by Gurdgrin, his left leg cut off at the knee – still he and Korhal took their turns digging to honour our fallen ally. I almost dropped the shovel during my turn, my back in a spasm, but not once did I allow myself to let out a sound. It was Varen who lay down the short pirate's body into the hole and Daxon who buried him.

'I wish we had a coffin for him,' Gurdgrin sighed, evoking nods from the others.

'Wouldn't it have been more fitting to bury him at sea?' I asked.

'It's not our way,' Korhal answered. 'Most pirate crews do, but not the Iron Stallion. For us we believe our lives are lived at sea, constantly going from land to land with no real home. So when we die we return to the land, our journey over at last.'

'That's nice,' I said with a warm smile. 'My father…'

'Yeah?' Korhal pressed, all eyes on me.

'Well, he died at sea.'

'Is that so?' Wes said, stroking the stubble at his chin with the stumps of his missing fingers.

'Yeah,' I sighed. 'He was a sea-merchant. Died in a storm. We never got his body back.'

'I'm sorry Yodrick,' Akaya whispered, her hand soothingly rubbing my arm. 'That's terrible. How come you never mentioned it?'

'You never asked. And honestly I haven't told that story in…a long time.'

Korhal was giving Wes a look, and a strange one at that. A chill went down my spine despite the sun beating down on us. Our attention was turned away by Daxon dropping the shovel, the job done.

'Who wants to say some words?' Daxon asked.

Varen unsurprisingly led the charge, his fondness for the short pirate obvious by how he tended to his body in the temple.

'It was seven years ago when Daxon sent me out to recruit some new talent for the Stallion; I travelled from city to city in search of someone extraordinary. Now I came across some great fighters, don't get me wrong, but none stood out as being a good fit.

'It was in Gillia I saw him – I still had one good eye then you see. He was in a pit-fight, outmatched by a dozen men taller and stronger than him. He played the situation tactically, armed with only a single knife.

'He cut at their legs, he slashed at them when they weren't looking, and all without drawing too much attention – though he certainly had mine. When the bodies started stacking up, it came down to him and some bulking brute with a great-sword. He didn't stand a chance. But I watched him launch that knife, with more confidence than I'd ever seen in a man.

'He missed! The Wargal you all know today was actually a terrible shot back when I met him, in fact his throw was so bad it almost took out a spectator. So of course this brute knocked him to the ground, but before he could finish him I jumped down and stopped the fight. Wargal was so thrilled at being saved he joined the crew as soon as I offered. Maker rest his soul.'

The others stepped up too, all sharing their favourite memories with the pirate. Gurdgrin's was about the time they managed to get an entire guard squad drunk. Wes's was about how they once stole a ship together, just the two of them. The stories went on. I was laughing at some of them, we all were. I felt as if I knew the man after a while, and was thankful for it. It came to me.

'I obviously didn't know Wargal long, but he certainly made an impression,' I started, showing my still-scarred hand from our training session and getting a few laughs. 'So I'll share a memory from earlier today. When the fight started he made the first move and as you all know he got a few arrows in him because of it. I stayed back from the fight, doing my best to keep the guards away from him. But when I saw Brongrim on his knees, I didn't know what to do.

'When I glanced back he clearly knew what I was thinking and he gave me a simple nod, encouraging me to leave him to save his ally. Even on his knees, he was willing to sacrifice himself for someone else. That's all I have to say.'

Brongrim was smiling at me, the others nodding along with closed fists against their chests. Daxon stepped up, the only one who hadn't spoken.

'Well put lad,' he said, moving into everyone's view. 'As pirates we rarely use last names – it keeps us safe and protects any family we might have back home. But I knew Wargal's. I don't know if it was because he was drunk that night or because he trusted me, but he told me it all the same. It was Eadoin. Wargal Eadoin. In Gillia where he's from, the name means friend. Not warrior, not sailor, but friend. It suits him well. If I didn't know anything else about Wargal, that would be enough. But he was also brave, intelligent, and one of the strongest men I've ever met. So rest well – friend.' We all bowed our heads and had a moment of silence to honour our fallen ally. 'With that I think we're done, so let us head back to the ship and be away from this awful city.'

'What about the sea-guard?' Mamorhah questioned.

'We took care of them.'

And that they had. When we got back to the pier, dozens of dead guards lined the way to the ship. Harzenkar was there and Akaya could not resist the temptation to give him a quick kick as we passed.

We drank that night. Everyone told more stories as we ate until our stomachs were full while washing it down with fresh mead. Brongrim sat beside me, constantly making it clear how thankful he was to me for saving him. Somewhere between the fourth and fifth rounds of mead he handed me something. Resting in my palm was an arrowhead.

'It's the one I used for my first kill,' he told me. 'I hadn't eaten in a week, but while hunting I saw this rabbit. I shot at it, but the arrow flew high and missed. By a hundred to one chance it flew between the trees and hit a deer right in the eye. Consider it a thank you for saving me.'

'Brongrim, I can't…'

'Take it,' he cut me off. 'For luck.'

I smiled and slipped the arrowhead into my pocket, and that was that.

I retired earlier than most, for Daxon promised me that tomorrow he would personally show me how to use that axe.

Oh goodie.

Chapter 7

The Black Book

Morning came, and I threw myself out of bed at the first light of dawn. My body ached much less, though I still had trouble bending certain ways. I had hoped for a few days of recuperation, but that had been optimistic. My axe was propped against the bedside wall for easy access; with it in hand I rushed to the main deck where Daxon stood waiting. He held an axe of his own, far less decorated than mine but sturdy all the same.

'Are you ready?' he asked with a cold, calculated expression as I approached.

'Let's do it,' I affirmed.

'As you may have started to gather, you must use an axe differently to how you use a sword.' I nodded. 'However, you can slice like a sword as easily if not more-so with an axe. Hacking is all well and good but most sharp axes can cut through armour, so keeping them sharp is a good idea.'

'And how do I do that?'

'There is a grindstone far below deck – I imagine you will spend a fair amount of time there honing your blade.'

Daxon grabbed the haft with both hands and held his weapon sideways. With a nod he urged me to copy him.

'Long weapons like this require two hands to wield properly, so you are quite locked down. Learn to use the hilt to block.'

Without warning he swung at me. I clumsily raised my axe but closed my eyes, and a second later it clattered to the floor.

'Awful,' he berated as I retrieved the weapon, 'Again!'

The second time I kept my eyes on his attack, but his swing was too strong for me to keep hold of the haft. The third time I blocked it successfully, but when he tried a second swing from a different angle I could not change stance quickly enough.

'This is hopeless!' Daxon spat. 'You'll never be good with that axe, might as well give up now.'

The captain began to walk away.

'No!' I cried after him, he turned back with a raised brow. 'I managed to kill those guards didn't I?'

'A stroke of luck,' he countered. 'If you were actually a decent fighter you wouldn't have allowed yourself to be stabbed despite having such a powerful weapon at your disposal.'

'They surrounded me!' I argued.

He dropped the weapon and strode towards me, cracking his knuckles. I squared up to him, though those terrifying eyes bore into me. A quick kick to the shin sent me toppling as he swiftly disarmed me. I managed to retain my balance, but a new pain erupted through my cheek and I fell. It was the second time he had ever struck me.

'You want to know what to do when you're surrounded?' he snapped. 'I'll show you.'

He gave a quick call to Wes and within minutes most of the crew were around us. Akaya steered the ship and Korhal was up in the crow's nest but all others were front and centre.

'Our young boy here reckons there was nothing he could have done yesterday once he was surrounded, I need help to prove him wrong,' Daxon explained.

'Cut the kid some slack,' Wes petitioned. 'He did good yesterday.'

'*Good* does not cut it. For the most part he was the only one with a decent weapon there, he should have slain twice as many guards with that thing.'

He had me step back as everyone was organised into a circle around him, all with weapons drawn. He stood in the centre with his less glamorous axe and closed his eyes, breathing.

'Don't go easy!' he instructed the others.

On his command they charged in. Brongrim stood back and fired an arrow, still a little unbalanced by the wooden stump which replaced his leg. The captain ducked beneath it and struck his first attacker – Gurdgrin – who was coming at him with hatchets raised. He hit him hard in the chest with the back end of the haft while spinning around to swing the deadly steel straight into Wes's sword. A split second later he ducked Varen's long blade. As they all closed in he rose back up, striking the flat of the blade into Wes's head as he spun the mighty weapon around with both hands and knocked everyone back.

Mamorhah, who had been standing back, took this opportunity to dive in with his duel blades. They were both aimed at different points, yet both hit nothing but wood as Daxon twirled his guard deflecting both. An arrow soared as Brongrim got his second clear shot, but even as it was loosed Daxon ducked, slicing up with the axe blade and cutting the arrow in half mid-flight. He charged at the archer, multiple arrows released at him in quick succession but all blocked either by the haft or the flat of the axe. He smacked the bow from Brongrim's grip and knocked him down with a swift kick to his good leg.

All others rushed to surround him, though no attacks prevailed. Even when they all charged in at once, Daxon kept on turning and shifting his guard to block every attack. Never did he spill a drop of blood, nor did he try to – he simply knocked them all down over and over again until they had had enough.

'Despite what you just saw, this is a highly trained crew,' Daxon barked at me. 'One of the best in fact. But a good axe-wielder can take on ary number of enemies. The length and versatility of your weapon is its best attribute, never forget.'

'Where did you learn to fight like that?' was all I could say.

He glanced at me, pulling lips back over clenched teeth. 'From an old friend,' he sighed. 'Now it's your turn.'

'What?'

'Go easy on him lads.'

With those words he left, as the crew surrounded me. I lifted my weapon trembling and prepared for the worst.

I was black and blue by the end of it, countless cuts across my body gave me a similar appearance to Gurdgrin. Daxon's initial schedule for me was replaced with one of constant axe fighting – though as in his original plan that night I met up with Varen in his quarters as he began to run me through my letters. His quarters puzzled me, filled to the brim with books and parchments and writing implements which surely would be of no use to him. Little else could be found in the room.

The blind man was patient at least, as well as sympathetic to my pain – after all a great deal of it was from him. He would write down letters and make me copy them, telling me which each one was and what sound it made. Obviously he could not judge my own writing, which I was grateful for as it was scratchy and messy compared to his.

I picked up the start of it quickly, remembering the basics from when I was young, though struggled on the rules. I spoke each word carefully, breaking it down into the sounds and trying my best to write down the letters correctly. He maintained it did not matter, as long as somebody knew what it meant. Hours ticked over doing this, until my hand shook simply from holding the quill for so long.

'We can stop for a while if you wish,' Varen suggested, clearly sensing my discomfort.

'Yes please.'

I dropped the quill and stretched out my palm, cracking each of my fingers.

'I apologise again that you had to endure such pain this morning, especially after yesterday, but we were all following orders,' Varen explained.

'It's okay,' I eased him. 'Can I ask you something?'

'I'd be worried if you didn't,' he chimed, grinning. 'Questions allow us to obtain knowledge, and knowledge is key.'

'It's about Daxon.'

'Oh?'

'I was just wondering; why does he carry a sword if he's so skilled with an axe?' I enquired.

'An old friend of his always carried an axe,' the man said simply.

'The one who taught him to fight like that?' I pressed.

The old man nodded. 'They were close. I suppose the captain never wanted to tarnish his memory by using the same weapon he used.'

'His memory?' I pondered. 'Is he dead?'

The old pirate's face loosened, his lips pulling into a thin line. 'I'm afraid so.'

'What happened?'

'Murdered.'

He said the word so bluntly that my body shook a little.

'By who?' I pressed.

'I would answer but I believe I only agreed to answer one question and you seem to have had more than your fair share.'

The response was snappy, and I did not expect it. Silence descended on us until eventually we carried on with my studies. We went for an hour more, calling it a night after that. I returned to my quarters and thought hard about everything. So many things made me question what was happening – it seemed everyone knew something I did not, which was to be expected of course but it still unsettled me. What was more, some members of the crew appeared to know more than others – Varen being one of the former. It was all very suspicious indeed.

The next morning, I trained with Korhal instead of Daxon, though he was just as ruthless. Even with his left hand he was deadly with that machete and it almost took my head off more than once. We went for hours until we were both sweating, but while I was covered it cuts and bruises he had only a scratch or two. I needed to get faster. I ate lunch on the go while swabbing the deck, almost thankful for the hot, soapy water on my battered hands. While working I got a good view of Wes and

Akaya sparring up towards the bow. It was hand to hand, and while Wes was quick and sneaky he was nothing compared to our female ally. It brought a smile to my face as she seemed to glow in the midday sun.

By the time the main deck was clean it was time for dinner which I ate with the others in the banquet hall. I drank mead like the rest and dined on the same food as everyone else, listening to Wes's crude jokes and watching Gurdgrin get hammered. While I rarely spoke unless spoken to, I felt involved. Again I reported to Varen as we carried on with my writing, but this time he gave me no leeway for asking questions of Daxon, so instead I spent our breaks finding out all I could about the others – where they were from, how they joined the crew.

Wes was from Okonia which explained his fighting style, it was known as the city of rogues and rodents. Akaya was of course from the land furthest away, in the Kingdom of Akrul – not ruled by our king nor governed by the laws of Issehai. Brongrim and Gurdgrin were cousins which despite the names I never would have guessed. When I thought about it they did have similar features, and both were from the snow-ridden lands of Saransa to the far north which explained the complexion.

And so began what came to be my routine. Each morning I would train with a different member of the crew, eat lunch while cleaning the deck, – occasionally also helping to open and close the masts while we sailed – eat dinner with the crew, and study with Varen before going to sleep. In all of this time I rarely saw Daxon. He was never on the main deck and he took almost all of his meals in his quarters. When he *was* around, he treated me with disregard and turned his nose up. Any free time I got was spent sharpening my axe and polishing it to a fine shine, only to be dirtied the next morning while fighting with the crew.

After a week of sailing I was feeling a little seasick, so was thrilled when land finally came into view. However, it was Daxon, Korhal, Wes, Akaya and Varen who took to the city of Gulderneck; leaving me on the ship with Brongrim, Gurdgrin and Mamorhah. I pressed to go, but Daxon would not even give me the time of day. So off they went, leaving me to simply carry out my daily routine. Brongrim was good company at least. After I saved him in the battle we had developed a sort of friendship. He would often keep me company while I carried out my chores, and during our training sessions he went easy on me.

On this occasion however he had too much to do, which left me to my own devices once my work was done.

I scoured the ship in search of distraction but soon found myself having explored the entirety of the Stallion and still being left with nothing. As I was beginning to give up I noticed something unusual in the armoury. In the back corner – a place where nobody would naturally look – the wall seemed different. I moved over to it, tracing my fingers along the point where it changed. I tapped lightly and quickly noticed a section was hollow.

As I kneeled to examine it more closely, I spotted a keyhole. It was the kind of thing nobody would notice unless they were looking for it, but there it was. The surge of adventure grasped me, and I was immediately grabbing Brongrim's arrowhead to jimmy the lock.

The hidden door swung open, a dark corridor stretching out before me. Without a thought I walked down it, grasping the wall for guidance. There was a creek, a slam, and everything was thrown into blackness. The door had closed behind me. *Guess I'm not going back that way.* I followed the cold passageway,

91

smashing my face against the ground as I came to unexpected stairs. I followed them up to what appeared like another doorway, light shining around its edges. I hesitated, my heartbeat quickening with uncertainty. I threw off my doubts and pushed it open, falling out of a wardrobe. It did not take me long to realise I was in Daxon's quarters. *This must be an escape route.*

After the initial shock of being somewhere I should not be, I tried to enjoy myself. I sat down in his chair, found and adorned his captain hat and smiled as I mimicked the role of Daxon. His room was twice as large as any other, with the front half acting like an office and his sleeping chambers in the back with a sizeable bed and silk sheets. I lay down on them for a moment, savouring the feeling of smooth fabric against my skin.

Returning to his desk, I half-heartedly browsed through the papers there, taking a closer look as I realised they held some interest. The name *Farrow Bloodneck* (I recognised the letters from the lessons with Varen) was scrawled over most of them. Reports of his deeds, a few vague descriptions, some personal writings from Daxon – all laid out before me.

Daxon was vague with the physical description, only mentioning dark haunting eyes. The term *Elder Blade* was also written several times, numbers written and crossed out a dozen times and the number eleven circled boldly. My breathing intensified for I knew this was information not meant for my eyes. I stood, ready to leave and forget all of this. The crew would surely be back soon and I needed to get out.

As quickly as I had stood, I sat down again almost against my will, intrigue pulling at me. A small black book sat at the top corner of his desk, dishevelled and battered. I flicked it open to again lay eyes on the captain's own writing, but more of a continuous stream of thought as opposed to the other scribbled ramblings.

I have tried to distance myself, but I fear it is becoming too difficult. Ever since Wes got him that axe---

My hands trembled, my heart pounding so loudly I was sure all of the ship could hear. *Was this about me?* I carried on eagerly.

--he has been more of a reminder. He looks so much like him, especially those eyes. He grows stronger every day; the crew all say that. They say he is a natural and one day he might even surpass me. I should be happy; it was always the plan. So why am I so frightened? Perhaps he simply reminds me too much of my old friend. Or maybe he reminds me of Ekrin. Either way, I don't look forward to the truth coming out.

The passage finished there – it was the most recent in the book. I flicked back for further clues to what the pirate was talking about.

I've found him. Farrow Bloodneck, there's a name I hadn't heard in a long time. Working with the Dramiculo now it seems, and wants to kill me for whatever reason. Let him try! I grow more powerful with each battle; he can't even hope to understand the strength I possess now. Yes, he is strong, he has those sorcerers to thank for that, but he's nothing compared to me. I'll find him and crush him with my own hands, and finally get my vengeance.

I flicked through more pages, but was interrupted by footsteps. They were approaching rapidly. Slamming the book shut I dashed back for the wardrobe, lingering there and peeking out of the cracks as I watched the captain enter and take a seat. He grabbed his quill and began writing. I stifled my breathing as best I could, hoping to slip out once he left.

A tickle in my throat made me strain against the urge to cough. He stayed there, shuffling around his notes and adding things to them. I backed up to the stairs and descended them slowly, repeatedly glancing back at the faint light. I came to the door where I had entered, but in this blackness I could not find a way to open it. I tried with the arrowhead again, but the door remained shut. Out of options, I was forced to return back towards Daxon's quarters, terrified and holding my breath completely now. I had no idea what torments he would put me through if I was caught.

I peeked through the cracks again, this time not seeing him. Temptation to rush out was strong, but I waited in case he was still in the room. Then I heard the sound of water hitting water – he was having a piss. Taking this chance, I dashed out of the room, quietly closing the door behind me. A chuckle sounded from beside me and I turned to glance up at Wes's smug face.

'Was wondering where you'd gotten to birdie,' he sneered.

'Don't tell him,' I blurted out.

The pirate simply laughed. 'Don't worry kid, we're on the same side...for now.'

With those eerie words he strode away, whistling a jolly sea shanty.

I was distracted during my studies with Varen that evening and I knew he sensed it.

'What did you do today?' I asked at the earliest opportunity.

'Just scouted for information,' the blind man told me.

'Get anything good?'

He was used to my questions by now, and often answered them without a second thought – even when his only answer was telling me not to ask certain things. We had built up a certain rhythm and I now spent my evenings learning more than letters and numbers. At this however he took pause, stroking his stubble with a wrinkled hand.

'Farrow is close,' he uttered. 'We should be able to close in on him in about a week.'

'What then?'

Another pause. 'We kill him.'

'Just like that?'

'Just like that.'

The force behind his voice seemed unusual for the normally relaxed pirate.

'Is he truly that bad?'

'He's the worst,' Varen said. 'He relies on beings who practice the ancient arts – dark stuff it is. They give him great power, power which he uses to do terrible things.'

'Sorcerers,' I recalled.

'How do you know that word?' my teacher narrowed in on me.

I panicked – though lucky for me Varen could not see how wide my eyes were.

'Just something I heard in an old story,' I lied. 'I didn't think they were real.'

I let out a sigh as he nodded along, seeming to believe me.

'I didn't either,' he grimaced. 'Not until I saw them in action. They gave Bloodneck strength, inhuman strength – the likes of which most men only dream of. The last time I met him was when I lost my first eye. He's a forced to be reckoned with, but Daxon will stop at nothing to destroy him.'

'How can the captain fight such a man?' I questioned.

'I can't say lad; in truth I've already told you too much. Just know our captain has a few tricks up his sleeve. Now, let's get back to your studies.'

I agreed, and that was that.

Chapter 8

Blood and Oaths

was awoken as the ship heaved from side to side. At first I thought we were under attack, but my window showed me a moonlit storm. Waves crashed into my cabin window over and over, rain pouring down so heavily I thought it may sink the ship. I rushed from the safety of my bed and up to the main deck where the rest of the crew were already trying to stabilize us. The force of the storm was staggering. It was difficult even to walk against the mighty gale. Akaya and Korhal were up on the ropes, trying to lower the sails. I rushed to Daxon's side at the wheel as he heaved to turn the ship with the help of Mamorhah.

'Anything I can do captain?'

'No!' he cried back above the roar of the storm. 'We have everything covered here, go back below deck!'

Begrudgingly I turned back, glancing up at my allies up in the ropes. Akaya appeared to be struggling, like she was caught or something. I had only taken a step forward when I was thrown back, smashing against the deck. It must have been a wave as most of the others were down too. Korhal had been thrown to the deck though seemed to be fine as he staggered to his feet. Akaya however was upside down, her ankle tangled in a rope as the wind prevented any opportunity at adjusting herself.

With what most would describe as a death wish, I sprinted to the ropes. I swiftly ascended, sparing no time with making sure I was secure – instinct took over.

Lightning blinded me.

I was young again, stone and slate beneath my hands in place of ropes. Those I called friends were either side of me, shouting out insults as we raced to the top. Old Lundrip stood up there, tutting as we heaved ourselves onto the roof.

'You need to be quicker than that if you ever want to join us!' he scolded, turning his back and disappearing down into an alley.

The light faded and I was back on the Stallion again, the pouring rain making the ropes dangerously slippery. Still I climbed without second thought, coming closer to Akaya. Beneath I heard shouts from the rest of the crew, but could not distinguish their words over the sound of the storm. I got to Akaya, reached out and grabbed her shoulder, pulling her close enough to grasp the ropes. When she had a tight grip I moved to her foot, tangled tightly between several loops in the rope. I began to pull at them, but before they came loose the ship rocked again and I went flying into the air.

Darkness.

When I came to, Akaya stood over my bed. It was like the first time I saw her, and like that time I appeared to be naked.

'What happened?' I groaned as I sat up.

A quick glance to my window told me it was daytime and that the storm had passed.

'You were thrown overboard,' she stated. 'Varen dived in to save you.'

'But he can't see!' I hollered. 'Is he okay?'

'He's awake,' she told me. 'But he's sick. The rapids were tough but he managed to grab you, it was the chill that got him. He hasn't warmed up since, no matter how many layers we put on him.'

My stomach sank. 'Will he live?'

Akaya shrugged. 'We don't know. At this point it seems the old timer wants a quick death, but Daxon is adamant he'll pull through. He jumped in after you both and dragged you back onto the ship.'

'Did he get sick too?' I queried.

She shook her head. 'He's just angry – you disobeyed his orders and now Varen is paying for your mistake.'

'I was protecting you!' I argued.

She smiled. Not like the sarcastic sneer I had seen before, but a genuine smile. She leaned over and planted a soft kiss on me cheek.

'I know,' she whispered in my ear. 'And I'm grateful.' She kissed me a second time and pulled away. 'When you feel up to it I'm supposed to escort you to the captain.'

I dreaded the thought, but agreed all the same. I was about to get up and dress but Akaya still lingered.

'I need clothes,' I told her bluntly.

'I know,' she said, the devious smile returning. 'But the captain says I'm not to let you out of my sight.'

She seemed pleased with herself when I threw away the covers to reveal my nakedness, and even more so when my cheeks turned red. I turned away from her prying eyes, but not before she took the chance to gaze at my manhood. She giggled and I blushed more. Her giggling stopped however when she saw my back; I suddenly became very conscious of the scars there. To my relief she did not ask and so I got dressed in silence.

Daxon opened the door less than a second after Akaya knocked.

'Thank you for bringing him,' he said in a low tone. 'You may leave us.'

She bowed her head and left. I was guided to a seat and he sat opposite; I glanced around the room – not having been here since four days prior when I snuck in. The little black book was out of sight and the captain moved the papers on his desk as his gaze bore into me. Despite what Akaya had said he was a little pale and he kept sniffing up snot a few times each minute.

'What were you thinking?' he started us off.

'I was protecting a crewmate,' I fired back at him, calm but determined.

'And because of your actions, another crewmate almost died.'

'I didn't ask Varen to jump in after me, nor did I expect him to,' I countered.

'That is not the point!' he growled, standing, his fists slamming onto the desk. 'You disobeyed a direct order from me and because of it Varen is now bedridden. You were irresponsible, you rushed in too quickly, and you were ignorant of the possible consequences!'

'And if I hadn't been, Akaya may have fallen to her death!' I argued, realising I was now shouting back.

'That's it,' Daxon spat. 'You're free to go.'

He turned his back on me and waved a dismissive hand.

I faltered. 'Wh...what's that supposed to mean?'

'I mean we took you without consent, we kept you like a prisoner and now you're free to go,' he said blankly, his back still turned. 'You're too much of a liability to this crew to carry on as a recruit. When we next drop anchor we'll set you up with some money and a job with one of our contacts. You'll be free to go about your life and forget you ever met us.'

He must have expected me to leave, for he stayed silent for a while.

'No chance.'

'What?' he asked, his fist clenching.

'There's *no* chance I'm leaving,' I told him. 'I've *trained* here. I've made *friend*s here. I've *killed* people for this crew – I forget how many. I've watched a good man die and avenged his death with the blade of my axe. Away from this ship I have nothing – no family, no friends. Frankly I've been happier as a prisoner here than I ever was in Cranwell. So call me a liability if you want, sentence me to swabbing the entire fucking boat every single day if you want, but don't expect me to pack up and leave because I'm telling you now it won't happen.'

I had barely finished my rant when Daxon lunged forward; all I saw for a flash of his fist and then I was on the ground with what felt like a broken jaw. I turned towards him clenching my fist but barely a moment after the first strike I felt his fist clenching around my neck. I clawed at his fingers as I felt my windpipe collapsing, *surely he wouldn't*. He lifted me to my feet, then higher still until my toes barely touched the floor. My chest heaved, yearning for air but unable to obtain it. Then, as suddenly as this encounter had begun, he released me and I collapsed to the floor, my insides burning as I gasped for breath.

'You're on *very* thin ice,' he spat after a few moments of silence.

I was clutching at my neck, still barely able to breathe as each breath felt like I was swallowing one of Gurdgrin's hatchets.

'What…happens…now?' I enquired, coughing and spluttering after each word.

'Get the bucket, you said you'd clean the entire ship and that's what you'll do.'

I opened my mouth to argue but he hit me with a deadly glare. He was serious and I had to be on my best behaviour now more than ever.

The rest of the crew seemed to disappear for the next few hours as I began swabbing the main deck, my hands quickly becoming raw and washed out. From nothingness there came a noise, the faint patter of footsteps coming closer. I spun my head around as Korhal swung his enormous machete. I threw myself away from his blow as the blade cleaved the bucket in two and sent water everywhere. I was only alive because of how clumsy he was with his left hand.

'What are you…' I started, but was cut off as he rushed me for another strike.

My axe was back in my room and I was unable to defend myself as the green-haired pirate charged me with venom in his eyes. I ducked his blow and pushed him with all of my strength before rushing back to my original position, lifting half of the bucket and holding it in front of me like a shield. Korhal regained his footing and came for me again. I threw the wood up to catch his steel and managed to throw him off centre enough that he slipped in the puddle of soapy water. His blade went flying from his hand and I leapt to the ground after it.

As we both stood and squared up I held the enormous machete aloft using both hands, amazed he had the strength to wield it with one.

'Now will you tell me what you're doing?' I yelled at the man.

Without responding he strode over. I held the blade out, fully expecting another attack. When he was within a few feet, he simply held his arm out. I gave him a confused glance.

'Blade please,' he spoke in an unfeeling tone.

I did not move for a few moments, finally handing the weapon over to him cautiously. He sheathed it and walked away, saying nothing more and leaving me confused and angry.

Once I had simmered, I found a new bucket and filled it. I finished swabbing the main deck after a few more hours, only stopping to grab some bread from the food hall. That place was empty too – in fact I had seen nobody at all aside from Korhal since beginning my chores, not even in the crow's nest nor at the ship's wheel.

I moved on to the lower decks, scrubbing the floors outside of the bed chambers and expecting to hear some voices there which of course never came. I was passing Mamorhah's room when the door flew open and I turned. There was nobody at the doorway so I moved closer in intrigue. As soon as I peeked my head through the door a booted foot sent me flying back into the wall. There Mamorhah stood, his twin blades unsheathed as his eyes locked onto me.

'Sorry to do this lad,' he said as the demon blade came for my throat.

I turned just in time, the steel only slightly touching the side of my neck and lodging itself into the wall. I felt the sting of a cut and the hot blood on my already bruised neck, but there was no time to think about it. Before the enormous pirate could pull his weapon free from the wall, I mustered all of my strength and struck him hard in the stomach. Admittedly it would have been stronger if I was not still weak from my dip in the ocean and the confrontation with Daxon, but it was at least enough to stagger him.

As his hand came loose from the demon blade I yanked it out myself with both hands in time to parry the next blow from the angel blade. I stabbed at him with his own sword, getting easily parried but doubling back and managing and sharp slash at his side before he struck me with his free hand. I went down but still clung to the weapon – the depiction of the demon practically staring at me with its crimson eyes. He hit at me in my lowered position but I managed to block his strike and kick at his shins.

In frustration he kicked the sword from my grasp, sending it flying down the corridor. He raised the angel blade, white and pristine and about to be covered with my blood. In one final desperate act I closed my eyes and kicked at his crotch. The death blow did not come, and instead I heard a groan. His weapon dropped to the floor and he was clutching at his groin with both hands. I retrieved the two blades and held them to his throat as he continued to make sounds of agony.

'I yield,' he grunted. 'You certainly got me there ya bastard, good job kid.'

He managed to compose himself, taking the weapons and leaving like Korhal had. I put my hand to my jaw where Mamorhah had struck me – it was right where Daxon had potentially broken my jaw and as I moved it I felt the bones clicking against one another.

Something was going on here and I wanted to know what. *What was it? Try to kill Yodrick day?* I rushed to Daxon's quarters and pounded on the door, though no matter how loud nor long I knocked there was no response. The only thing I could do was continue my chores, though I made a quick detour to my own chambers to grab the axe in case of future attack.

The next was Gurdgrin whose hatchet missed my face by less than an inch. I rapidly grabbed my weapon which was propped against the wall and deflected his next two. The following one flew low and cut against my leg, but as I rushed him through the corridor I was able to knock him to the ground and he too yielded.

Limping around with blood still running slowly from my leg, and with my jaw feeling like it was going to fall off, I thought I might die.

I was taken by surprise when something hard hit me on the back of the head. I was dazed for a moment and turned towards a blurry version of Akaya as another fist struck me in the face. My nose burst, though I managed to lift my axe and fend her off. Instead of beating her in combat, she simply seemed to get bored after five minutes of fighting and turned tail. She had definitely went easy on me; that first punch could have killed me if she had wanted it to and that was without even equipping her gauntlets.

Wes was ruthless with his attacks which came as I was finishing scrubbing the food hall. As his jagged blade slashed against my side I cried out, 'What's going on here?' but he simply grinned and gave no answer. He laughed as we battled to and fro, His speed often getting the best of me and inflicting injury after injury. Finally, I managed a good swing right into his shoulder, and after that he yielded and left.

I journeyed down to the armoury, Brongrim was fletching arrows. He was right in front of me, unlike the others who had all ambushed me when my attention was turned.

'Yodrick,' he greeted me pleasantly. 'It's nice to see you.'

'Please tell me you're not going to attack me like the others,' I begged.

He stood, a little off balance on his wooden leg, and grabbed his bow.

'Sorry mate,' he said as he knocked an arrow and fired.

I lifted up the nearly-empty bucket and shielded myself from the arrow. The force of the projectile knocked me back a step, the second getting caught in my makeshift shield. The third hit my thigh and I groaned out in pain as I rushed him. Another three were fired before I reached him, one catching my shoulder. As soon as I was at him I dropped the shield. He reached for his dagger but I kicked his good leg out from under him and he toppled easily. When it was clear he would not persist, I held a hand out to help him up.

'Can you *please* tell me what's going on here?' I pleaded.

'Head on up to the main deck,' he instructed me. 'I'll finish up your cleaning and meet you up there soon.'

I was filled with frustration, but went up regardless. The sun was beginning to set. The entire crew were there, including Varen who was being held up by Gurdgrin. Each of them cast a long shadow in the light of the orange sky. They wore their usual attire, though as well as their regular weapons were seven long, curved daggers. Daxon stood at the head of the group.

'Let me guess, I'll have to fight you now,' I tutted.

'No,' he told me. 'You have already proven yourself. Strip your shirt and sandals.'

The other members of the crew formed a circle around me, Brongrim coming up shortly after with a similar dagger at his hip. I obeyed, shaking despite the lack of cold. I stood facing the captain in nothing but my breeches, covered in injuries from the others and aware at the sharp steel now pointed towards me.

'We stand here in light of the dying sun to welcome another soul into our ranks. The eyes of the maker watch over us all, so speak no lies.'

'By the force of the Stallion!' the others chanted in unison.

My mind told me to flee, that something was amiss here, to change my mind and take up Daxon's earlier offer of leaving. My body stayed still however, my eyes firmly glued on Daxon's.

'We wish to honour Yodrick as he joins our brotherhood, if he has the aptitude.'

'May the Stallion ride!' they choired.

'Bring forth the blood!' he commanded.

Mamorhah carried out a jug, laying it down before me and returning to his place in the circle. I glanced down, the tint of the light not shielding my eyes to what it was.

'We have seen his spirit as he has fended off attacks from all of you. Now we shall see if Yodrick's stomach is as strong as his ambition. Yodrick, drink the blood of the Stallion.'

'Drink. Drink. Drink,' they all called.

I could barely stand, and blood was still pouring from several parts of my body. Struggling to lift the jug to my lips, I slowly poured the liquid down my throat, the blood still warm. It was rancid, and I felt my body trying reject it as it seemed to slither slowly down into my stomach. I wanted to hurl it back up but I forced it down, tears coming to my eyes all the while. The entire time I kept my eyes forward, fearing what would happen if I failed to correctly take part in this ceremony. Once the last drop was down, I placed the jug back on the floor. I thought for a moment it might all come back up, but I was able to swallow it down.

'His stomach runs strong!' Daxon called. 'Now Yodrick, with the blood of the Stallion running through you, will you endure the test of iron?' I nodded. 'Cut him!'

The words chilled me, though I calmed my breathing and stayed focused as one by one the crew approached and slashed my bare flesh with their daggers. I wanted to cry out so badly, and by the final cut from Daxon himself I felt as though I may pass out.

'Now, young Stallion, repeat the words that have governed this crew for decades. "I am blood of the Stallion, and as such I will ride the sea until my death when I may return to the land. I will love none but my crew, I will shed no Stallion blood. My mistress will be victory; my family will be the hunt. I will take no prisoners, nor will I slaughter a man on his knees. Honour binds me, in this life and the next."'

I repeated the mantra word for word, evoking a short nod from Daxon.

'Who other than me would name our new crew member?' Daxon posed.

I glanced to my left as Wes stepped forward.

'I would,' he said enthusiastically.

'Go on,' the captain said.

Did I see a shudder?

'I name him the Blood of the Stallion,' the rat-like pirate said – he paused, a sly grin crossing his lips. 'Yodrick...son of the pirate captain, Darkskull.'

I glanced around rapidly, looking for explanation in expressions. Everyone else seemed to be doing the same – only Varen looking sombre. A‹aya stepped towards me, eyes wide. Her hand reached out as if to caress my cheek, but she gasped and pulled it back. Excessive murmurings filled my ears, only to be broken with the sound of ringing steel as Daxon unsheathed his blade.

'Scoundrel!' Daxon cried, narrowing in on Wes.

He still smiled, and his long jagged blade came out too, pointed towards the captain. 'You tried your best to keep it hidden but I was too clever for you!' he laughed. 'Go on, tell them all what you did. Tell everyone why this boy is truly here!'

'Traitor, I'll have you hanged for this!' the captain countered, his lips pulled back in a snarl.

'Do your worst.'

'Ship on the horizon!' Brongrim interrupted, pointing out towards the setting sun. True to his word, one was approaching at breakneck speed. Its mast was a headless woman, its flag a bloodied shield.

'The Headless Maiden!' Akaya cried shrilly, pointing eastwards. 'She's coming right towards us!'

Right on cue, the opposing ship was approaching at breakneck speed; the billowing flag sporting a shield spattered with blood, and the mast portraying a crude, decapitated figure of a woman.

'Farrow,' Daxon grunted through gritted teeth. *'Finally.'*

Chapter 9

The Headless Maiden

Within moments we were at war. Flaming arrows beseeched the deck while Brongrim and several of the others fired dozens right back at them – the ships all the while coming closer together. Daxon grabbed my shoulders.

'Look lad, I know your mind must be racing and I have a million things to say to you, but right now I need you to get that axe of yours.'

I nodded and was off, down below deck where you could still hear the commotion of what was going on. I slung myself into my cabin, grabbing both weapon and a shirt, and charging back out. Wes stood in my way.

'Come on!' I called. 'We need to get back up there!'

I went to rush past him but his arm blocked me.

'Not so fast Yodrick.'

'If this about what you said earlier, it can wait for now.'

'No,' he grunted. 'It's not about that. No matter what happened up there, you *did* become a member of the Stallion; and as such you need to understand why we're fighting this battle.'

'Can you at least explain it on the way?'

'I suppose I can, but you better listen carefully.'

We ran back to the main deck where the battle was only truly beginning. Steel met steel as grappling hooks were flung and enemies flocked to our decks. I rushed into the field of fire without hesitation, my axe swinging left and right, hacking into my foes. All were clad in chainmail with standard steel swords – no match for the crew. These were only foot soldiers however, obvious from how quickly they went down.

'With me!' Daxon called as he leapt the gap to board their ship. Mamorhah was over next, then Akaya, followed by Korhal and Gurdgrin. Brongrim stayed however, firing arrows at those trying to board the Stallion. I grasped his arm.

'Leave me mate, I can't exactly jump that far with the wooden leg and someone needs to protect Varen and the ship.'

He marked the words with another arrow into an enemy's face. I gave a small smile.

'Take care of yourself, my friend.'

'You too,' he chimed. 'Do me proud lad.'

'Well if you're quite done saying your loving farewells we better get moving!' Wes urged, pushing me on forward. 'Bron – once we're over steer the ship away. Keep close but don't let any more of these bastards board.'

Once Wes and I were on the Headless Maiden we cut the ropes and the Stallion veered out of reach. More footmen attacked but within seconds they were dead at our feet.

'You've truly gotten the hang of that thing,' he laughed.

'I'd hope so after how much training you've all put me through.'

We were further behind the others who surged through the dozens of men opposing us. Daxon led the charge, cutting down anyone and everyone unlucky enough to get in his way. Blood splattered the deck, though not a drop seemed to tarnish his sword.

'Remember when Yakal said something about an Elder Blade?' Wes asked me, stabbing a charging enemy through the neck with his jagged sword.

I grunted an affirmation as I knocked down a straggler with the haft of my weapon and buried the blade of my axe into his gut. It seemed we were getting all those too afraid to attack the main party, meaning easy pickings for us.

'Well that's what Daxon's sword is.'

'And this is important because...'

'It's important because the Elder Blades are said to be the most powerful weapons in the world,' he snapped as he flung a knife into the back of a wayward fighter, knocking him off the ship.

'How can a weapon be more powerful than another?' I questioned.

The rest of the crew had delved down to the lower decks, and the hatch was quickly being swarmed with the grey of chainmail. I ran forward, swinging my axe into two foes and getting stabbed by a third in the process. Gritting my teeth, I smashed the hilt of my axe into his face once, twice, three times. He was unconscious, or dead, it did not matter.

Another half dozen blocked my path, trying to follow the team down the hatch which I could not let happen. I remembered Daxon's demonstration and twirled my weapon full circle, knocking back and even killing some of my enemies.

I fought them off over and over only to find more took their place. Bodies piled up around me into walls of flesh and blood. Soon any who challenged me had to climb over their fallen allies to reach me. A pain formed in my gut. *How many had I killed now?* Now covered with cuts – some deep enough to keep a constant stream of blood flowing – I glanced over the top of the pile of corpses but Wes was nowhere to be seen. More of the steel-clad foes were approaching and for the first time in a long time I appeared to be alone.

I dived down into the open hatch, pulling it closed behind me. The lock would not keep me safe forever, though it would do for now. Hopefully those still on the main deck would be too cowardly to follow. I surged through the darkness, tripping over yet more bodies as I held my axe ready. Light filtered in further down the narrow passageway, lit torches lining the walls. All was silent aside from the ringing in my ears. A shadow against the flames appeared. I spun around and swung, though the attack was blocked. I backed up a step but an enormous blade came towards me, stopping only inches from my throat.

'Yodrick,' a voice stammered.

A closer glance at my opponent revealed that it was Korhal, his green hair black in the dim firelight.

'Korhal,' I sighed, my chest pained. 'Where are the others?'

'I saw you holding the entrance and I went back to help, but you seemed fine on your own,' he grinned, a sparkle in his eye followed by a grim shadow. 'Unfortunately by the time I decided to leave you, the others were gone. What about Wes?'

'No idea,' I told him. 'Lost him back up there.'

'Something feels off about this.'

'Off about what?' I questioned, seeing the slight twitching in the stump of his right arm.

'It all seems too easy, fighting off these footmen, getting down here. Sure there's a lot of them, but not a single experienced fighter amongst them.'

'You make a good point,' I said, thinking about the situation. 'Maybe Farrow is trying to lure us into a false sense of security.'

'Could be, could be,' the one-armed pirate tutted. 'Either way, we need to find the others.'

Off we went, scouring the lower decks for any sign of conflict. At one point I thought Korhal had turned on me as he swung around with machete in hand. As the separated head of an enemy rolled against my foot however I soon realised what had transpired. That man was the first of about a dozen – single fighters waiting in the dark recesses of the ship to ambush us at any chance they got. We were more cautious after the first however; listening for the faintest of sounds, checking around every corner. One even got a hefty slash on Korhal who, of course, quickly dispensed of the pest. Nonetheless, my ally was left with a long line of blood over his torso.

Eventually, with no other encounters other than the odd lone attacker, we found ourselves back at the hatch to the main deck. It was still locked without any signs of attempted entry.

'I guess we go back up?' I suggested. 'Maybe try to find Wes?'

'Yodrick, about Wes…or more specifically about what he said…'

'Daxon already told me we would talk about this later,' I told him, though even in this darkness the analysis on his face was unmissable.

'I'm afraid this may not be something which can wait. Aren't you curious to hear about your father?'

'Look!' I spat at him with sudden aggression. 'I don't understand what Wes said or why he said it, but you have the wrong person! I know who my father was, okay? He was a sea-merchant called Jarthal Alton, not some pirate captain called Darkskull! He died almost eleven years ago at sea and I never saw him again!'

'Eleven years,' Korhal muttered as I was regaining my breath. 'So not long before Daxon became arguably the most famous pirate in the world by allegedly going from town to town slaughtering innocents.'

'Just shut up!' I cried.

'Yodrick, I'm not trying to hurt you, listen to me.'

My fists clung so strongly to the haft of my axe that my arms shook and my knuckles turned white. 'My father was a good man...' I sobbed, tears streaming down my face.

Korhal sheathed his blade and rested his hand on my shoulder. I felt too weak to shrug it off.

'Yes, he was...' the pirate whispered. 'In more ways than you know.'

I glanced up at him slowly. 'Y...you knew him?' I stammered.

He met my eyes and nodded slowly. 'Jarthal. I knew him back before he went by that other name. Now I know he must have done it to protect you.'

My weeping intensified, my hands trembled uncontrollably and the axe fell from my grip.

'He was truly a pirate?'

'Yes Yodrick, he was. And a great one at that.'

'Wes...Wes said Darkskull was a captain.'

'Captain of the Stallion, before Daxon was.'

'How did he die?'

Silence.

'It…it was…' Korhal stuttered. 'It was all Farrow's fault.'

My eyes flashed open and my jaw locked. I threw off Korhal's arm and picked up my weapon.

'Yodrick, what are you…'

'I'm going to kill him,' I cut him off. 'I'm going to find the bastard and kill him for taking my father and ruining my life!'

I surged forward, my ally tailing behind as I threw open the hatch and clambered onto the deck, the first light of dawn beating down on us. My heart stopped when I found nobody there. Some of the blood remained but most of it, and even the corpses, were missing. There was a low chuckle and a robed figure moved into view. He was tall, with ebony skin and long, tied back hair. Dark hair, darker eyes. He had to be my man.

'Farrow!' I cried, charging towards him with my axe.

He pulled his lips back in a grin and waved a hand as I was closing in. Everything slowed down and I could hardly breathe. Each stride took ten times as long, though my dark-skinned opponent moved normally.

'What have you done to me!' I cried.

'Oh, foolish boy,' he laughed. 'Don't you recognise sorcery when you see it? Oh, of course you don't. After all, we are a dying breed.'

With the flick of his wrist I went flying back, landing at Korhal's feet.

'Yodrick are you hurt?' he gasped as he helped me back up.

'Wh…what just happened?'

Daxon, Akaya, Gurdgrin and Mamorhah burst up out of the hatch.

'Sursaroh!' Daxon yelled. 'Tell me where your master is, damned fiend!'

'Oh, captain Daxon,' he said, low and mocking. 'How nice to see you remember me, and nicer still to see that Elder Blade in your hand. Speaking of which, congratulation on achieving your rank, Farrow told me all about that.'

'Where is he?' the captain barked.

'Not here if that's what you're asking,' the sorcerer laughed. 'Didn't you guess by my conjurations?'

'What do you speak of?' Mamorhah demanded.

Sursaroh cackled manically. 'Oh, how foolish you all are. Look around! Don't you notice anything unusual?'

Everyone glanced around at the scene before us – I caught Daxon's expression as his eyes widened with immediate terror.

'No, it can't be!' Daxon yelled. 'There's no way you're *that* powerful. There were hundreds!'

'Oh, is that all?' our enemy sighed. 'I must be having an off day. At full strength it's more like thousands.'

Realisation struck me. The enemies we faced, the men in chainmail, none of them were real. *How is that possible?*

'You'll never get away with this, sorcerer!' Akaya cried out, but as we readied ourselves to attack, the robed man waved up his arms and six soldiers appeared before us – this time in full plate mail and helmets.

I staggered back, my body shaking.

'Stay calm everyone,' Daxon called. 'They may look stronger but they're all just as fake as the others.'

I raised my axe, though my legs quivered as I faced this conjured foe. It lifted a greatsword and swung at my chest. Leaping back, I raised my axe up high and came down on its shoulder with force. It shuddered slightly but made no indication of pain even as I sliced back the blade. I charged in again, this time sweeping low to take out its leg, but the blade simply buries itself into the flesh without consequence. While I was stuck there, the flat of its blade came up and struck me hard in the face. I fell back, blood gushing from my face and the axe still buried in its meaty leg.

It came over me, sword aloft. I rolled out of the way as steel cut into the boards of the deck. I snatched my weapon and got back to my feet, standing defensively. A yell distracted me and I turned towards a weakened Mamorhah on his knees. A sudden kick to the back smashed my head into the floor. I groaned, hearing the swoosh of the steel behind me but unable to react.

Nothing came of it.

When I turned no enemy stood there, it seemed all were gone. Instead, a haunting cry sounded. Across the deck stood Wes, his jagged blade buried into the sorcerer's side.

'You demon!' Sursaroh called as black blood flowed out of the wound.

We turned to approach them, but within a second our foe pulled himself free from the blade and disappeared in a blaze of smoke. Daxon strode to Wes, unfaltering and intimidating. I worried for a moment he might kill him but instead the captain extended a hand. Wes frowned but took it anyway. They stood there for a moment, arms embraced, Daxon said something but I was too far away to hear.

'The villain has escaped,' Daxon called to the rest of us. 'It seems Farrow was never here and this was all a trap. Our mission remains the same however, we are to find Farrow and kill him.'

'And how are we going to do that?' Mamorhah spat, still in bad shape. 'When you first told me about Farrow you said he had two of those sorcerers on his side. How can we possibly face that?'

Daxon grimaced. 'I will admit, Sursaroh's power was hugely underestimated. We will need to form a new strategy but for now we must get back to the Stallion.'

Once back on board, Brongrim greeted us with grim news. Varen had worsened while we were gone and now lay unconscious without much hope of him waking. Everyone took the news hard, even I who had known the man for the shortest amount of time. Wes and Daxon disappeared to his quarters while everyone else headed for the food hall for a drink. I h went to my quarters instead, unwilling to take part in any sort of merriment, not even to drown my sorrows.

Farrow has to die! I thought over and over, unable to rest. Mamorhah was right though, I could not imagine how we would fight against those sorcerers – the thought of Sursaroh's magic sent chills through my body. So caught up in my thoughts, I never heard the footsteps and only noticed the figure at my door when I glanced over.

'Akaya!' I blurted, panting, 'You startled me.'

'I wanted to check you were okay.'

'I'm fine,' I lied, waving a dismissive hand.

She entered the room and moved closer.

'I did some research,' she said. 'Looked back into some old records.'

'What about?' I asked.

She leaned over onto my bed and held out a sheathed dagger.

'It's a little late by my estimate, but happy birthday.'

I counted the days in my head and realised she was right. I had been on the verge of sixteen when the Stallion first took me and had been so preoccupied with training I forgot about it.

'Thank you,' I said, taking the fine blade.

'It was one of Wargal's,' she said. 'He kept a will and left half a dozen of them to me. I think it must have been his little joke since he knew how much I hated using weapons. Still, I think he would have been happy for this one to go to you. It was the one you used when you first trained together.'

I smiled at the thought and unsheathed the weapon, staring at it before carefully placing it next to my axe.

'I don't know what to say.'

'Then say nothing Yodrick. You're a man now. Even if not for reaching the age, you became a man last night when you officially joined us.'

She lifted up off the bed and turned to close the door.

'What are you doing?' I asked, my confusion intensifying as she took off her coat.

'I never got the chance to thank you for saving me,' she said, biting her lip. 'I don't want to miss the chance this time.'

Even as she spoke I noticed my groin hardening. She slowly unbuttoned her blouse, revealing the lacy red bra beneath.

'Have you ever been with a woman Yodrick?' I shook my head. 'Good, just do what I say and I promise you it'll be amazing.'

'Okay,' I sighed, sitting up on the bed.

'Strip.'

The single word sent heat through me, and I rushed to get out of my shirt and breeches, sitting there in my underwear. She threw off her blouse and in one fluid motion dropped her skirt. The leggings came off just as quickly, and she stood there in her undergarments. They matched and I could hardly contain the erection trying to free itself.

'Strip,' she repeated, leaning over to do it for me, lightly tugging at the fabric until it slid from my legs, revealing what was beneath. She grinned when she saw it, lowering down until her lips touched it. I let out a gasp, evoking a light laugh from her. It made me nervous, but before I could dwell on it her mouth engulfed my member. I groaned, warmth unlike any I had ever known flowing over every inch of my body. She sucked lightly as her tongue coiled around it and my eyes rolled back. I have no idea how long that part lasted but remember feeling so empty when she finally pulled away.

'Now it's your turn,' she whispered, stripping what was left of her clothing. She lay on her side next to me, kissing my lips hard. I sunk into the kiss, feeling her tongue press against mine and her hands on my face as she pulled me down to her groin. She instructed me on what to do with my mouth and tongue and soon she was moaning. I continued to do my best until she shuddered, pulling me on top of her. She swiftly guided my member to her entrance, and suddenly I was inside of her. Pleasure erupted through my entire body, shaking, groaning. She grabbed my naked backside and pulled me in further.

I began to thrust as per her instruction, and soon we were in a rhythm. Our moans merged into one another, the world around us disappearing and our love-making becoming the only thing that mattered. She flipped me over and got on top of me, raising and lowering herself onto my throbbing penis. I grabbed at her dangling breasts and she bit back a scream as I pinched her nipples. She shuddered again, more intensely this time. I could feel her muscles tightening around me as she cried out. The tightness sent something sensational through me and I slipped into an orgasm of my own. Finally, after weeks of pining over her and her beauty, Akaya had returned my affections. She was mine.

When it was over she collapsed on me, both of us breathing heavily and in synchronisation with each other. Tiredness washed over us and we drifted into a deep sleep.

Chapter 10

Truth Revealed

The sound of the door opening woke me up. It was Akaya, fully dressed and failing to silently leave my chambers.

'Where are you going?' I asked sleepily.

'Look Yodrick,' she sighed, turning back to me. 'Last night was great but I don't want you reading too much into it.'

I sat up, pulling the covers around my nakedness. 'What do you mean?'

'It was a one-time thing.' Even as she said the words I felt my heart drop. 'We're crewmates and it wouldn't be right for us to continue this.'

I got to my feet and walked to her, no longer caring I was nude. I dropped my hands to her hips and held her loosely. She was taller but not by much, and in the moment she let me remain there I felt like a real man.

'It wouldn't be complicated,' I tried to reassure her, but her expression told me no.

She pushed my hands away and clenched her fists.

'I'm sorry,' she said. 'I was worried you'd get the wrong idea; I should've made it clear before anything happened. What happened last night meant nothing. It was just sex. Nothing else.'

And so she left, the door swinging shut behind her. I climbed back to my bed, feeling suddenly deflated. I had been a fool to imagine I could ever have her. Women like Akaya could not be tamed. *Never mind,* I told myself, *plenty more pirates on the sea.*

I would have stayed in bed the entire day sulking but a knock at the door pulled me from my miserable pit. I hurriedly dressed and opened the door to face a stern Korhal.

'Captain requests your presence on the main deck,' he said robotically, turning to leave without delay.

I followed, wiping the moisture from my face. Everyone was there aside from Varen and I joined the group while trying my best to avoid eye contact with Akaya. Daxon stood before us, nervously pacing. He watched me with heavy eyes, laden with dark bags. *Had he gotten any sleep last night?*

'I have assembled you all here to pay penance for deceiving you,' he started, 'Especially you Yodrick.'

His gaze met mine and I swear a tear rolled down his cheek.

'If you mean the Darkskull thing then get to it!' Mamorhah interrupted. 'I'm sick of feeling like I'm not in the know.'

'Fine.' Daxon continued, 'As some of you know – namely Wes, Akaya and Korhal – there was a captain before me who went by the name of Darkskull. However, Korhal, Wes and I knew him as Jarthal and he was Yodrick's father.'

'And that's why you were so adamant about taking him with us,' Gurdgrin interjected.

The captain's eyes flashed to mine again. 'That was...part of it.'

'What happened to him?' Brongrim asked. 'Yodrick's father I mean.'

'He died.'

'How?' Brongrim pressed.

I stepped forward and turned to my friend. 'Farrow killed him,' I said, evoking a sneer from Wes. 'Korhal told me.'

All eyes were on the green-haired pirate but Daxon regained the focus.

'I'm afraid Yodrick that that's not quite true.'

My jaw dropped and I took a step back, my leg shaking a little.

'But...Korhal said...'

'What I said is it was Farrow's *fault*,' the pirate corrected. 'Which I honestly believe.'

'Thank you for your words my friend, but there is no use cushioning the truth,' Daxon sighed.

I turned to the captain.

'What do you mean?' I asked him.

I caught glimpse of Brongrim, Gurdgrin and Mamorhah whose curious expressions matched my own but I doubted they had the pounding in their chests I had. It was so loud I was sure everyone could hear it.

'I killed your father.'

Everything turned silent. His lips moved but I heard nothing of his following words. My peripheral vision showed outraged reactions of Brongrim and Gurdgrin though if they said anything I did not hear it. My hands were shaking and I slowly fell to my knees. I grabbed at my hair and pulled, though in that moment I felt nothing. Sound began to return but acted as a constant humming murmur.

'Shut up!' I snapped, my eyes darting up to the captain. 'Tell me why you did it.'

'Yodrick,' Akaya's voice sounded; she was next to me with a hand on my shoulder. 'Please just calm...'

'Tell me!' I demanded again, throwing off her grasp.

Daxon's eyes widened, his hand moving to his blade. He unsheathed it.

'For this,' he said. 'It is an Elder Blade, one of only a handful in the entire world.'

My teeth gritted and I pulled myself to my feet.

'You killed my father...for a sword?' I growled.

'Yes,' he sighed. 'The Elder Blades are fused with a magical energy, they...'

'Enough!' I cried. 'You said he was your friend, but you killed him! You took my father away from me! You ruined my life! My mother killed herself because of you!'

'Yodrick,' Korhal said this time. 'Please...'

'No!' I yelled, tears flooding down my face – my fists clenched and I stepped forward, pointing an unwavering finger at the man before me. 'You once claimed you were nothing like Farrow, but from what I know now you're worse than him. You said it yourself, *all fear Daxon, the dreaded pirate,* right? Well I do not fear you, but you should fear me! You took everything from me, and I swear by the maker you will burn like the monster you are!'

My breathing was heavy. Every inch of me ached from how hard I was tensing.

'That's enough Yodrick,' Wes said, moving to me and laying a hand on my arm.

At the feeling of contact, I shirked him off and punched him right across the face. He went down hard, cursing as his knees smashed against the deck. I narrowed in on him.

'And you knew all of this!' I cried. 'But still, you said nothing! You used me to play your own games, you're as bad as he is.'

With that Wes was back on his feet, his face inches from mine.

'I'll have you know I loved your father like a brother,' he spat. 'And I fought by his side as Daxon betrayed him and took the ship. That's more than I can say for Korhal, Akaya or even Varen.'

I shuddered, turning to those he had mentioned. When I looked at Akaya I felt nothing but disgust. I gagged at the thought of what we had done, when all the while she knew she had been a factor in my father's death. She glanced away when my eyes met hers.

'Darkskull was not strong enough,' Korhal retaliated. 'We did what was best for the Stallion!'

'You broke our most sacred rule,' Wes grunted, approaching him and drawing the long jagged blade. 'You spilled Stallion blood.'

'You seemed to have no problem with joining us after,' Korhal countered, unleashing his katana.

'That's enough!' Daxon called.

'No,' I said, once more facing the captain. 'It's not.'

My axe was back in my chambers, but Wargal's knife was at my hip. As I drew it I only prayed that the deceased pirate had not known about any of this. Before I could quell the rage I was rushing at Daxon. He grabbed for his sword but he was not quick enough and my blade sliced against his hand. He recoiled and stepped back but once more I was on him, slashing furiously.

'Yodrick, stop this,' he pleaded, dodging a potentially lethal blow to the neck.

'Not until you've paid for your betrayal!'

He kicked the blade from my grip but I carried on with my fists. He lifted his guard to block the flurry of strikes, though I would not relent. I kept hitting until my knuckles bled but in all of this he never fought back.

'Listen, just let me tell you why...'

'I know why!' I snapped, catching him in face. 'For some stupid sword!'

I lunged and he swept to the side, letting me tumble to the floor. I was back up in an instant, straight back at him.

'You killed him!' a word coming out with every punch. 'You monster! You evil, corrupted fiend! You're a bastard! I hope you end up with Farrow, you deserve each other!'

His boot was against my chest and I was toppling backwards with flaming pain in my chest. He stood over me, eyes bloodshot and shaking, his fists clenched so hard his entire body was quivering.

'Enough!' he grunted through gritted teeth. 'We'll settle this properly. Korhal, get his axe!'

'But captain...' the pirate argued.

'Now!' he spat.

Within the minute Korhal was back. I was on my feet and furious as my weapon was handed to me. The crew were all ordered not to interfere under any circumstances. Daxon unstrapped his sword belt and handed it off to Akaya, instead picking up the axe he had used to test my skills. At Wes's command we commenced and that was all I needed to hear. I was on him in a second, swinging with all the fury I could muster.

Daxon blocked each strike against the haft before stepping up and kicking me in the shin. I faltered but managed to jump back before he landed his following overhead blow.

I used my height to my advantage, staying lower than him and swinging at his knees. I kept his block low, and on my sixth strike spun the weapon and caught him hard on the forearm. He recoiled, blood pouring from the gaping wound. He momentarily held the weapon in one hand while he clutched the other to his injury. Then he slicked his thick hair back with the blood and grimaced, spinning and striking at me with momentum. My guard barely held up, and as I retreated, he caught my hand and chopped off the end of one of my fingers. I bit back a cry and charged him, using the hilt of the axe to keep him at bay while I struck at him with the steel.

It went on like this, neither of us showing any sign of slowing down. I was fast, but he was faster. He got three more hits on me – my leg, my left wrist and a shallow cut on my shoulder. I only managed to get strikes on him with dirty tricks and none of them serious.

The only sound on deck was the clashing of weapons, the crew all remaining silent and when I faced them their expressions were stern. Even as I fought, I remembered how much I had admired this man, how much I wanted to be like him. He had given me a new life, but that did not make up for him taking my old one away.

I redoubled my efforts. I was faster, stronger, though still could not break his guard. All of this training had not helped, not against him. His gaze bore into me, as if his eyes were saying *give up, give up now*, but I would not. I came in with a firm overhead strike, the haft of his axe blocked mine and we stayed there for a moment. I tried to turn the weapon, but he turned with me. Our faces were only inches apart, both of us with gritted teeth as we pressed against one another.

'You killed him,' I cried once more as I spun around him and sliced my blade across the back of his thigh.

He staggered, going down for only a moment. I charged but he anticipated it. Everything seemed to move slowly as axe his outstretched; in that brief moment I could not stop my foot coming down. Before my feet had even settled into the lunge, he swung against my front foot and in seconds I was toppling over, my weapon flying from my hand. He was over me just as quickly, his own axe discarded and punches raining down on me. My nose and lip burst with metallic blood, though his knees pinned my arms and I could not stop him.

'That's enough captain,' Wes said, grabbing his shoulder after what felt like an eternity of pain had passed.

Daxon snapped his gaze to the intruder, but as he turned back to me he gave a gentle nod and stood. My hands went to my face and pulled away covered in dark crimson.

Daxon stood over me and scowled. 'Come back when you're a man and can follow up on your words!' he spat, turning and striding away.

Rage gripped me again, though even as I tried to move my body would not allow it. It was Wes who helped me to my feet. He and Brongrim carried me to my chambers where they bathed me of the blood and let me rest. I did not protest, nor did I yelp when the scolding water hit my open wounds. I felt numb.

'For what it's worth I'm sorry,' Wes said – Brongrim had disappeared a while ago, and he sat beside my bed while I lay simply breathing. 'I may have submitted when we lost the fight, but I never forgave Daxon for killing your father. He was my friend, the rightful captain of the Stallion, and I cared for him deeply. I think Daxon expected as much, probably why he made me first mate – so he could keep an eye on me.'

'Why are you telling me all of this?' I groaned.

He shrugged. 'I'm not sure,' he admitted. 'Daxon ordered we ditch you at nearest land which will be as early as dawn so it's not like I'm going to see you again; I guess I just didn't want you to completely hate me.'

'The only one I hate is him,' I sighed, the wound in my leg acting up again.

'He does have his reasons. Long, complicated, and sometimes unfathomable reasons which I won't try to convince you of, but reasons all the same. Still, I don't blame you for wanting him dead. Lord, I want him dead most of the time. His obsession with Farrow is frightening but it's the only thing that stops me slitting his throat while he sleeps. Despite how much ill will I have for him, I know he's without a doubt the best person to take down that son of a bitch.'

'Fuck his reasons,' I cursed. 'And fuck this Farrow Bloodneck. I don't give a shit about either. All I care about is him and what he did. Mark my words Wes, this won't be the last time we meet. I'll get stronger, stronger than Daxon could ever hope to be. I'll find this ship again and I'll punish him for killing my father.'

'I like your spirit!' Wes chimed. 'But I hope you know what you're getting into. When you leave this ship you don't have to look back. You could start a new life, be whoever you want to be. Not many people get that chance.'

'I don't want a new life. I want vengeance for the life I lost; the childhood I missed, the parents who never watched me grow up – all because of him. I'll watch him burn and I'll laugh as the flames engulf him, or I'll go to the maker trying.'

When morning came Wes escorted me to the edge of the ship. We had docked in Blakereath, a trading city like Cranwell but on a much larger scale. Brongrim was there, also wishing his goodbyes.

'Take care of yourself lad,' he said, drawing me in for a strong embrace. 'I'm sorry about the way things turned out. If I'd known...'

'There's no way you could have,' I cut him off. 'Don't blame yourself.'

I felt around in my pocket, the arrowhead he had given me brushing my fingertips.

'It's a shame Varen hasn't woken up, he would've wanted to wish you goodbye.'

'I'm glad he's not here, he was one of the ones who betrayed my father. I don't think I can forgive him for that.'

I got only a solemn nod in response.

'Daxon wanted to just throw you out with nothing, but I think these are much better suited with you,' Wes said, handing me Wargal's dagger and the axe with its head heavily wrapped.

'I appreciate it,' I told him. 'I promise they'll go to good use.'

A small smirk was exchanged between us.

'And here,' he said, handing me a purse of coins. 'Consider that your pay for the time you served on the Stallion. Use it to get yourself started with whatever new life you choose to lead.'

He knew from last night I was serious about not starting fresh but I thanked him for the money all the same. I grasped his arm and gave him a firm nod, bidding them both farewell and crossing over to the dock. They lifted anchor and within minutes the Iron Stallion was sailing away. *I'll see all you again soon.*

I marched on into the crowds of Blakereath. Wes had suggested I start anew, but that implied I did not know what my next step was. On the contrary, I knew exactly what I was going to do. I turned back towards the harbour with eyes on an old dishevelled ship, tied up next to a sign which read, *For Sale*. Now all I needed was a crew, and where better to find one than a place like this?

Chapter 11

Blakereath

I began by outfitting myself like a true pirate rather than a lowly cabin boy. The tailor was an old, short-tempered man who wanted rid of me the second I walked in his door. It was only when he saw my gold that he gave me the time of day. I laid eyes on a brown leather coat – nothing said intimidation like it. I had it fitted along with a black bandana, some dark trousers and boots (the good kind with sturdy soles) and walked out of there a figure to be reckoned with. The rest of my day I spent in the nearest tavern, a rundown place called *The Sunken Sails*. It was a pirate tavern true and proper, a weapon on everyone's hip.

I drank little but made sure to keep buying drinks for the innkeeper and the barmaid. This would be the best place to gather a crew and in case that went south I wanted the owners on my side. I sat alone at a table, not many were in at first but I persisted, buying drinks and keeping to myself. As the day passed by more and more flocked in until the place was heaving. I ruled out the larger, older men – none of them would ever follow my orders without challenge. Unfortunately, their sort made up the majority of the occupancy, so it was slim pickings. A few stood out however.

A young boy, younger than I perhaps. He stood beside one of the larger men at the bar and had a knife at his hip. He was slim, all of his features dark. His eyes were darting around the room and his hands shook as he sheepishly sipped his beer. Eventually his gaze landed on me, though quickly flicked away when I stared back. There was also a boy at a table a few over from mine, eighteen perhaps but alone like me. He was broad with noticeable muscles and already six empty pint glasses around him. And a man – older than I was looking for but intriguing. He was tall and slender, his face half shrouded by a hooded cloak. He was at the far end of the bar, nursing a rum and cracking his knuckles every few minutes.

I approached the first, supporting my still-injured body on the wrapped axe. Stopping at the bar next to him I ordered another drink, taking a hearty swig and turning to him.

'How old are you, lad?' I enquired, trying to mimic the authoritative tone of Daxon.

He turned to me with wide eyes, mouth agape. The man beside him cut in before he could form a response.

'Why you talking to my nephew?' he grunted.

His skin was darker than the boy's and his eyes darker still as he clocked me with a powerful stare.

'Just being friendly,' I said blankly. 'What's it to you?'

His glass hit the bar with a thud. 'I don't want any rotten kids getting to him, I'm responsible for him ya hear?'

'Loud and clear,' I said, turning away and taking another swig. 'So lad...'

'Are you playing games with me kid?' the boy's uncle cut me off. 'I told you to shut your mouth.'

'And if I don't?' I challenged, his brow furrowing.

'I'll cut out your tongue so you can't speak again!'

I laughed, strong and confident. It was fake of course, and I was glad the coat covered most of my body to hide my shaking.

'I'd like to see you try.'

Within a second he was in my face, his nephew shoved out of the way. I sipped lightly at my pint, not bearing him any attention even as his hand grasped my shoulder. I kept drinking.

'Listen here you little punk!' he spat, but before he could continue the barman was there.

'I'll have no fighting in *my* place!' the old timer declared.

'Fine,' my opponent sneered. 'We'll take it outside.'

I knocked away his hand and finished my pint. Before I could decline his offer however, several others gathered behind him. My eyes darted between them and the innkeeper who appeared a little frightened. I nodded, and without a word led the way out of the tavern. It was getting dark now and the streets were cold. My aggravator was joined by two others, all armed. His nephew stayed near the door, watching. They all unsheathed their blades but I held up a hand to stop them.

'What's your name?' I asked.

'Why does it matter?' my opponent barked.

'I think you should always know the name of a man you're about to put in the ground,' I called back in mock confidence.

They all laughed.

'My name is Melik,' he grinned. 'What about you kid?'

'You don't need to know,' I told him. 'After all, you're not about to put *me* in the ground.'

I unravelled the cloth and the blade of my axe shone in the moonlight. Melik strode forward, his two goons behind.

'That's a mighty fine weapon,' Melik said. 'I'll enjoy taking it from your corpse!'

In a second he was at me. Without thinking I swung the axe in a wide arc, making them all leap back. I kept my distance, using the extra reach of my weapon to keep them in check. The one on the left flanked to my side and I turned to parry his thrust, spinning back straight away to block an oncoming assault from Melik. My flanker took the chance to get a quick cut in at my side. I turned and cracked the haft of my axe against his face. As I felt the sting of blood I knew I was in over my head. Most would not have been able to hit back that quickly; these men were trained fighters.

As the three tried to surround me again I spun to my right and slashed at the third opponent before changing my stance and swiping around at the two others, catching Melik on the arm. They rushed me, faster this time. As I parried one the other two cut at my sides and I was only able to get away by hacking at them furiously. A figure appeared at my side.

'What are you doing?' Melik yelled at him. 'You have no business here!'

I glanced to the newcomer – it was the hooded man from back inside the tavern, except his hood had fallen back to reveal a shaggy blond mane and a scruffy beard.

'Three against one didn't quite seem fair,' he chuckled, throwing his coat open to reveal a blade at his hip. 'I thought I'd even it up a bit.'

'Thank you,' I whispered under my breath.

'Don't mention it,' he replied, equally as quiet.

Melik and his goons charged forward, but with a flash of steel one of them was disarmed. I must have blinked, for I never even saw my companion move. He held a rapier in hand, a flimsy weapon by anyone's judgement though it had sent a broadsword flying into the dirt. I rushed into the fight as Melik leapt at the stranger, stopping them from double teaming him as the third of our opponents rushed to retrieve his blade. With my attention now focused on one opponent, I made easy work of blocking the incoming strikes while dealing out my own punishment. After a few nasty cuts into my opponent's flesh he began to back away.

It was victory...almost. As one fell back, the other came forward with blade in hand once more. I glimpsed the blond who was caught up with holding back Melik, his blade faster than any I had seen. Still, their ringleader was beginning to gain the upper hand purely through brute force. As the third fighter approached I rushed him, using the haft of my axe to push him back. He tried to hold his ground, though I quickly sent the blade flying away once more. At the sight, I swiftly spun around and caught Melik in the back of the leg. He went down, my ally taking no time in swatting the sword from his grasp. I grabbed him by the back of the collar.

'Go on!' he growled. 'Kill me bastard!'

'I will not kill a man on his knees,' I declared, my gaze shifting to his nephew who stood by the entrance looking afraid – about a dozen had joined him to watch the fight. 'Nor will I spill the blood of a man who is protecting his family.'

The hatred in Melik's face appeared to melt away. 'So what? You're sparing me?'

'This time. You come at me again and I'll put you in the ground.' I turned to the crowd and raised my voice. 'That goes for any of you. Take no heed of my youth, for I am a pirate true and proper and will kill anyone who gets in my way.'

The three men retrieved their weapons and took Melik's nephew as they retreated into the night.

'I suggest you find a new place to drink!' the blond man called after them, turning to me with a grin afterwards.

'Thanks again for helping me,' I told him. 'What's your name?'

'Arkin,' he grunted as he returned the blade to its scabbard. 'What about yours great pirate?'

He smiled mockingly. *No,* I thought, *I can't let anything link me to that old life.*

'You can call me Darkskull,' I told him.

'That's a mighty flashy name you've picked out for yourself,' he hollered. 'I hope it does ya well.'

'Have you ever considered...'

'Joining a crew?' he interrupted. 'Unfortunately not. I've got a good life here. Also, it would probably get in the way with my guard duty.'

I almost stumbled back at the words.

'You're a guard?' I gaped.

'Don't worry,' he consoled me. 'It's not against the law just to *be* a pirate here in Blakereath, so you're safe. Also, I owe you one; I've been meaning to beat some sense into that meathead Melik for months now.'

'He's always like that?'

'More or less, thinks he owns the place. And I quite like drinking here so I'm hoping he'll have the sense to stay away.'

'Here's hoping,' I echoed.

We made our way back in to the delight of the patrons who seemed equally as glad to be rid of Melik. Arkin bought me a pint and we sat together, chatting.

'Your accent,' he pointed out. 'Not much of a change but it's certainly different. Where ya from?'

'Merrywood,' I lied.

'Oh, terrible business been going on there,' his gaze lingered on me.

'I wouldn't know,' I told him, 'Haven't been back home in a while, part of doing what I do, ya know?'

He nodded. 'Look, I said this before but I don't want you worrying.'

'I'm not…'

'Let me finish. I might be a guard but I believe your business is your own. Just don't go killing people and I won't have to say anything. You seem like a nice lad; I can't see myself in the pirate life but if I find anyone I'll send 'em your way.'

'Th…thank you,' I muttered. 'I appreciate it.'

'Call it my gratitude for scaring off that piece of shit.' He finished his pint. 'Well, that's me off, up early tomorrow.'

'Thanks for the drink.'

'No worries lad. I'll see ya around – Darkskull.'

He smiled to himself as he threw up his hood and walked out. It felt lonely once Arkin was gone, but he was far from the only one to buy me a drink that night. It turned out everyone had been getting sick of Melik throwing his weight around.

The night went on, free drinks piling up in front of me, coming faster than I could drink them.

I cannot remember exactly when I passed out, but when I awoke it was to the innkeeper – Sid – throwing a bucket of water over me. I was on the tavern floor, nobody in the place aside from me and him.

'Sorry lad,' he said as I thrashed around, startled. 'Didn't want to wake ya, but Gelda thought there might be somewhere you needed to be.'

'There isn't,' I groaned as he handed me a towel. 'Just got here.'

'So you haven't got a place yet?' he enquired, I shook my head. 'Well, if you need it we have a room upstairs. It ain't much but it's yours if ya want it.'

I dried myself and stood, smoothing out my clothes.

'I don't have much money,' I told him mournfully.

'I didn't ask for any,' he said, my eyebrows raising. 'We get a tonne of riffraff here – bad for business. And while most folks here respect me, I can't put up a fight like I used to. Gelda gets scared sometimes.'

'That's terrible but what can I do?'

'Well you sure handled yourself well last night,' he countered. 'All I ask is you stay down here when we're busy and scare away the trouble. You do that and the room is yours, free of charge for as long as you stay.'

'That's all?' I pressed.

'That's all,' he confirmed, offering his hand.

I grasped it and smiled. It was agreed. Sid showed me up to the room which already had my axe in it – I must have dropped it at some point. It was smaller than my quarters back on the ship but not by much, and definitely much larger than my makeshift home back in Cranwell. Neither Sid nor Gelda lived here but they used the larger room as an office which had a bed in it for rare occasions. My room had clearly not been touched in years, dust clung to it like a leech and the mattress was old and worn. Still, it was better than nothing.

Gelda brought me up some breakfast once I was settled in; while I ate she stitched up my wounds, receiving the odd gasp or groan from me. I had not realised how many hits the trio had gotten on me until every inch of them had been poked with a needle.

'Heard you're a pirate,' the plump barmaid said as she pierced my skin for what felt like the hundredth time.

'That's right,' I mumbled with a mouth full of food.

'It explains all of these scars,' she tutted. 'I haven't seen wounds like these in a long time.'

'Occupational hazard,' I retorted.

'I know a couple of young lads who hang around by the shipyards,' she told me. 'Both good fighters but in need of some discipline. Sid overheard you talking about finding a crew, I could introduce you.'

'Names?'

'Dirk and Thalkrin.'

'How old?'

'Fourteen, the pair of them.'

'Family?'

'Dirk is an orphan, Thalkrin's father is still kicking but he's a piece of shit. They live in an abandoned place somewhere with a bunch of orphans so I hear, but I know where to find them.'

'Promising,' I muttered. 'But don't bring them here. I'll scout the city later today and find a place. I'll meet them there tomorrow.'

'Okay,' she said. 'I'll hold off until then.'

I thanked her and she left the room, leaving me to my thoughts. It was as good a start as any – I had a place to live, potential recruits and (if last night was anything to go by) a blossoming reputation.

After a short nap I wandered around Blakereath, making mental notes of where certain shops were and where I could find work if my money ran out. The smell of the sea was strong in the air, sending me back to Cranwell, if only for a moment. Except this was not Cranwell, it was bigger, which meant more outfitted guards and cleaner streets – for the most part. The larger streets all led into the town square, twice as big as any I had seen.

Dozens of stalls were set up in the centre where you could buy anything from necklaces to lanterns. Around the sides of the square more shops faced in – blacksmiths and bakers, fletchers and florists, and in the centre of it all a fountain.

It was white marble and gleaming. The stonework depicted a king, maybe *the* king, though I did not know his name. It was the same figure I had seen back in Merrywood. Water streamed around his standing likeness as he he d a blade in hand like a true warrior. So much detail was in the sword, its long blade stretching almost over the fountain itself. The stone had been moulded so precisely, the pattern on its pommel oddly specific. It was almost as if the king himself had only been second priority and the sword of utmost importance.

'Mister! Mister!' a voice interrupted me.

A filthy man in ragged clothes rushed up to me.

'What is it?' I asked, taking a cautious step back.

'Nobody will listen to me!' he cried. 'My sister is hurt. She needs help and I can't carry her on my own.'

I nodded and ran with the man into an alley. His sister was there, as filthy as him and lying on the ground.

'What's wrong with you?' I asked, approaching.

A sudden impact hit my back and sent my face into the dirt. I flipped over. The woman was getting up, knife in hand, several others appearing out of the shadows.

'Good work *brother*,' the woman chimed. 'We've caught ourselves a rich one by the look of him.'

I scanned the scene. The alleyway only had one way in and out. Five figures surrounded me all armed with knives as I slowly got to my feet, internally cursing myself for leaving the axe back at the tavern. Wargal's knife was at my hip, hidden by my coat, but I knew I was not good enough with it to fight off all of these thugs.

'Looks like a pirate,' one of them called. 'We best be careful.'

'Please,' laughed the one who had led me here. 'He's just a boy. He can't do no harm.'

Again that smell of seawater hit me, and I tilted my head up to take it in better.

I fell onto the cold, hard ground of Cranwell for the fourth time that day, my body aching and my pride just as hurt. It was not helped by incessant disappointed tutting.

'Not good enough,' Lundrip spat, snow settling on his shoulders.

'I can't do it, there's no way up there!' I yelled back at him, followed by a sharp strike to my face.

Red splattered against white and I got back to my feet.

'There is always a way.'

I held my hand to my bloodied mouth, crimson flowing over my palm. When I looked up from it my teacher was gone and his soft whistle sounded from the rooftops.

I leapt into action, turning and cutting the man behind me with my blade as I retreated further into the alley. They gave chase but I was quicker. Leaping against the building on my right I clung onto a crack in the stonework. Pushing off of the wall with my legs I managed to clamber onto the adjacent one, clinging to the top of it as I pulled myself over. I jumped down into another alleyway but I was far from safe, the thieves already beginning to hoist themselves over.

I sprinted through the passageway, my gaze shifting frantically to find the best escape route. The alley twisted and turned, never letting back out onto the main street. Their voices and footsteps were getting louder, closing in on me. I saw it. To the untrained eye it was simply the ledge of a boarded up window but that was not what I saw. I jumped up onto it, about five feet from the ground, turning and leaping across to the roof of the single storey building opposite. My grip was flimsy, my hardy clothes weighing me down. Hands grabbed my ankles, tugging at me. I kicked frantically, pulling desperately at the edge of the roof.

'Hey!' another voice called, and the hand receded.

Once on the roof I was away without turning back. I climbed to a second storey building to be safe, though they did not seem to be perusing me.

The city below spread for a mile at least end to end. Further in land there stood a stately home, gated up with a dozen guards outside. There was nothing like that in Cranwell, but then again there was nobody of importance in Cranwell. We had our mayor of course, a fat old bastard who lived a half mile outside of town and never bothered with us. Maybe Blakereath's mayor (or whoever lived there) was different.

The city had everything and was full from top to bottom. That meant unfortunately it lacked the one thing I was looking for – space. No matter how long I looked I could not spot anywhere I could use as a training ground in the entire city. Disappointed, I climbed back down and headed for the tavern.

Chapter 12

Thief

'There's nowhere for us to go!' I groaned to Gelda as I nursed my drink.

'You could always train them here,' she suggested, I sighed and shook my head.

'You and Sid have done enough for me already, it'll only bring you trouble if things don't work out with these boys. No, I need somewhere more isolated.'

'Sorry son, not much I can do about that.'

I gave her a weak smile and sat as she got back to work. More people were beginning to pile in, many who had not been here the night before. I listened in and heard Melik's name thrown around a lot; I realised there was no sign of him. *Good riddance.*

The broad boy I had eyed yesterday was here, this time chatting to an older patron and five empty glasses on their table already. With Sid and Gelda doing their best to keep up with the surge of new customers, I sat lonely watching the door for any sign of Arkin. When he showed no sign of showing I watched the boy, waiting for an opportunity to join him.

I was out of luck. The older man talked to the boy for the next several hours and still no Arkin.

I wanted to leave, and I would have if not for my promise to Sid. Eagerly watching the drunkards, I actually hoped for any dispute so that I might have some excitement that day. Then I saw her. She was alone now and nowhere near as intimidating. She did not notice me and I turned my face away, trying my best to listen in as she sat a few stools down from me and ordered a drink.

'I don't want any trouble from you,' I heard Sid tell her.

'Would I do that to you?' she said with a laugh.

'How did you get the money?' he asked.

'A good, honest day's work,' she chimed, chuckling under her breath.

'This is no joke Deline!' Sid spat. 'Where are those thief friends of yours anyhow?'

'Likely in the cells by now.'

'What happened?'

'Got caught. We were in the middle of robbing this kid and a guard saw us. The others fought, I took the day's loot and ran.'

I had not noticed I was clenching my fist until my fingers began to hurt. I stood and moved into the seat next to her, axe at my side.

Facing forward I ordered another pint. 'Didn't recognise you without your knife pointed at me.'

My gaze stayed onwards but I could tell she was shocked when she realised who I was. The blade came out, aimed at my stomach.

'What about now?' she growled. 'What are you even doing here?'

'I live here,' I said simply. 'And I don't want the likes of you in my home.'

Her hand shook for a moment and I swiftly knocked the knife from her grip. She bent down to grab it but I caught her arm.

'Get off me!' she cried, but my grasp stayed firm.

'What's going on here?' Sid questioned.

'This is the woman who tried to rob me today. You told me to keep out any trouble and that's exactly what I'm doing.'

'Dad, tell him to get off me!' she yelled.

I pulled back, glancing from Deline to Sid and back again. 'Dad?' I muttered, shocked.

It was Deline's turn to be cocky.

'Yes Darkskull,' Sid grimaced. 'Deline is my daughter.'

It was cold outside and I paced back and forth for a while cursing before Sid came after me. I had not meant to walk out and I hated giving that horrid woman the satisfaction, but I was at a loss.

'Lad, please come back inside,' he begged, 'There are so many people in there, I don't have time to keep an eye on any trouble.'

'I can't believe this!' I yelled. 'That woman in there has pulled a knife on me twice today, and you're saying she's your daughter?'

'Deline wasn't always like that,' he sighed. 'She was a good girl growing up. Always helped me with *The Sunken Sails* and kept her nose out of trouble. I always thought I'd leave the tavern to her one day and she seemed eager to take it. She was made for bar work that girl, so friendly and charming.'

'Not from what I saw,' I grumbled.

'Please lad, don't hate her.'

'Don't hate her?' I exclaimed. 'She and her companions chased me through back alleys with knives in their hands, who knows what they would have done if they caught me?'

'She wouldn't have hurt you!' Sid insisted. 'She's still a good lass at heart, but she changed after her mother died. Started spending time with the wrong crowd and all that. I tried to get through to her but I was busy with the tavern, I could hardly afford to hire Gelda and even with the two of us I was swamped with work. I lost her to those miscreants, but she's still my little girl.'

I could not be angry at Sid but that did not mean I had to like his daughter. After all she had held me at knifepoint and tried to rob me.

We went back in together, with Deline giving me a devious grin as I passed by and sat at the end of the bar. My mood was ruined and I wanted more than even now to simply retire to my room. The night went on and there was no real trouble – a couple of disputes between customers which I managed to calm before they escalated but nothing else.

More patrons bought me drinks for taking care of Melik, though none stayed around long enough to chat. Eventually *The Sunken Sails* began to empty out. By the time I remembered about the boy I wanted to talk to, he had already left. Soon it was only a few drunkards playing cards in the corner, Sid and Gelda cleaning up the place, and Deline who was still at the bar.

I turned to her and away again when I realised her eyes were on me.

'What are you still doing here?' I grumbled, refusing to make eye contact.

'Just finishing my drink,' she said. 'And wondering why my father employed someone like you to stave off trouble.'

'What do you mean *someone like me?*' I spat back.

She laughed. 'Somebody's sensitive. I just meant you don't look like you have much experience.'

I pushed myself up and faced her, our eyes meeting. 'I have experience!' I grunted. She averted her gaze and took a swig, ignoring me. I moved behind the bar so she had no option but to look at me. 'How many people have you killed?' I asked her.

For the first time her eyes widened with what appeared like doubt. She shook her head briefly and clocked me with a confident stare.

'More than you,' she muttered.

'I doubt it, but I wouldn't know.' She raised an eyebrow. 'I ost track when I was sailing the seas with Daxon and his crew.'

'Like I'm supposed to believe *you* know Daxon,' she laughed.

'Believe what you want,' I told her. 'I can tell by your eyes you never killed anyone.'

She looked down, finished her drink, and stood to leave.

'You're going?' Sid chimed in before she reached the door.

He was across the tavern and had a broom in hand.

'Sorry dad, have places to be.'

He approached her. 'Please, stay the night. You said it yourself, your friends are in the prison, there's no need for you to dash off like this.'

She began to argue, but stopped as her eyes turned to me, a small smirk crossing her face. 'Actually, you know what dad? I think I think I will stay, thanks.'

Sid beamed and Deline smiled as she saw me gritting my teeth.

Gelda went home soon after and I wasted no time in retiring to my room. I heard Sid and Deline laughing downstairs and buried my head into the pillow. I was about to finally drift off when I heard them coming upstairs. There was a knock and Sid popped his head into the room.

'Darkskull, I got some blankets so me and Deline are going to sleep in the office tonight. I've left some supper downstairs if you get hungry.'

I nodded and thanked him, all the while cursing myself for letting that woman get to me. There was silence for a while, but not even half an hour later there was another knock on my door.

I mumbled a sleepy, *'What?'* and Deline came in.

I sat up rapidly, my face beginning to boil. She had blankets and a pillow under her arm.

'My father snores so I'm going to sleep in here tonight.'

'Fine,' I groaned, though it had not been a question.

I pulled my trousers to me and got up.

'What are you doing?'

'You can have the bed; I'm going for a walk.'

She seemed surprised as I threw on the rest of my clothes and strode out of the room. I realised shortly into the walk that I had made a mistake. It was cold in Blakereath at night, perhaps even colder than Cranwell. I was uncomfortable, and had nothing to do. I walked still, trying to clear my head. I debated walking around until morning to avoid that awful thief. I was tired though and my head hurt. I returned to the tavern soon after and sat downstairs eating the supper Sid had prepared for me.

Finally, I swallowed my pride and went back to the room. I gathered the blankets and lay down on the hard wooden floor.

'You can't possibly be comfortable down there,' Deline's voice came after a few minutes. I grunted and flipped over, eyes away from her.

'You want me to say I'm sorry?' she spat, the sound of her feet hitting the floor behind me. 'Well I'm not okay? You looked wealthy and you're not exactly intimidating – you were a perfect target.'

'Whatever,' I groaned. 'I wouldn't expect any regret from the likes of you.'

Her hand grasped me, *had I gone too far?* She grabbed at the covers and threw them off me, forcing me to sit up and turn around to face her. Her eyes shone in the faint light – the only part of her that was visible.

'What do you mean *the likes of me?*'

'Just that I have low expectations for a thief.'

She tutted. 'You're a pirate, you mean to tell me you've never stolen before?'

My mind flashed back to Cranwell and all of those people who I pickpocketed.

'I've never surrounded someone and held them at knifepoint for the sake of a few coins,' I spat back.

'You claim to be a pirate who has killed people! Don't try to hold any morale value over me when you're a murderer!'

'Scoundrel!' 'Killer!' 'Murderer!'

'It was in self-defence,' I argued. 'And you've probably killed people, doing what you do.'

Her eyes dropped, her face gradually becoming clearer in the dim light. 'Once,' she muttered, barely a whisper. 'And it was an accident.'

It was cold that day. Icy. Easy enough for anyone to slip, especially so high up. All I did was push him – on a normal day that would have been it. But no. He fell. He fell and he never got up again. Despite it all I still pocketed the ring. I wore it even now.

'My first time was like that,' I admitted without thinking.

'What happened?' she pressed.

I shook my head and hoped she could see the gesture in the darkness. 'What about you?'

'Chalk it up to a mugging that went wrong, back when I first joined the...*group.*'

'The thieves you mean,' I blurted bluntly.

'They're more than that,' she protested. 'They're my friends, my family.'

My fist clenched. 'They're not your friends,' I spat. 'They probably didn't even realise you ditched them. The only family you still have is in the next room, and you don't even give a shit about him!'

Her mouth opened as if she would argue, but it closed just as quickly. Defeated, she returned to the bed without another word. It was not meant to be an attack on her, the story just hit close to home. I grabbed the blanket and went to sleep.

Chapter 13

Fresh Meat

Her brows furrowed and I swear I caught glimpse of a grin as her eyes flicked to me.

'Actually dad I think I'll stay a bit longer.'

Those were the words which I dreaded to hear. I thought that after last night she would stop messing with me but clearly her fun was far from over. We were eating breakfast – sausages Gelda had made for the four of us. I was almost finished, having gotten up earlier in an attempt to avoid the wretched tyrant before me. Now at her proclamation I could not bring myself to finish the food, and in fact felt a little sick.

Deline was a piece of work, still dirtied and in her ragged clothes from the day before. I knew it was hypocritical to judge, after all I had surely been worse within the last month, and worse still when I was living in Cranwell.

'But what about your thief friends?' Gelda questioned. 'Won't the scoundrels want you there when they get out of their cells?'

'That's enough Gelda,' Sid sighed. 'Who Deline chooses to associate herself with is none of our business.'

'It's fine,' Deline interjected. 'They're not my friends anyway.'

A quick glance towards me and I shivered.

'So Darkskull,' Sid said, changing the subject. 'What do you plan to do about this no-training-space predicament?'

'I'm not sure.'

'Training space?' Deline enquired.

Before I could stop him Sid explained my situation to the thief. She laughed, and my fist clenched.

'So you're going to teach some rotten kids how to fight?' she chuckled. 'What are you basing your experience on? Some alleged companionship with Daxon?'

'Yes,' I barked, gritting my teeth.

'Bet even *I* could give you a run for your money.'

I stood, knife already in hand. Gelda gasped and Sid groaned but Deline smiled and pulled out her own blade.

'First blood?' she asked, a wide grin across her face.

'Suits me.'

'What if someone sees you fighting?' Gelda interjected.

'Don't worry,' Sid calmed her. 'We don't open for a while, plus it'll do those two some good to settle their dispute.'

I nodded to the older man and the two of us moved into the centre of the tavern as the elders moved tables and chairs out of our way. Without delay she was upon me, swiping the air as I dodged the incoming blow. She turned, the blade of her knife shining even in the dull light of the tavern. She swiped again, this time narrowly missing my sternum. I picked my opportunity and leapt at her. Even mid-strike I noticed her eyes flick to my wrist. I swiftly pulled my hand away as her own knife cut across where my hand would have been.

'You're quick,' she praised.

'You too.'

The words were by me stooping and swiping at her legs; she leapt back, her blade batting away my own. Despite myself I could not help but smile. I watched her stance. No matter how we moved, her feet always planted themselves firmly – no exploiting that. Her eyes watched my hand closely, always quick enough to pick up on the smallest of hints. In all honesty I had no idea how I was still in this fight; my reflexes were not as good as hers. *It must be from pure instinct.*

Every time I lunged in, her blade threatened to find my wielding hand. I saw no way to get close enough, meanwhile she had been an inch away from victory several times now. I backed up to clear my head and glanced for a moment at my own blade. *Of course!* How stupid I must have been not to think of it, this was *Wargal's* knife. That meant it was made for one thing. When she next came in I parried off to the side easily. She spun away from my reach and directly into my trap. As she was turning I let the knife fly. The steel skimmed across her exposed arm, leaving a line of blood in its trail.

'Cheater!' she accused.

'We never made a rule against it,' I laughed, her face reddening.

'That was a dirty move. I'm starting to think you truly are a pirate.'

My smile remained while Sid tended to his daughter's wound with a wet cloth. She went for a walk not long after, her father going along to make sure she did not run off again.

'She's right, you know?' Gelda commented. 'That was an awfully crafty thing to do.'

'You should see me when I have more than just a knife,' I hollered, the older woman laughing along.

'Well I'm glad you took that rotten daughter of his down a few pegs!'

'You don't like her?'

She shook her head and sighed. 'Always saw me as a threat, like I'd steal her father away or something. Never occurred to her that Sid is almost old enough to be *my* father. No, that girl is trouble. Always will be.'

I thought on that for a while. Gelda was right, Deline *was* trouble. Trouble which I did not want nor need. Though with Sid wrapped around her finger and me with nowhere else to stay, it seemed like I was stuck with her – at least for now.

When they got back she had returned to her tormenting nature. Every word I said she tried to contradict, each talent I had was outdone by her. She read better, she wrote better, her reflexes were quicker. She spent the rest of the day disturbing me and sat beside me all through that night to prevent any conversation prospects with the other patrons.

Again, there was no trouble at *The Sunken Sails* which meant unfortunately no escape from my tormentor. That night Sid went home and she slept in the office, though simply the thought of her presence stopped me from getting a good sleep that night. This routine went on, the two of us at each other's throats at every opportunity. I wandered the city as often as I could, partially to get my bearings but mainly to escape *her*. At nights I worked the tavern, deterring any trouble before it had a chance to properly start. Only getting into one real fight and only hand-to-hand.

Before I knew it, a week had passed – arguably the most tiresome week of my life. In my daily traversing of the city I had spotted several more potential crewmates and done my research into them. It did not however fix the problem of nowhere to train them. I was even considering going back on my principles and bringing people to the tavern, at least it would let me get out onto the sea with a crew and away from Deline.

'Haven't gotten yourself into too much trouble I see!' the voice called, and I was happy to see the familiar face.

His hood was up which shadowed some of his features, but the voice was alone would have been enough.

'Arkin!' I greeted the man, grasping his arm with a smile.

He was a sight for sore eyes, especially with Deline sat next to me, being irritating as usual.

'Nice to see ya again lad!' he cheered. 'Who's this lovely lady beside you?'

I followed his eyes to Deline and scoffed. *Her? Lovely?* I suppose she was much more presentable than last week, with new clothes and the dirt scrubbed out of her. The hair appeared brown now as opposed to black and her pale skin was devoid of its previous ailments. Still, far from lovely. She extended her hand to the guard tenderly which he took and kissed gently.

'I'm Deline,' she said, applying a lower, more flirtatious tone to her own voice. 'Pleasure to meet you.'

'Arkin,' the blond said. 'And I assure you the pleasure is mine.'

He kissed her hand again before reluctantly releasing it.

'I'm going to get some air.'

As I went to stand however, the guard grabbed me.

'Darkskull, hang on there. I found a few people who might be of interest to you.'

I sat back down, turning my back fully to Deline to face Arkin. 'That's fantastic, but recruits are the least of my worries these days.'

'How so?'

Deline coughed abruptly and loudly from behind me, but I played her no attention.

'I've searched the whole city and can't find a good place to train them.'

'You should have just came to me!' he laughed. 'There's an olden building in the north-east quarter which we use to train new guards. Place is all but abandoned most of the year – I could loan you a key.'

My face lightened.

'You're a guard?' Deline spat in disgust, her eyes moving to anywhere in the room but on Arkin.

'Shhh,' I silenced her, turning back to my friend, 'You're sure that would be okay?'

'Of course,' he chuckled. 'Just try not to damage it too much and it'll be fine.'

I grinned, ear to ear. Finally, what I had been looking for, and Arkin said it was repayment for helping with Melik. We worked out the logistics and I ended up paying for our drinks the rest of the night as an extra thank you. He bid me farewell that night, saying we would meet again soon. I got Gelda to spread the message to Dirk and Thalkrin the next day, then I hit the streets myself. Arkin dropped by later to give me the key.

'Tell your guys to meet me there at noon tomorrow?' I asked him.

He affirmed it and I slept that night knowing I was making progress. Not even Deline's constant criticisms could dampen my mood.

They were late. Every last one of them. Every few minutes I checked the doorway in case they were waiting outside, but there was no sign of them. The place was good, a little rundown but overall a good practice area. It had high windows so nobody could spy on us, and only the one entrance. Most of the building was a single room, still full of practice dummies and targets. I found a few weapons in the back, nothing fancy but there was a range back there. Mostly rapiers though.

Unwrapping the steel of my axe, I turned to the nearest dummy. *Might as well get some practice in.* Most of the figures were armoured, in plate mail nonetheless. I took a few swings, keeping focus on my stance. The creaking of the door made me spin around eagerly.

'Oh, it's just you,' I grumbled. 'What are you doing here?'

'Came to watch,' Deline chimed. 'Doesn't look like you have much of a turnout.'

'They'll be here,' I snapped back, returning to the target.

I got in another few swings before she distracted me again, this time with an exaggerated sigh. 'If you're so bored then leave!' I barked at her, but as I spun around faces were peeking into the doorway.

'We could come back later?' a boy asked, but I put aside my anger and encouraged them in.

Two boys and a girl, all fairly well dressed but a glint of mischief in each of their eyes. I recognised none of them.

'Tell me your names,' I urged; they all seemed nervous.

'Come on, out with it,' Deline chimed in.

I shot her a stern expression.

'I'm Perkyn,' said the boy who had spoken before.

He was the tallest of them and the brawniest. None could be older than fourteen. His skin was tanned and his hair a fiery red which fell to his shoulders. Around his neck hung a simple pendant, bearing the likeness of a golden hawk. The girl (who stepped forward next and introduced herself as Felima) was similar in appearance which made me think they were siblings. Her hair was much longer however, falling slightly shy of her waist and tied back in a loose ponytail. The third was sheepish. He was smaller than the others, with dusty brown hair and huge doe eyes. He hesitated.

'I...I'm Laricko.'

I assessed the three of them. Perhaps some potential in each of them, though I was unsure. Perkyn seemed battle-ready as it was, but the other two I was uncertain of.

'So you're the ones Arkin sent me?' They nodded; I tutted. 'I expect a more vocal response from my recruits, but we will get to etiquette later. First I need to assess your skills.'

How would Daxon handle this situation? I was trying to imitate his demeanour as best I could. *No,* I thought, *I'm nothing like him, I have to do this for myself.*

'Excuse me, mister...'

'Darkskull,' I told Perkyn. 'And none of this *mister* business. You can call me by my name, or simply *captain*.'

162

Deline began to laugh. 'Only thing *you* are captain of is cheating in knife fights.'

'That's enough from you,' I threatened with an outstretched finger. 'You were saying lad?'

'Just wondering why a supposed "captain" like you, is recruiting kids like us.'

'It does all seem a bit fishy,' Felima added. 'After all you don't look old enough to be a pirate captain.'

That struck hard and Deline's continued sniggering only put me off further. Still, I breathed deeply and composed myself.

'If you want to doubt me, feel free,' I sighed. 'Nobody is forcing you to be here. If you want to get out of this city and explore the world, with endless opportunities at your fingertips, then put your faith in me. If not, I'm sure you all know where the door is.'

I waited, half expecting all of them to leave. But they did not. They stayed put. I heard muffled clapping from the doorway.

'Looks like we got here just in time for the speech.'

Two more boys had entered. I did not recognise these neither, which led me to my next assertion. 'You must be Dirk and Thalkrin.'

They entered and crossed over to us. Despite the similar age they appeared so much older than the trio – it was something about the visible scars and the unkempt stubble beginning to form beneath their chins. They introduced themselves. The taller of the two was Thalkrin, though that was one of only a few things which set them apart. Both had ebony skin, with dark eyes and hair, though

Dirk's was shorter. They dressed similarly too, in layers of torn clothing overlapping one another.

'We waiting for anyone else or are we gonna get to training?' Dirk encouraged eagerly, though more of a grimace than a smile on his face.

'I had invited a few more, but it looks like they're not going to show,' I muttered.

I moved to lock the door, but as I was closing it a hand from outside stopped me. The face of Hadivik met me – the blacksmith's apprentice who I had found in the city.

'Sorry I'm late,' he called out. 'Boss wouldn't let me out of the shop until I sharpened every sword in the place, the bastard.'

'Get yourself in here.'

He was the oldest of them at sixteen, though his physique was that of a full-grown man. He had bulking muscles from working the forge all day, with minor burns and cuts covering a good portion of his shirtless body. He greeted the others as I closed and bolted the door, giving a judging glare towards Deline as I did it. It seemed like she was staying.

'Let the training begin!'

Chapter 14

Allies

soon had them kitted up with weapons from the supplies, however limited they were. Fortunately, Dirk and Thalkrin had brought their own daggers and Hadivik had brought his own weapon of choice – his blacksmith's hammer. It was sturdy enough, double-headed and had a decently sized grip.

'Each of you get in front of a practice dummy, let me see how you'd take on an opponent.'

They did as I instructed and went to town on the figures. The trio were equipped with standard broadswords as they had no weapon preference, though it was clear from the get go only Perkyn was decent with the blade. Laricko and Felima were both slow and sloppy, each of them dropping their weapon at least once. I shook my head and approached the timid boy.

'Keep a firm grip on your weapon,' I instructed. 'Hold it further up the hilt. No. Like this. There, now you've got it.'

Despite my corrections he was still sloppy, though when I suggested another weapon he seemed persistent to keep at it with the broadsword. When I corrected Felima she voiced that she would prefer something lighter; I switched her broadsword for a rapier and she seemed to be at least slightly better with the thinner blade.

Perkyn and Thalkrin only needed slight adjustments in their stance while Dirk was an all-round natural with a blade. With only a dagger he had managed to find the chinks in the plate armour and sunk his weapon into the fake opponent multiple times. His stance was as perfect as any I had seen. I would have bet my left arm that he could have given Wargal a run for his money. Hadivik was the most interesting to me however, his blunt weapon smashing repeatedly against the steel with constant vigour. His form was off and his movement was a little slow, but lord was he strong.

'How long do we have to do this?' Perkyn groaned.

'Until I tell you to stop.'

My response was met with a sigh from Laricko and Felima.

'Can't handle the strain rich boy?' Dirk laughed from beside Perkyn.

'I can handle it just fine!' the redhead grunted, broadsword clashing against armour. Both boys attacked harder with their respective weapons, glancing at one another every few seconds. I stood back and admired their enthusiasm.

'You don't want to break that up?' Deline tutted, now beside me.

'A bit of healthy competition is good for them.'

And I seemed to be right, neither of them slowed and I believed they were pushing each other to strike harder and faster; I could not say the same for everyone. After only ten minutes Laricko was faltering, his blows sloppy and ineffective. I leapt between him and his dummy and caught a strike on the sleeve of my coat, knocking it from his grip. His doe-like eyes met mine.

'Sorry...captain.'

Tears appeared to well in his eyes.

'You're not suited for a broadsword,' I told him. 'Not until you can build up more strength at least. Go out back and pick another weapon.'

To his credit he bowed his head respectively and quickly ran out.

'Typical rich kid.' Dirk scoffed.

My hand caught Perkyn's shoulder as he was raising his sword. Our eyes locked and he glanced down.

'That's what I thought. Get back to work.'

As I turned back to Deline she had a cocky smirk directed at me. The timid boy returned shortly after with a bow, evoking an audible laugh from Dirk and Thalkrin which I could not dispute.

'Lad, it takes a lot of practice to be an archer,' I told him quietly.

He nodded enthusiastically. 'I know captain, but I'm willing to try.'

I had not the heart to put him down, so instead directed him to a target away from the others to avoid accidents. I watched as he knocked his first arrow, which on release fell from the bowstring and to his feet. The others were watching, most with smirks.

'Get back to work!' I ordered.

I moved around, observing them. *We have a lot of work to do.* Deline had taken to sitting on a stool and sharpening her knife on a whetstone I pulled up my own stool and relaxed next to her.

'Something to say?' I shook my head. 'Not exactly the best the best crew in the world.'

I agreed with her for once, and if to emphasise her point a moment later I heard the clash of blades. Spinning around I was not surprised to see Dirk and Perkyn standing an inch apart, dagger pressing against broadsword.

'What's your problem?' Perkyn spat through gritted teeth.

Within a second I was between them, throwing both of them back by their collars.

'I could ask the same of both of you.'

'I have no problem,' Dirk replied, a sly grin shining. 'I'm just not overly fond on posh bastards like you three playing at fighting.'

I stopped everyone and gathered them around, aggression on the faces of more than the two boys.

'Clearly I've gone about this wrong,' I sighed. 'I wanted to test your skills first, but I have no use for them if you're at each other's throats.'

'What do you expect us to do?' the fiery redhead spat.

Without a word I pulled Deline away from her dwindling and into the circle, with many complaints and profanities coming from her. I drew her closer to me and whispered something in her ear. She pulled back and grinned, darting out to the back and returning with a broadsword.

'What's going on?' Felima asked.

'I want the six of you to fight the two of us. Whoever manages to draw blood will act as my second in command and have power over the others.'

The faces of the two boys lit up with determination. Deline and I stood back to back and it started.

The first charge was better than I had anticipated. Thalkrin and Dirk branched off to either side of me and I was aware of Perkyn edging closer. Dirk was the first to leap in, a snarl on his face as he lunged with his knife. I caught the small weapon against the haft of my axe and knocked him back with a merciless kick. Behind, I heard Deline parrying Hadivik and Felima.

168

Perkyn was the next to jump in at the sight of Dirk's failure, though Laricko loosed his first straight arrow of the day – directly into his friend's shoulder.

'Switch!' Deline called and we spun around one another in time for me to swat aside a rapier strike while she parried the incoming knife from Thalkrin.

I smiled to myself, it was good timing. As I swung my axe in large arcs to keep Hadivik and his deadly hammer back, I could hear obscenities coming from Perkyn and the sorrowful apologies of Laricko. Felima disappeared from view, *likely to help her brother,* and was replaced by a fighting Dirk who had his gaze set on me. I hated fending off smaller weapons with the axe, it was not a good match up for me. Still, I managed to bat away his arm a few times. As he lunged in past my guard, Deline's sword came out of nowhere and knocked it from his grasp. Hadivik kept his distance as I used my free hand to strike the orphan hard in the chest. Thalkrin was also disarmed.

'Stop,' I called.

Felima was keeping pressure on Perkyn's wound and Laricko was crying by this point. Both the ruffians were unarmed and Hadivik dared not approach on his own. *What a disgrace. They were...*

'Pitiful!' Deline beat me to it. 'Absolutely pitiful.'

Dirk bared his teeth in a snarl. 'Not my fault the two of you went in on me,' he spat.

'There are *six* of you,' I pointed out. 'And yet only two of us. Still, we remained unharmed while all of you have been defeated. Even if Deline and I were some of the greatest fighters in the world – which we are far from – the six of you should have managed to at least inflict a scratch.'

'Looks like the little boy did,' Thalkrin sneered.

Perkyn was indeed still bleeding, though it seemed to have slowed.

'Enough. The point I made is that unless you can work as a team you're all useless to me. In battle, you are as responsible for your allies' lives as much as your own. Deline and I don't get on well, but we clearly understand better than the lot of you.'

'Fuck this,' Dirk spat. 'I'm out.'

He picked up his blade and headed for the door.

'You leave and you admit what a coward you are.' He stopped, his back still turned to me. 'Nobody got anywhere by just walking out on things, sometimes we have to do the hard things in life to get what we want. I'm telling you now, I can make the lot of you into a great crew that will one day be revered throughout Issehai. This crew needs a good fighter like you Dirk, if you can swallow that awful pride of yours and step it up that is.'

He was hesitating.

'What about you Thalkrin?' Deline chimed in, turning to his friend.

He did not seem the brightest of the bunch, but when she asked he nodded.

'I'm no coward. I'll be a part of this crew. Anything to get me away from Blakereath.'

'I guess I'm staying too then,' Dirk sighed, walking back to us.

'You won't regret it,' I said with a smile, though he went to Perkyn who, though injured, still raised a guard as he approached.

'I'll do what Darkskull says and play nice with you rich bastards, but don't expect me to like you.'

'Same to you,' the redhead spat.

It was not ideal, but it was progress. For the next few hours I had them at the dummies again, slashing and stabbing and bludgeoning until their hands were raw. Laricko never seemed to recover from his guilt but he still shot at the target again and again.

Each time he would empty the entire quiver, sometimes hitting the target once or twice but for the most part not at all, then he would retrieve the arrows from around the room and start over. I tried to guide him, even holding his arms where they should be, but he was simply too weak to draw the bow properly. Deline was chuckling.

I, of course, thanked her for the help with my demonstration and she, of course, mocked me for the kindness.

Though she added, 'We do make quite a good team.'

We sat side by side and shared a comfortable moment, not filled with teasing nor resentment for once.

'Well,' I broke, 'I suppose you're a decent enough fighter – for a thief.'

'And I suppose you're okay with that axe – for a cheat.'

The scorn burned, but I managed to laugh along.

'Ex-thief,' she corrected.

'Excuse me?'

'You called me a thief. That's not me anymore.'

Deline's face was straight, her eyes soft. Gone was the scruffy woman I had met and in her place sat someone who appeared presentable. The clothes were simple, yet worn well by her. Leggings, cut-off breaches, a long sleeved shirt of dark cotton. Her skin was still rough, though her long hair (tied back in a loose knot) made her appear almost pretty.

'So you're not going to steal anymore?'

'I wouldn't go that far,' she chuckled. 'But it's certainly not going to be how I make a living from now on.'

'What changed?'

'Being back at the tavern I think,' she sighed. 'Living there again, seeing my dad every day. I couldn't bear to go back to my old habits after all of this; all he has done for me.'

I nodded and sensed a sincerity in her words.

'So what do you think you'll do?'

'I'm not sure,' she told me. 'Maybe work at the tavern once you're gone.'

I smiled contently, watching my recruits hard at work. *Is there room for another?* I considered the woman next to me who was clearly good with both a knife and a sword. On top of that we seemed to work well together – the demonstration alone proved that. *Was this somebody I could rely on in the field of battle?* The answer to my internal question surprised me, as it was *yes, yes she was.*

'There's always room for another on the crew,' I proposed.

Silence.

'Nah, I think I'm good,' her response came. 'The whole pirate's life thing isn't for me.'

I understood, I was still unsure whether it was entirely for me either, though the thought of Daxon deterred me from moving on to something else.

The recruits were beginning to tire, not one but all of them. Perkyn and Dirk obviously fought through the pain, still side by side trying to outdo one another. *As long as they can work together,* I thought, *perhaps this can work.*

'Captain,' Felima whined, 'Can we please stop now?'

'Fine,' I muttered after judging they had had enough. 'Stop what you're doing, we're done for the day.'

Sighs of relief rang out, and the recruits began to file towards us. All except one.

Laricko was still at work, his dusty brown hair stuck to his brow with sweat. Arrow after arrow he fired, mostly in vain. Still, he continued nonetheless.

'Laricko,' I called.

He spun, bow pointed to the ground. 'Yes captain?'

'We're done for the day.'

'If it's all the same to you captain, I'd like to keep practicing.'

I nodded.

'Very well.' I addressed the others, saying, 'You've all done some good work today, get some rest and be here for dawn tomorrow. I expect nobody to be late this time. When you come into this hall next, the real work starts. Understood?'

'Aye captain,' Perkyn led, followed by a few murmurs of something similar.

'I'll let you get away with that for now,' I told them. 'Next time, I'll teach you the meaning of respect. You may go.'

They all filed out, Perkyn and Felima shooting back a concerned glance towards Laricko who was too occupied to notice. The door slammec shut after them, and I once more sat beside Deline.

'Kid at least has spirit,' she said, watching along as time after time the small, timid boy missed his target.

On the few occasions per round of arrows that he hit his mark, his face would light up for a second, pride practically glowing from him. The moment was fleeting however, for almost always his following shot would miss terribly and humble him once again.

'Definitely,' I affirmed.

Both of us watched for a while longer, but the day was drawing on and Laricko showed no sign of stopping.

'My dad will want you back at *the sails* soon,' Deline pointed out.

I stood and strode to Laricko, taking care to walk extra loudly in case I frightened him and ended up with an arrow in me.

'Lad, we're going to have to head off now.'

'That's okay,' he answered. 'I'm fine here.'

'You sure?' I enquired.

He smiled and nodded and I decided I could trust him with the keys. He seemed determined to improve his skills, and I was not about to rob the boy of that small pleasure. I told him to lock up after he left and be there extra early to open up and he bid us farewell.

'You sure nothing bad will happen?' Deline pressed as we closed the door behind us.

'Let the boy have his fun,' I told her. 'After all, he doesn't seem the type of lad who would purposely disappoint us.'

As we strode into the night I was confident with my position. I knew Laricko would not go looking for trouble, it did not occur to me however that trouble may be looking for him.

Chapter 15

White Sky

My night at the tavern was again uneventful, though with Deline and I now being civil it was not entirely boring. She even helped me to shut down the ramblings of a drunken oaf who was yelling profanities at nobody in particular.

I retired early, intent on being awake early enough to meet the recruits. Deline willingly covered my post down by the bar but said I owed her one. I dreaded to think what kind of favour she might expect from me.

It felt strange waking and leaving before dawn, when the last of the patrons were still leaving and the others were ready to go to bed. I had not slept much and when the early morning air hit me I felt sick to my stomach. Holding back the urge to vomit I continued, spear in hand, through Blakereath. The sun was rising by the time I got there, the streets practically empty aside from a few guards making routine patrols. They eyed me when I passed, attention drawn to my wrapped axe which I used as a cane.

Hadivik was there before I, though no sign of the others – not even Laricko. My eyes flicked around in all directions as I came closer, hoping to catch sight of him. No luck.

'Where is everybody?' I asked.

Hadivik shrugged.

I moved to the door and noticed it was open slightly. *Was Laricko here all night?* I entered the building, my hand instantly clenching around my axe.

'By the maker,' Hadivik grunted as he followed me in.

Every single practice dummy was torn to shreds, the armour all stripped and broken across the floor. Arrows lay snapped in half and the archery targets had been hacked apart. My eyes however did not take it all in at first, instead shooting to the trail of crimson across the floor leading into the back room. I rushed to where it led and, as well as most of the good weapons being gone, an injured Laricko lay there.

His clothes were bloody; his eyes were shut. I knelt down and put my ear to his chest.

'He's alive,' I sighed.

But when I came back up I felt a trickle down my cheek. I put my hand to it and saw red. It took me a moment to realise it was *his* blood. A pool of it was ranging from his collarbone to his sternum, dark and thick.

'He needs a doctor,' Hadivik said, laying eyes on his fragile frame.

'Go into the city and find a medic, anyone who can get here on short notice,' I ordered.

He fled without so much as an '*aye captain*' but that was the least of my concerns. I stripped Laricko of his shirt, ripping the fabric and tying t as tightly as possible around his chest to clot the flow. It had been a long time since I had to do something like this, and I had never been too great at it to begin with.

The old man's arm was broken, torn so much that the bone was on display. I had to stop myself from vomiting but Cerik had no problem administrating the bandages. The others were all out in the field, leaving the two of us. Lundrip was panting; taking every opportunity to spit insults at us. It was too bloody for me, and I winced at the sight of it. The man's other arm jutted out as he slapped the side of my head and told me to focus, Cerik echoing his words. I put pressure on the wound but the warmth of it unsettled me. Even in this cold weather his blood was as hot as fire. I closed my eyes and prayed for it to all be over.

'What's going on?' Dirk questioned, he and Thalkrin suddenly in the room with me.

'I don't know,' I told them. 'I got here and found him like this.'

'Looks like the kid got stabbed,' Thalkrin grunted. 'Whoever it was knew what they were doing.'

I turned to him, still pressing down on the wound. 'What do you mean?'

'It's the cut of a thousand torments,' Dirk answered. 'If you can strike them in exactly the right place, they'll bleed out for hours in agony before dying. The lad might be unconscious, but I bet you he's still in pain.'

'Who would do this?'

The two redheads came forward, heads low. Felima in particular seemed close to tears.

'The Blakereath Cobras,' Perkyn spat through gritted teeth.

Dirk smiled, followed by a bitter laugh. 'I'm impressed kid; I didn't think you lot had it in you to do business with the Cobras.'

Perkyn seemed as if he would go for Dirk but I held up a hand and asked, 'Who are the Cobras?'

'They're the most notorious gang in Blakereath,' Thalkrin said once it was clear that neither Perkyn nor Felima would give me a response. 'They sell hallucinogenic drugs, mainly to spoiled rich kids like *them*.'

'I guess someone missed a payment,' Dirk added.

Within a second Perkyn was on Dirk, fists flying. Felima tried to hold him back but was knocked aside with next to no struggle. The shorter boy blocked his blow and whipped out his knife, holding it an inch from the redhead's throat.

'That's enough!' I cried. 'Now I don't know what's going on here but it can wait until Laricko is healed.'

As if on que, Hadivik appeared in the doorway with a man behind him. The stranger wore a mask – the face of a horned demon with only two eyeholes showing any of his face. When he tried to speak it was muffled, but I got the gist of it as he leaned over the boy and opened a box of supplies.

'The cut of a thousand torments,' the man cooed, unwrapping the makeshift bandage. 'I'll need you all to stand back, this will be difficult.'

I nodded and moved everyone through to the main room. Felima was crying, and Dirk was still throwing mocking glances at Perkyn who was running fingers over his hawk pendant. I ran my fingers over my face and rubbed at my eyes. My head was pounding, almost as fast as my heart.

'Tell me what all of this is about,' I demanded.

Dirk tried to make some snide comment but I silenced him with a swift blow to the stomach. He was clearly not impressed but stepped down and kept his mouth shut. I pointed at Perkyn and asked again. He dropped his head and reluctantly told me everything.

He explained how he, Felima and Laricko were the children of some of the noble families of Rundali. Despite their sizeable fortune they were never contempt and sought adventure at every opportunity. When a new drug known as White Sky began to rear its head, the trio fled Rundali in search of an easy thrill. That was why they were here in Blakereath.

Felima added how deep they got, each dose of the drug only making them want more. Unfortunately, when their prestigious families found out about this, they cut the kids off – leaving them with no way of paying the Blakereath Cobras for the product they had already used. During the entire story Hadivik shifted awkwardly, his gaze on the redheads with what seemed like disgust.

'This is revenge,' Perkyn concluded, pointing through to his dying friend. 'And it's only the start. This was to teach us a lesson. They'll be back.'

I ran my palm across my brow. The doctor was still hard at work with Laricko and there was nothing anyone could do to help.

'You don't cross the Cobras,' Dirk sighed – the glare from Perkyn suggesting fists were about to be raised once more.

'We can fix this,' I interjected, trying to keep the focus away from Dirk's apathetic comments.

Most were hanging off my words, though Hadivik seemed unconvinced. His attention seemed elsewhere, anywhere other than on the conversation. I watched him and his gaze eventually found mine with a raised eyebrow.

'Problem lad?' I asked.

He shrugged, wiped sweat from his brow and breathed hard – almost as if he were forcing his discomfort.

'I don't think we should be getting involved with these people.'

Before I could dispute his argument, the doctor came back through.

'What's the word?' I enquired.

The medic's mask discomforted me, for it gave the man the appearance of a creature that would drag Laricko to the depths of eternal torment himself.

'The boy will live,' the doctor said, evoking expressions of jcy from Felima and Perkyn. 'He is unconscious however and I am not certain if he shall ever wake. If he has not woken by sundown tomorrow I would consider putting nim out of his torment.'

'No,' Perkyn spat at once. 'We will *not* give up on him.'

The doctor seemed taken aback, but shrugged.

'Either way, my work here is done. I've wiped my hands of the entire thing.'

I reached into my pocket and seized the purse of coins. I was getting drinks for free at the tavern now, so it was still hefty. I fished out a few coins and handed them to the doctor. 'For your service, and hopefully your discretion.'

He clearly understood and gave me a slight nod before walking away without a word. I turned back to the group.

'We're not "putting him out of his misery,"' Perkyn echoed.

I rested a hand on his shoulder and caught his eye. 'Don't worry lad, I don't give up on my crew. We'll find the bastards who did this and put a stop to them.'

'We?' Dirk enquired, a sly grin forming.

I nodded.

'If we're going to take them down I need every one of you.'

'Not me,' Hadivik replied. 'I never signed up for taking down the most powerful gang in Blakereath.'

Felima stepped towards him, eyes fierce with a new kind of determination.

'Actually you did,' she declared. 'You signed up for anything and everything when you joined this crew.'

'We haven't even joined!' he spat back, an anger deep within his voice. 'We're not pirates, we're recruits. Recruits who've only had one day of practice at that. I have no obligation to any of you.'

He turned and headed towards the door. I rushed after him, catching his shoulder. He violently shrugged me off, loosing his hammer from his belt and spinning around with malicious intent.

'I'm not going after them,' he cried again.

I held my hands up in defence.

'I'm not asking you to, but at least stay here and look after Laricko while we're away.'

His eyes darted from me to the other and through to the back room. Finally, he lowered his weapon and gave a solemn nod, walking in silence through to where Laricko lay. Again I wiped at my brow, head throbbing; only to be made worse by the rest of the group asking me what the plan was – a question to which I had no answers.

'I know where their hideout is,' Thalkrin commented, delivering me from my pain

The redheads stared at him suspiciously. He explained his uncle used to run with them and he had been there once or twice. With that issue solved another arose, for we could not simply charge in and take them down. I had experience in fighting multiple enemies, but not the others, not that I knew.

'We need backup,' I told them.'

'And where do you expect to find it?' Dirk sighed. 'You barely got *this* group together.'

It was a low blow but he was right. Deline came to mind but even with her our numbers were few. I deliberated it for a while before being struck by genius.

'The guards,' I exclaimed.

'Don't make me laugh,' Dirk grunted. 'The Cobras have been around for two years now and all the guards have done is sit on their arses.'

Perkyn was smiling however, already catching on. 'Darkskull has an in, though.'

I smiled back at the boy and confirmed, 'That's right.'

The plan was quickly set in motion. I sent for Deline and she reluctantly came. When the situation was explained to her however she seemed happy to help, explaining, 'I lost two of my friends to White Sky, always hated the Cobras after that.'

All that was left was to get the guards on board, so with hope in my heart I went to their barracks. The others came with me, already armed w th what we had left after the attack. Two guards stood either side of the entrance so I gestured for the group to stay back and approached alone. Swords came out as soon as they noticed me. I lifted both hands to reassure them, having purposely left my axe with Deline.

'State your business,' one commanded.

'I'm here to speak with Arkin,' I explained.

The other laughed, 'Oh are you now? Well when you see him tell him to actually show up for his post.'

My brow furrowed. 'What do you mean?'

'Lazy bastard hasn't been in for three days, pathetic excuse for a guard that one.'

'And when he does show up, he always causes some sort of trouble. Falling asleep at his post and letting wicked kids get away with breaking the law,' the other added, obviously referring to youths like the trio

'So where is he?'

'Probably unconscious on a tavern floor somewhere,' one scoffed. 'If not there, try his house. It's the last one on Ikrus street, I shouldn't be telling you but maybe you can get him to do his job.'

I bowed my head slightly in thanks, returning to my team as the guards continued their jibes about the man, laughing all the while.

'What's the situation?' Perkyn voiced.

It was difficult; I was finding out for the first time that a man I respected was a common drunkard. I ignored the question and those that followed, simply leading the group through the city.

Ikrus street was in the old quarter of the city, with more living in poverty and more guards to push them around. Every eye was on us, lawbreakers and law upholders alike watching intently. With weapons in our grasps and at our sides we made a cutting image, however it drew towards us a large deal of unwanted attention. Take the first guard that stopped us for example. He wanted to know what we were up to, so I told him we were simply visiting an old friend.

The man seemed to believe us well enough, after all every other person who passed was armed. He let us by after wasting another five minutes of our time asking pointless questions. He was not the only guard to stop us neither, so after over an hour we finally reached Arkin's home.

I checked the location, this was it. The last house on a street, with a sign reading Ikrus hanging on the wall. I gave a firm knock but got no indication of anyone being home.

'Where are we?' Dirk insisted.

'This is where Arkin lives,' I told him. 'He's our in. He can get the force of the guards behind us.' I finished under my breath, 'I hope.'

Again I pounded at the door, louder this time. Still nothing.   peered through a low window, but there was no sign of the man.

'Leave it to me,' Thalkrin sighed.

Before I could stop the youth, he was scaling the brickwork and diving into an open window on the second floor. After a minute the door swung open from the inside. In the doorway stood Thalkrin, supporting a semi-conscious Arkin against his shoulder. He stunk of beer.

My eyes were quickly snapped away from the scene as I heard the heavy footsteps of armoured guards. They were at the other end of the block and fixed sight on us as the young boy dragged the blond from his home.

'Shit,' I cursed. 'Take him back to the training room, I'll keep the path clear for you.'

The others piled in, supporting the drunk guard as they darted into an alley. They had barely gotten out of sight as the guards rushed over to me.

'Hey, what were you doing with Commander Arkin?' one voiced, his hand already grasping the hilt of his rapier.

'Commander?' I blurted.

'Yes, the man you were just hauling out of his house,' the other spat, releasing his blade from its scabbard. 'Where did your friends take him?'

I still had my axe in my grasp and I considered fighting my way out, but that would cause a scene. If I wanted the guards' help I could not in good conscience slaughter two of them in the street.

'Arkin is a friend of mine,' I admitted.

They laughed. 'Ha, a guard captain, *friends* with a kid like you.'

'I'm not a kid,' I warned.

My self- control was fleeting as my temper reared; my right palm gripped the haft of my axe until it burned.

'Well how do you supposedly know Arkin?' one continued.

'Met him at *The Sunken Sails*.'

They exchanged a look and one nodded.

'Aye, sounds about right, he does drink there from time to time,' he said to his companion. 'What was *your* business there?'

'I work there,' I told them. 'Check it out later if you want, but right now I need to get back to him.'

They muttered words quietly to one another for some time, finally agreeing to let me go, saying, 'We'll let this slide for now, but if we find you're lying there'll be the maker to pay.'

I nodded and hurried off back to the training room. Arkin was fully conscious now, sipping some water as Felima and Perkyn gathered alongside Hadivik to check on Laricko. The guard met my eyes when I entered.

'Darkskull,' he cheered. 'While my home is much more comfortable, it's always a pleasure.'

He was slurring slightly and he looked awful. His eyes were bloodshot and never focused on one spot. On top of that he smelt dreadful. He must have never changed outfits after his last duty, for he was still in his guard uniform – rapier and all.

'They filled you in?' I asked.

He shook his head. 'They just said you needed me.'

I went on to explain the situation to Arkin, who seemingly tried his best to stay focused on my words. When the speech was done he simply lay his head in his hands and sighed.

'I wish I could do more lad, I truly do, but the guards have lost all respect for me.'

'As they should,' Dirk cut in. 'Look at yourself man, you're a mess.'

I scolded Dirk but Arkin waved a hand.

'He's not wrong my friend; I *am* a mess,' he groaned, sipping more water.

'Still, surely you have some influence. Those guards back there said you were a commander,' I pressed with unyielding motivation.

'Commander I may be,' he said, 'But that doesn't make any of them respect me. I may be able to round up about a dozen of the greener guards, but no experienced member will follow me.'

I considered his statement and gave a regrettable nod.

'They'll have to do,' I sighed.

Two street kids, two ex-addicts, a hungover commander, a thief, a team of guards barely out of training, and me – the most inexperienced captain in all of Issehai. Together we would attempt to take down the largest gang in Blakereath.

Oh joy.

Chapter 16

Into the Mouth of the Cobra

A dmittedly the guards Arkin had rounded up looked better than I had expected, though as they practiced a few swings while I gathered my thoughts my opinion of them changed. Perkyn held a better stance than most of them and Felima was already quicker with a rapier.

'They're not great, but it's the best I can do,' Arkin said from beside me.

The man's hangover had subsided and he was back to his rational self. That was important. I needed him to be entirely focused for what lay ahead of us.

'If I were you, I'd get rid of whoever trains the new guards,' I quipped, watching the disorganisation.

We had managed to secure more men than Arkin had initially thought – fourteen of them in all. Each one of them clueless to Arkin's reputation and simply wanting to please their commander. They all knew the mission, though none of them knew they were acting outside the hand of the law.

'So we head out tonight?' my friend asked.

I nodded. 'Aye, hopefully get them when they're sleeping. Take them by surprise.'

I cast a glance to the back room where Hadivik was still watching over Laricko. The young blacksmith had not spoken a word to anyone since we returned. Deline was showing some of the guards a few fighting techniques, though entire weeks of training could not prepare this group for what we were up against.

I insisted Dirk and Thalkrin arm themselves with more than knives. We had little left in the way of weapons, but each managed to scavenge up a blunt cutlass. The guards all carried rapiers, as did Felima and Arkin. Deline and Perkyn wielded broadswords and I held my trusted axe. Having no archers would surely prove difficult, though I was clueless to what the Cobras would have. Thalkrin had made out they used a large variety, I hoped for our sakes he was mistaken.

When the light of day began to disappear, we headed out into the streets of Blakereath. There were twenty-one of us, all battle ready. We split into groups of three to avoid unwanted attention. I was with Felima and a guard called Lynrik – a man barely in his twenties with a scratchy beard and an overhanging gut.

Thalkrin's team led the way, far into the old quarter where we stopped in an alleyway. He reached down and heaved up a large slab of stone, which to the casual observer seemed to be part of the ground. Beneath it however was a hole which stretched down into darkness and metal railings acting as a ladder.

One by one we descended, covering up the hole once we were inside. It was pure darkness until Thalkrin struck a match and lit a torch which hung on the wall. We followed his lead as he knew where each torch was, lighting more of our way as we followed the underground tunnel. Most of us had our weapons readied, walking as silently as possible.

There were many crossroads which soon appeared to make up an underground labyrinth. Over a dozen times Thalkrin stopped, trying his best to remember which way to go. With so many choices and seemingly only one right way, I imagined one could get lost down here for months if they knew not where to go.

'We need to split up,' Thalkrin said in hushed tone as we came to yet another decision; this time there were three paths. 'All tunnels from here on lead to the Cobras' base, but go to different parts of it – the quarters, the armoury and the supply room. They link up, but if we want to be efficient we should attack from all sides.'

I agreed with the lad and we quickly drafted up a plan. The seven teams split up and proceeded down each tunnel, one team at a time so we did not make too much noise. My team took lead of the rightmost tunnel towards the armoury. It was our job to take out anyone in there and leave someone behind to bar the door so the gang could not reach their weapons.

The road ahead was long and dark, and these final tunnels had no torches to light. However, dim firelight sparked in the distance ahead of us and muffled steps came closer.

'Who's there?' a voice called in the darkness.

I stiffened. Whoever it was, we needed to take him out before he alerted the others.

'It's Gordrik,' I lied, giving him the name of Thalkrin's uncle.

'Gordrik? I thought you left us,' he said in confusion as he approached. 'Wait a minute, you're not...'

But before he could finish his sentence I leapt forward and swung my axe at his neck. He managed to duck it, dropping the torch and sweeping behind me, pulling out a knife. I raised my guard, but I had not needed to. A spot of blood appeared on his torso, and he collapsed to the ground. Felima was behind him, pulling her rapier from his back. The lit torch still burned upon the stone tunnel floor and in the dim light her face dropped.

'First kill?' I asked her.

She nodded, though I had known it already. Her hands were shaking, though I had no time to comfort her. We needed to move on. Her and Lynrik stepped over the body, and the guard picked up the discarded torch. I thought about what the other group would think when they reached the corpse we had left.

Finally, we came to a wooden door where we waited for the others to catch up. Deline headed the second group with two guards whose names I had forgotten.

'When we get in there, take no mercy,' I told them. 'We kill anyone in there as quickly as possible, then proceed through and join the others in the quarters. Felima, Lynrik, the two of you stay behind and barricade the door behind us. Understood?'

They agreed and without delay we charged through to the armoury. It took me a moment to get my bearings and in that moment a knife found my shoulder. Instinctively I swung my axe and took down my attacker. The other five surged into the room, but the enemy was already upon us. I parried an incoming attack but an arrow hit my calf and I faltered. Deline dashed in to finish off my opponent and together we rushed the archer. She managed to duck his next shot by an inch and we made quick work of him.

A punch to my back had me spinning around and a man with metal gauntlets struck at me again. I bashed aside his arm with the hilt of my weapon and sliced down into his shoulder. He fell back and Felima's rapier came out of nowhere to pierce his neck. Her eyes flashed as she stood over her kill, but was unaware of the incoming attacker. I charged him before he got to her, forcing him back into the wall. He tried to raise a knife but I pulled out my dagger and stabbed it into his hand. His weapon fell to the floor and my blade found his throat.

Two more fell to the swinging of my axe and by that point the victory was ours. Ten men bearing the crest of the cobra lay dead, but only four of us stood. One of Deline's group had been hacked to bits, and Lynrik sat against the wall, alive but injured. I dashed over to him and checked the wound in his leg.

'It doesn't look good,' I told him, evoking tears from his eyes. 'I can slow the blood, but you'll most likely be dead in a few hours.'

I ripped off the sleeve of a fallen enemy and wrapped it around the gaping hole in his thigh.

'Pass me that bow,' he sobbed, gesturing to the dead archer. 'I can still hold the room.'

'You're a good warrior,' I told him. 'Your sacrifice will not be in vain.'

'I'll stay with him,' Felima said. 'We'll stick to the plan. I'll barricade the door and we'll hold the armoury as long as possible.'

She was hurt too, nothing major but a cut ran across her cheek drenching her face with blood. It seemed she was limping too but I could not be sure. In truth we were all injured, but I pushed aside my own pain and focused on the task at hand.

Deline, myself and the guard took a moment to prepare ourselves, then charged through to the main quarters – Felima bolting the door behind us. The battle was already in full flow, the rest of our party and dozens of enemies fighting tooth and nail. I came behind two unsuspecting Cobras and made quick work of them. Arkin was moving faster than lightning as he picked apart enemies with his rapier.

Arrows were flying and I followed the source to an archer keeping out of the way. I rushed for him, hoping to catch him unawares, but he spotted me. I tried to dodge his first shot but it struck me hard in the hip. I gasped, faltering and narrowly avoiding the next which would have caught me in the eye. Another arrow hit me in the back of the leg as I tried to continue; I turned around as the second archer loosed an arrow into my back. The two closed in on me while I screamed out in pain. I closed my eyes and saw the faces of Daxon and my father. I had to keep going, I had gotten out of worse situations than this.

Cerik was flaunting the ring in front of me. Lord that made me mad. We were on top of the baker's, right next to the town square.

'That's mine!' I cried. 'I was the one who almost got caught.'

Cerik laughed as my face turned red. 'And I was the one who slipped it off his finger,' he sneered.

I lunged at him, managing to snatch it from him. I gleamed but he struck me. His fist knocked me back but I managed to hold onto it and slipped in onto my finger. He pushed me and so I pushed him back. I had not meant for it to happen, but he slipped. Before I knew it he was falling from the rooftop.

Those fingers pointing at me. Those accusations. I had never meant for it to happen.

Lundrip found me quickly enough. I had only been running for a few hours when one of the others grabbed me and brought me before him. The crows had strict rules about these things. Killing a clansman was punishable by death, but the old

R. B. S. SNAITH

man took pity when he heard the story. I got eighty lashes – more than anyone had ever gotten. Each was more painful than the last, cutting into my skin more and more.

I passed out after twenty but they made sure to keep me awake so that I felt every bit of it. After forty they even stitched me up so that I did not die of blood loss before it was over and even still they got me within an inch of death.

After that they disbanded me and threw me out in the street to die, cold and in agony. Somehow I managed to survive it though. Left for dead, but still fighting. I recovered. I got stronger. I thought maybe I was immortal.

I felt far from immortal now, the arrows feeling like searing fire burrowing into my body. I knew I still had to do something but right now I was waiting for the merciful release of death.

'Stop!'

The voice surprised me, echoing through the sounds of battle and bringing everything to silence. I opened my eyes. The archers had stopped in their tracks and (like everyone) had their eyes focused on the speaker.

She was tall and fair skinned, adorned in the finest silks I had ever seen. She walked out onto the field of battle; nobody aside her dared to move. I got my first glance at the devastation. Bodies littered the ground, allies and enemies alike.

'What is this commotion?' the woman continued, slow and deliberate.

She seemed unfazed by the death all around her.

'These slimy bastards attacked us mistress,' one of the Cobras spat.

She tutted. 'Is that so? Who is the leader amongst you?'

None of my companions moved. I struggled against the pain and rose to my feet, the arrows burrowing deeper as my muscles contracted.

'I am,' I groaned, coughing up blood.

She seemingly floated towards me, her dress trailing out behind her. 'And who are you?' she whispered, a mere foot away.

'My name is Darkskull, captain of the greatest pirate crew in Issehai.'

She glanced around at what was left of my team and laughed, 'Your *crew* seems to resemble a washed out group of nobodies.' She narrowed in on me and asked, 'Why have you ventured into the mouth of the cobra?'

I realised how snakelike the woman was, fitting the name of her gang. Her silks were green and yellow, trailing behind her like a tail, and the way she spoke was like a hiss.

'You organised an attack on one of my crew and left him to die in agony. We came here to take you down and stop The Blakereath Cobras from ever doing this again,' I threatened.

'You mean the young timid boy from Rundali,' she hissed, whipping her gaze around and settling it on Perkyn. 'I remember this one too.'

As she approached him he lifted his blade but was seized by two of the Cobras. I rushed towards him but was grabbed and disarmed by the archers.

'Let me go,' Perkyn demanded, struggling against his captors.

The pendant around his neck shone in the dim light, though unlike the animal depicted Perkyn was no longer the predator – he was prey.

'If I'm not mistaken you also cheated us,' she said.

'Please,' I yelled, 'Release him and his sister from what they owe. I will be in your debt.'

The *mistress* seemed to assess the situation, clicking her tongue against her teeth.

'So be it,' she sighed. 'All three of them will be released from their debts, in return for a future favour.'

'Thank you,' I started, but fell to silence when she pulled out a knife.

Her eyes met Perkyn's and she grinned. 'For this one however, consider death your release!'

In one swift motion she sliced the redhead's throat. I screamed and struggled against the archers, but I was too weak.

'You bitch,' I cried, screaming until my throat was dry.

'Consider this a mercy,' the woman cackled. 'I'll contact all of you when I require my favour. Now get out.'

Felima burst through the door and lay eyes on her brother. I caught her expression before I was pulled away – one of horror. I heard a scream and the aggravated cries of my allies being dragged away like me; I struggled as hard as I could, but felt myself weakening. Within only a few moments my sight began to falter and everything became black.

Chapter 17

The Golden Hawk

As the light of morning hit me, my first thought was that I was in a gutter. I was in a gutter and somebody was slapping my face. I groaned and the slapping stopped.

'Darkskull,' Arkin's voice called.

'Aye,' I grunted. 'I'm awake.'

I sat up, bloodied bodies all around me. The memories came flooding back and a tear came to my eyes. Young Perkyn was dead because I got in over my head. How stupid I must have been to think I could take down the Cobras with so few allies. Felima was facing away from me, sobbing quietly into her hands.

'Where are the guards?' I asked.

'Dead,' Deline spat, coming from behind and sitting in the gutter beside me.

'All of them?'

'All of them,' Arkin confirmed. 'The redhead says Lynrik died while they were holding the room.'

'He did well,' I said. 'He was brave until the end.'

'The others fell during the fight,' Arkin continued. 'Lord knows what I'll tell my superiors, how I deceived fourteen new guards into a suicide mission.'

I was relieved Dirk and Thalkrin were still alive. My axe was missing however, likely still in their hideout. I checked for my dagger which was still tucked safely into my belt, and Brongrim's arrowhead was still in my pocket, for which I was thankful.

'Is anyone hurt?' I called to the full group.

Dirk came forward and lifted up his shirt to reveal a long gash across his torso.

'Got this in the fight.'

'Does it hurt?' I asked.

'I'll live,' he said bluntly. 'Can't move my right arm though, think someone must have cut a nerve. Thalkrin is having some trouble moving his fingers too, but aside from that everyone is alright. Well, except for…'

He gestured towards Felima who did not appear to be physically injured but was still beside herself over the death of her brother.

'We need to get out of Blakereath,' Deline said, surprising me.

'I thought you wanted to stay here and reconnect with Sid,' I said.

She ran a bloodied hand across her brow.

'The woman said she would contact *all* of us when she wanted a favour. If I stick around, it'll only put my dad in danger.'

'Aye,' Arkin chimed in. 'And as soon as people find out about what went down with the guards, the lot of us will be put on the block.'

'Maybe you're right,' I sighed. 'After all I never intended to stay in Blakereath, I just wanted to find a crew.'

'Well you've found one,' Arkin said jokingly, though with a hint of distain.

'You're saying you'll take me up on the offer then?' I enquired.

The man nodded and despite the mood I gave him a soft smile.

'You can count me in too,' Deline said.

'Yeah, us too,' Thalkrin said on behalf of himself and Dirk. 'Anything to be done with this shithole.'

Felima noticed the pause in conversation and turned to us. I thought she would be furious with me for what happened to Perkyn, but to my surprise she choked back a sob and nodded.

'Count me in,' she agreed.

'Truly?' I voiced.

'Of course,' she said. 'All of this happened because of *us*, if we had never gotten involved with the Cobras then Perkyn and all of those guards would still be alive. I need to atone for what I've done, me *and* Laricko.'

'Laricko,' I muttered, remembering the boy's condition. 'We should get back to him and see how he is.'

The others agreed and helped me to my feet. It seemed out of everyone I was the most beaten up. I could not bend my back and my right leg hurt too much to walk on. As well as that my hip ached in the cold wind and the wound on my shoulder made it difficult to use my left arm. I made it through the streets with Arkin and Deline supporting me from either side, no longer having my axe to rest on.

Guards gave us questionable looks but Arkin told each of them to mind their own business.

'I'll miss having this level of control over people,' he said in passing.

Back at the training room a tired Hadivik was waiting by the door. He opened his mouth to say something but closed it again once he glanced over us.

'If you haven't guessed, it didn't go well,' Dirk told him, heaving his bloodied self to the ground.

'Where's Laricko?' I asked.

'Here' came a voice from the back room.

Felima and I both sprinted towards the voice, as well as I could at least, and it was true. He was awake, slumped against a wall and appearing to be in a great deal of pain, but at least he was awake. The redhead leapt onto him, wrapping her arms tightly around him and only pulling back when he cried out.

'Lord you had me scared for a while there lad,' I told him.

'Hadivik filled me in on everything. What happened? Where's Perkyn?' the eager boy questioned.

Solemn looks crossed both my face and that of Felima. The girl began to tear up, only managing to sob, 'He's...he's...'

'He's dead,' I finished for her.

My eyes were fixed on the boy, expecting him to cry or lash out. To my surprise he did neither, he simply nodded and said, 'Okay,' asking me to leave the two of them for a moment.

I did as he asked and closed the door behind me, only then did I hear him crying. It broke my heart but I had to be strong – for my team. I needed to focus my frustration on something; I came across the young blacksmith.

Marched over to him I pointed a finger.

'You let us down,' I accused. 'We needed all of the help we could get in that fight and you stayed here like a coward.'

'Lay off the boy,' Arkin countered. 'If I could change the past, *I* wouldn't have gone into that death-trap.'

'People died in there,' I continued, ignoring the commander. 'If you had come with us, maybe one of them would still be here.'

'Or maybe *he* would be dead also,' Arkin interjected again.

'Just tell me one thing,' I ordered Hadivik. 'Tell me why you didn't join us today.'

I knew from the heat in my face it must be bright red and at this point I was yelling. Hadivik stood, coming face to face with me – only an inch apart.

'You want to know why?' he growled at me.

'I'm sure we're all interested,' I spat back.

'They killed my family!' he screamed. 'All of them. My parents, my grandparents, my sister. All of them, wiped out. I am the last survivor and I refused to go because I will not let them wipe me out too.'

I took a step back, the fury gone. It all made sense now – why he tensed up at the mention of the Cobras, why he had said we should not mess with them, all of it.

'I'm sorry,' I whispered, expecting the worst.

He sat back down, head in hands.

'It's okay,' he told me. 'You didn't know. But if it's all the same to you captain I'd like to get out of this city once and for all.'

The others backed up his words in a chorus of agreement.

'Sounds good to me,' Laricko said from the doorway.

He was being supported by Felima but he was upright and moving which was all I needed. Everyone grabbed their weapons, leaving me with only my dagger. Together we staggered out of the training room like the last survivors of a war, bloodied and broken.

'We'll need supplies,' Deline voiced.

'And a ship,' Arkin added.

'I'm sure he at least has a ship,' Deline laughed back, dropping her jaw when she saw me shaking my head.

'There's a cheap one for sale at the docks. It's a bit banged up, but it'll do for now,' I told them.

'Do you at least have enough to pay for it?' Felima asked.

I reached into my coat and pulled out the purse, counting out fifty silver pieces, not exactly ship-buying money but perhaps I could haggle.

'Maybe,' I replied. 'But definitely not enough to buy supplies as well.'

'I have a little saved up back at my place,' Arkin voiced. 'I was saving it for booze but if I stay long enough for a drink I might be hanged before I get to finish it.'

'You got much?' Dirk asked, with what I could not help interpreting as a sinister grin.

'More than our esteemed captain over here,' he laughed. 'I'll rush home and grab it, you lot get supplies and meet me by the docks.'

He darted off and Hadivik took his place supporting me through the market. It was still early hours with most shops and stalls only now opening. The group sat Laricko and I down by the fountain and I dished out the coins for the others to grab what we needed. Dirk and Thalkrin scurried off in search of food; crackers, bread rolls, anything which we could stock up on. Felima went for equipment; tools, a map and ropes for the ship, a sharpening stone and medical kits. Hadivik went for extra clothes and Deline for drink – water and mead alike.

'You hanging in there lad?' I asked Laricko.

He nodded, saying nothing, though his eyes told me he was far from okay.

'Happy to be putting all of this behind me,' he said and that was something I *did* believe.

With the return of the crew and our supplies readied, we headed for the peer to meet Arkin. He was already waiting aboard the ship with a smile.

'The man drove a hard bargain for such a piece of crap,' he called out to us, laughing.

We boarded the dishevelled vessel with distain on all faces bar mine and Arkin's. We were laughing hysterically and the others simply stared at us.

'Well done Darkskull,' Arkin chuckled. 'You're now the fine captain of the worst ship on the sea.'

'Oh don't be so absurd Arkin,' I mockingly scolded. 'We're not even at sea yet.'

Again we were laughing, so much so we never noticed the guards approaching.

'Commander Arkin? Is that you?' one called.

Dirk, Laricko and Thalkrin were hoisting the anchor while I made my way towards the helm.

'You can take your commander title and shove it up your arse,' he called back to them, an enormous grin on his face. 'I'm a pirate now.'

I took the wheel and ordered Deline to lower the sails. The strong sea-wind took hold and we were away within minutes, Arkin's taunts echoing through the harbour as we moved out of their reach.

The ropes up above were shoddy at best, so once we were well out of the way of Blakereath I commanded the others to tighten up the sails with our new equipment. None of them knew what they were doing, but then again neither did I. It took them a while to figure it out but for what felt like the first time in a long time we had no time pressure. Sailing the ship was easy enough, especially as we had no set destination. I leaned my aching body against the wheel and sailed into the open sea until Blakereath was out of sight.

When the crucial work on the ship was done the others gathered around me. A small crew of eight (myself included) for a small ship.

'What now captain?' Laricko chimed.

'We need to make a name for ourselves, establish some connections and maybe recruit a few more crewmates.'

'Aye but to make a name for ourselves we need an actual name,' Hadivik pointed out.

Murmured agreements sounded all round.

'So what name should we give to this scrap pile of a ship?' Arkin posed.

'The Shabby Sailor,' Dirk suggested.

'The Rotten Death-trap,' Felima laughed.

'Here's an idea,' Deline said, casting a quick glance towards Felima. 'How about we name it after Perkyn? I mean, he never got a chance to be a proper part of the crew, so let's honour his memory.'

Felima smiled, a tear rolling down her cheek. A couple of them were nodding but everyone turned to me for approval.

'It's a great idea,' I said solemnly.

'Wait,' Dirk cut in. 'And this isn't just because I didn't like the kid – he fought until the end and I respect that. But *The Perkyn* isn't exactly the catchiest name.'

'It doesn't have to actually *be* his name,' Deline argued. 'Maybe something that reminds us of him.'

'Yeah,' I agreed. 'Like that necklace he wore, of the gold bird.'

'The golden hawk,' Felima said simply. 'Back in Rundali he paid a jeweller to make it. It's from an old legend.'

'I know the one,' Arkin cut in;

'When all mankind shall fall to fate,

And Darkness comes forth, tall and great,

From parts its weapon shall be forged,

With utmost ire, this world engorged.

Then to escape this monstrous wrath...'

He stopped and Felima finished;

'The golden hawk shall show the path. He was always obsessed with idea of the legendary hawk.'

'Well it sounds like a good name to me,' I determined.

'Definitely beats Rotten Death-trap,' Laricko chuckled.

It seemed everyone was in agreement and thus from that day our ship was known as *The Golden Hawk.*

Chapter 18

Prejudice

We had been sailing westward for three days. After grabbing a map and getting my bearings it seemed our best option was to sail around the Western Point. There we could dock and take our time to get the ship properly fixed up and maybe start spreading our names. My goal was not clouded however; I had known as soon as the salty air hit me once more I had spent too much time in Blakereath. My goal was to find the Stallion and face Daxon again, but both I and the crew were far from ready.

My injuries had begun to heal, though I still staggered when I walked. Something about sailing comforted me though, it seemed to heal me faster though I knew it was all in my mind.

Arkin was feeling seasick and had been vomiting pretty much since we set sail. I had left him to his own devices, as I had with the others. Most of them had never been on a ship before, so I was giving them time to settle in. I showed Deline how to steer the ship to allow myself a few hours of sleep each night, but other than that I had not asked anything of the crew.

'Greetings all, your friend Arkin has returned,' the guard called as he made his way onto the main deck, still looking green.

The others were scattered around the ship, so only a few caught his words. Deline was nowhere to be found, as usual. Hadivik was working on weapon designs below deck. Dirk and Thalkrin were up in the crow's nest, not keeping a lookout, simply watching the world go by – it was their first time away from the city. Felima was below deck somewhere, likely still mourning Perkyn like she had been since we set sail. Laricko on the other hand was taking the loss much better and spent a lot of time shining the bow he had taken from Blakereath – he said he would be practicing, though he had no arrows.

The blond approached, coming up to join me at the stern as I manned the wheel.

'Looking good captain,' he chuckled.

'You holding up alright?' I asked.

'Aye,' he replied. 'Just finding my sea legs...and my sea stomach.'

I smiled at that, the man was good humoured but there was something which I needed to address.

'Arkin, I appreciate you coming on board with us but I need to know I can rely on you.'

His smile faded and his face turned stern and serious.

'Of course you can Darkskull, what's this...'

'It's about the drinking,' I cut in. 'It got you into trouble back in Blakereath and I don't want it getting you into trouble here. If we get into a scrape I need you by my side, not passed out below deck. Am I understood?'

For the first time he looked at me not only as a friend but as a captain. He was taller, older, more experienced, but he still bowed his head slightly and gave a firm, 'Yes captain!'

Once that business was over with, he got to work sharpening the few blades we had aboard of his own accord. By the time he was done the sun was growing dark, and the crew gathered around to test out their steel. I watched on as Dirk and

Thalkrin crossed cutlasses, each strong and quick but Dirk a little stronger. He was using his left hand, still unable to move his right arm, but it looked second nature. From the way their eyes blazed as they struck and parried I could tell this was not their first time sparring. The clash of blade on blade rang out over and over, neither willing to relent. Finally, Dirk took his companion by surprise with a forward faint before swooping around and touching the blade to his rips.

Next was a less intense fight, more like Arkin showing Felima how to properly use her rapier. If anyone could teach her how to fight with such a flimsy weapon it was him.

'What do you say Arkin?' Dirk called. 'Fancy taking me on?'

The guard rose to the challenge and they came face to face. Arkin waited patiently for Dirk to charge in recklessly, but surprisingly the boy stood his ground. He was a skilled fighter and knew how swift the man's blade could be. They stayed there at a standstill for what felt like forever until finally the guard's lack of patience overwhelmed him and he struck. The boy barely parried in time, the tip cutting across his face. Arkin swung back quickly, though Dirk ducked and landed a punch into his chest.

He staggered.

Dirk used the opportunity to launch his first attack, a downward slash which caught the man on the shoulder. It pierced his clothes, and by the sound he made I would bet it pierced his skin too.

'Hey, watch your contact!' I called out, but Arkin held up a hand.

'I'm okay,' he affirmed before sweeping side to side as quick as an arrow and cutting at the boy's hand.

Dirk took the lacerations without dropping his blade, but as he readjusted his grip Arkin struck at the cutlass and it flew from his grasp. Dirk cursed and retrieved his blade, Arkin grinning with pride.

In this time Deline had been sparring with Hadivik, but had easily bested him with the extra reach of her blade compared to his hammer. After her victory she stepped towards the blond and declared, 'I'm next.'

This duel was far more intense, both parties quick and practically untouchable, though I knew who would win before the fight had even begun. Deline was a good fighter, but she was reckless. Again and again she charged straight into Arkin's slashes, and did not learn from the punishment. She gave her all, but in the end he again came out on top.

'Well I guess that makes me the victor of all,' Arkin laughed cockily, flashing a grin around to the crew.

'Not quite,' Laricko argued.

'Oh, lad,' Arkin said. 'You haven't even got arrows for that bow of yours.'

He shook his head. 'I don't mean me. You still haven't beaten captain Darkskull.'

All eyes were on me, expectantly. My hands wandered, and I remembered I had no weapon aside my dagger.

'Here,' Deline offered her blade, practically reading my mind. 'Knock that smug grin off of his face for me, I'll steer the ship.'

I nodded and took the broadsword, giving a light grin. The sun was setting now, casting a reddish light across the sea.

'Let's make this quick,' Arkin said.

'Oh, it will be,' I fired back.

Everyone had their eyes glued to us. I spun the blade around in my hand, adjusting to the weight of it.

'I know you're good with an axe, but what about a sword?' Arkin enquired.

'Better than you might think,' I told him, but before my mouth had even closed he was upon me.

I deflected the first attack clumsily, no longer used to a sword. He came back at me even faster and I leapt away. I gripped the blade with both hands to make it more comfortable in my grip and prepared. As he came at me again I swept down to the left and struck his rapier with the flat of my blade. It shook violently but did not leave his grasp.

He countered with a slash to my injured leg which I was too slow to parry but I got him back with a strong cut to the arm. Back and forth we went, injuring one another more and more. The restriction from my left arm hindered me but I held my own against the man. I feared he might best me and it would look bad in front of the crew. Longer we went on, until almost all light died away. And finally...

'Land ahead!' Deline called out.

I sighed and bowed my head to Arkin.

'Another time my friend.'

I ordered Laricko up to the crow's nest to get what bearings we could in the dark. I sent Dirk and Arkin up the rigging to drop the sails and took the wheel from Deline.

'The rest of you, prepare to drop anchor as soon as we reach the docks.'

'Aye captain,' they all called back.

The sky was turning black, though luckily we still had a full moon to guide us. Slowly the city began to reveal itself – a mismatch of buildings and people in one of the most notorious places for trading in all of Issehai. As we pulled up towards the harbour it reminded me of Cranwell, full of hard faces and more than a little dishevelled. It was riving however, full of people even in the night.

When I gave the order to drop anchor and we docked at the peer, guards awaited us. Torches and fires in almost every window lit their faces and they could see us just as easily.

'Evenin' sir,' one said as we approached.

I was at the head of the group. The others all followed with their weapons sheathed – for now. The guards on the other hand had theirs drawn, long jagged blades which reminded me of Wes's sword. Their weapons did not exactly paint them as guards, and neither did their appearances. While all in chainmail and the city's colours, not one of them seemed particularly lawful. Half a dozen of them there were, with eight eyes and perhaps a few full sets of teeth between them.

'Good evening gentlemen,' I replied. 'You'll have no need for those swords, we're not looking for a fight.'

Back on the Stallion, the blades would be out already. Wes was short tempered and Daxon could be even more so. I grimaced.

'We'll be the judge o' tha',' another spat, his face covered in scars. 'How 'bout you empty yer purses 'n' hand o'er yer shiny weapons?'

'I'm afraid that won't be possible,' Arkin cut in.

His hand hovered close to his hilt and my gaze begged him not to. We locked eyes for a moment and he gave me a faint nod before stepping down. I fished into my pocket and pulled out a purse, it was the rest of our money and there was not much in it. I plucked out some coins.

'This doesn't have to come to violence,' I told them in my friendliest tone. 'How about we give each of you a piece of silver and you let us pass?'

They turned to one another and mumbled illegibly. The first speaker approached. I handed him the coins and he bit one of them. When he was certain it was real, he retreated to his companions and handed out the silver.

'You can pass,' he declared, but his eyes quickly settled on Dirk and Thalkrin and he frowned. 'All except those two.'

'What you just say?' Dirk spat, his fist around the hilt of his cutlass.

'We don't like your kind 'ere,' the scrawniest of them yelled.

Confused, I glanced towards the streets and as I suspected only those with pale and tanned hues walked happily from tavern to tavern. The few dark faces I saw were of those scuttling around, avoiding the attention of all others.

I shot daggers at the men before me, venom in my gaze.

I told them, 'They're part of my crew, you'll let them pass.'

Gone was the politeness from my tone, for I had no tolerance for this sort of prejudice. I recalled the man being beaten back in Merrywood and how I had done nothing.

'We don't want more mongrels in our city.'

'What did you just call me?' Dirk hollered, unsheathing his blade and dashing forward.

I managed to grab the boy before he got any closer. The guards took a few steps back and Dirk began to shout profanities at them.

213

'See what we mean?' another sneered. 'Animals, the lot of 'em.'

Thalkrin was at my other side and I thought I might have to stop him too.

'Captain, if it's helpful we could stay on the ship,' the lad sighed.

'Fuck that!' Dirk cursed, struggling to get loose. 'I'll cut every one of those bastards' throats!'

'Get those monsters back on yer boat 'fore we cut the lot o' ya to pieces,' their frontrunner said.

While holding Dirk back I turned to him.

'There are no monsters amongst us,' I told him. 'If you want to see a monster then ask for a mirror so you may cast eyes on a true demon.'

'Ya li'l cunt, who do ya think ya are?' he questioned.

'The name's Darkskull, captain of the Golden Hawk and the greatest pirate crew you'll ever meet.'

They laughed, all of them. I gritted my teeth and leaned down to whisper in Dirk's ear. He stopped struggling and I drew my dagger.

'What ya gonna do with tha' thing boy? Pick yer teeth?' the small one mocked.

'No,' I answered, striding forward. 'But I will put every one of you into an early grave if you don't let my crew pass.'

The frontrunner took the challenge and stepped forward with sword aloft. He jabbed as I came into reach but I swept to the side and stabbed my blade into his hand. He screamed out and dropped his weapon, blood streaming. The next charged in, so I grabbed my first opponent and spun him around. The second man's blade cut

214

straight into his ally's chest before he could stop it. He let out a dying gasp as I dropped him to the ground.

'You'll pay for tha',' the attacked cried.

'What for?' I enquired innocently. 'You were the one who killed him.'

'Enough,' another called from the back. 'Let's be done with this mess. Darkskull, yer crew may pass, assumin' none of ya speak of what's happened 'ere tonight.'

I nodded and gestured for the others to come forward, letting Arkin proceed to the streets first so that I could stay back to keep an eye on the guards. I watched their contorted faces as they glared at Thalkrin and Dirk, the latter glaring back. When I finally passed them I gave a cocky smile, saying, 'It's *Captain* Darkskull for the record.'

'Well that was truly something captain,' Hadivik praised.

I smiled. The boy had hardly spoke since our confrontation back in Blakereath and I was glad to be winning back his support.

'I think we all deserve a drink after that,' Deline commented and it seemed everyone agreed.

We did not have to walk far, for taverns lined the first street we came to. Everyone piled into the closest one, though I was pulled back by Dirk.

'What is it lad?' I asked.

His fury had abandoned his face, an inner sadness replacing it.

'I just wanted to say...thank you captain. What you did back there...well, it meant a lot.'

'Don't be stupid Dirk, you're a member of this crew. Any one of us would stand up for you, remember that,' I told him.

I patted him on the back reassuringly and guided him into the tavern. I felt victorious, though that feeling soon left as I realised the fight had only just begun.

As we walked to the bar, every eye was on Dirk and Thalkrin. Sneering and murmured comments of 'mongrel' and 'demon' filled the tavern. Everyone sat down at the bar, and as the bartended laid eyes on the two boys he scoffed. I did my best to ignore it, though I knew the lads were hard pressed to do the same.

'Eight pints my good man,' I said cheerily, throwing down some coins.

'Don't serve blacks,' he said simply.

My patience was wearing thin. I cleared my throat loudly, forcing the old man to look at me.

'I don't think you heard me sir,' I said louder. 'I asked for eight pints for me and my crew.'

'Oh I heard ya lad,' he said through gritted teeth. 'But the fact remains we don't serve blacks here.'

'And why not?' I yelled in his face, spit hitting his brow.

'Darkskull, calm down,' Deline begged.

'No,' I cried. 'I won't calm down. Not until every one of you gets a nice refreshing pint.'

'Okay, okay, relax,' the barman groaned. 'I'll give ya eight.'

All eyes were now on me but at least they were not on Dirk and Thalkrin anymore. True to his word the man poured eight pints and laid them on the bar before us. I took a long swig of mine, but before either Dirk or Thalkrin could do the same the old man spat a snot-filled glob into each of their tankards. Thalkrin sighed and pushed his away, whereas Dirk took his revenge by spitting into the barman's face.

In an instant, the man's hands were around the boy's throat as he called out, 'Black mongrel, fucking demon, mistake of nature.'

I reached for my blade but it was Laricko who got there first. He picked up his own tankard and rammed it into the man's face. He released Dirk and recoiled, giving me time to throw myself over the bar and grab the man by his collar.

'Get the fuck off me,' the elder cried, struggling against my grasp.

I reached back and picked up Dirk's tainted pint, hoisting the barman's head back and slowly poured the vile liquid over his face. He spluttered and coughed as it went in his mouth and up his nose. When it was empty, I did the same with Thalkrin's.

'Never dare to insult any of my crew like that again,' I threatened. 'Next time it'll be blood running down your face.'

Throwing him to the floor I turned back to my crew, telling them it was time to leave. I leapt back over the bar and drank the rest of my pint in one swig before snatching my coins back up from the counter. However, as I turned towards the door, a dozen were on their feet blocking the way. I gestured to the others and heard the sound of steel being unsheathed. The crowd moved aside quickly after that.

'Who *are* you people?' someone called as I began to lead the march through.

'We...' I started, but was cut off by Thalkrin.

'We're the crew of the Golden Hawk and if you mess with us we won't hesitate to end you,' he said.

I smirked.

'We won't tolerate your prejudice,' Dirk continued. 'So if you have a problem with us you can shove your words up your arses.'

Silence was all we were met with as we left the tavern.

'Not how I would've phrased it but certainly effective,' I praised the two of them once we were out in the cold night air.'

Dirk put a hand on Laricko's shoulder. 'Thanks for helping me out back there. Guess you're not as useless as I thought.'

It was a backhanded compliment but Laricko smiled nonetheless. It took us some time to find an inn which would allow people of Dirk and Thalkrin's physical appearance, but after several doorstep arguments we finally found a place.

We rented two rooms, men in one and women in the other. Unfortunately, that meant Deline and Felima had plenty of space, while Hadivik, Arkin, Thalkrin, Dirk, Laricko and I had to share. There were only two beds, so I asserted my authority as captain and claimed one. Thalkrin was quick and grabbed the other, leaving the rest on the floor. I had considered leading us back to the ship but was too exhausted for another run-in with the guards.

'You two okay?' I asked Dirk and Thalkrin.

'Well it's not the warmest welcome I've had but not the coldest neither,' Dirk replied.

'There are some people back in Blakereath like that, racists who hate us because we're black. You get used to it on the streets,' Thalkrin added.

'It's wrong,' Arkin said. 'I knew a few guards who would arrest people all the time just for the colour of their skin, didn't matter to them if they'd done anything.'

'A few?' Dirk laughed. 'From where I was standing it was most of them. And if you were only arrested you were lucky, I got plenty of beatings from guards. I could understand it when it was because of stealing but sometimes I was minding my own business.'

'That happened to my friend a few times,' Hadivik added. 'His skin was darker than the night and the guards never let him forget it.'

Arkin seemed shocked to discover this, as was I. Back in Cranwell there were some who would turn up their noses at the sight of a black face and a few who would go as far as violence, but it had never been a regular thing.

'It's not right,' I sighed. 'It's stupid and cowardly and racist and just plain wrong.'

'Unfortunately it's how the word works,' Thalkrin said. 'Some people are like that.'

'It makes sense that it's like that here,' Arkin groaned. 'The Western Point is the main docking point for people from Akrul so racism is second nature to them.'

I thought of Akaya who was from Akrul and she was certainly darker than I but not as much as Brongrim or Gurdgrin, nor Dirk or Thalkrin for that matter. The thought of her pained me, the betrayal still fresh in my mind.

There was little said after that and even after the others drifted off I kept thinking about it – about how awful the world could be. Finally, I wore myself out and I drifted off to sleep.

Chapter 19

Spoils of Beauty

'Stop right there,' a voice called and a moment later someone barged past me.

I practically leapt out of the way of the second person who was clearly chasing the first. Curiosity had its hold on me and I was soon running after them to figure out what was going on. The Western Point had dingy streets and was littered with thieves and violent criminals, all of which I noticed during this pursuit. No crime was hidden here, there was no point to it, for nobody cared.

As I began to close the distance between the other two runners, I noticed the chased was a black woman and her pursuer a guard. The woman made a wrong turn and the guard closed in on her, with me shortly behind.

'Now I've got ya, mongrel scum,' I heard the man say as he backed her into an alley.

From behind I only noticed his arm was moving down but I had no idea what he was doing – not until I heard the terror in the woman's voice at least. I unsheathed my dagger and went to intervene.

'Only one thing ya blacks are good for,' he was saying. 'Now be a good li'l mongrel 'n' don't struggle.'

Before he could get any closer to the frightened woman I grabbed him by the back of the head and hoisted him onto the ground. My eyes met with hers, those beautiful browns full of tears and despair. It pained me. She was younger than I had thought at first, less than twenty for sure.

'Get out of here,' I instructed.

Without hesitation she ran past the both of us and out of the alley, giving me a glimpse of a thankful smile as she did so.

'Oy, that one was mine,' the guard grumbled as he leapt back to his feet, pulling up his trousers.

I took no pause in throwing him against a wall and pressing my blade to his throat.

'You try to do anything like that again and you'll lose that cock of yours,' I threatened.

'Yer that mongrel lover everyone's talking 'bout, aren't ya?' he spat. 'Making quite a name for yerself, think yer a big shot right?'

I used my free hand to punch him in the gut; he groaned and doubled over. I readied my blade to cut him but realised I was shaking. If everyone was talking about me and the crew, we could not stay much longer.

'Darkskull,' a voice called from the street.

I turned towards Hadivik who was approaching down the alley. He had his hammer in hand and at the ready. The boy looked terrified and I knew instantly that something was seriously wrong.

'You're lucky. I'm going to leave you with your life, this time,' I told the guard.

He glanced up at me and in anger spat in my face. I wiped the vile substance away and brought the edge of my blade across his cheek, leaving a long red cut.

'I suggest you change your ways or I'll be back,' I said, punching him into the dirt and turning to my crewmate.

'Captain, they've followed us,' Hadivik cried.

'Who?' I asked, seeing the fear in his eyes.

'The Cobras,' he panted. 'They're here in the city and they're looking for us. It looks like they want their favour after all.'

'We better get the crew and get out of here as quickly as possible.'

Within the hour we were back aboard the ship with danger on our tail. I said my farewell to this horrid place. We had stayed for a full five days and in that time gotten nothing but trouble. That incident with the guard had been the seventh time I had saved someone from a hate crime and, like the fiend said, it had gotten my name around.

The only productive thing from this stop was we had grossly overpaid an elderly man to paint the ship's exterior a shoddy golden colour to match the name. Aside from that the money had gone on clothes for the crew – something to make them look slightly more like pirates and slightly less like common riffraff. Our funds were running short now and everyone knew it but, at that exact moment, money was the least of our worries.

'Lift the anchor! Drop the sails!' I barked, ordering everyone about.

I rushed to the tiller and awaited departure, casting glances to the pier, afraid of what would be there. Finally, the anchor was hoisted and the wind caught our sails. I turned the ship north and we pulled away from the city, several figures beginning to crowd the harbour behind us.

'You'll never escape us,' an unforgettable voice yelled out, high and snakelike.

I pushed all thought of her from my mind as we took to the seas, heading north until we were away from land and then north-east. The crew gathered around, all worried but still anxious to hear my next plan. When I could find no words, Deline took the stand.

'We can't keep running,' she told me. 'If they stay on our tail, one day we'll have to turn around and fight them.'

'Foolish,' Hadivik spat. 'I know better than anyone how deadly they are. I tried to warn you back in Blakereath but nobody listened and people died because of it.'

I paced back and forth, listening as the rest of the crew began to take sides.

'Deline is right,' I said finally. 'One day we will have to turn and face the Cobras. But Hadivik is also right that they are too strong for us right now, which is why starting sunrise tomorrow you will all begin your official training. No more fooling around and competing for pride, but real, strenuous training.'

There was a lull, so I let my gaze bear into each of them.

'I must be going deaf because I didn't hear anything,' I called out. 'I said it's time for some real, strenuous training!'

'Aye captain!' they responded in unison.

I hated pushing them like this, it was not who I aspired to be but it had to be done; I had to be their captain and I could not afford failure.

'Captain,' Laricko voiced. 'That's all well and good, but what about me? I don't even have a weapon.'

It was true. I had meant to go to the blacksmith's that day and refit us with new weapons but the Cobras appearing had been an unexpected occurrence.

'And we barely have the coins between us to buy one,' Thalkrin pointed out.

224

I scratched at my chin, feeling the patchy hair that was growing through thicker and thicker.

'I suppose we do what all pirates are known for then,' I voiced. 'We raid a ship.'

The crew seemed to be a little taken aback by that, much to my dismay. If we were to do something like this, everyone needed to be on board with it.

'You sure about this, captain?' Arkin asked.

I nodded. 'Aye. We're pirates after all, might as well act like it.'

Felima and Laricko appeared to be a little nervous, though I could practically see the gleaming in the eyes of Thalkrin, Dirk and even Deline.

'Thought you'd never held someone at knifepoint for the sake of a few coins,' Deline laughed, echoing the words from the first night we spoke.

'This is for more than a few coins,' I answered. 'This could be the difference between holding off the Blakereath Cobras until we can defeat them and being torn to shreds before we have the chance.'

The crew seemed to be realising I was not changing my mind about this and they all began to fall in line. Every mention of the Cobras appeared to send a shiver down Hadivik's spine, which was understandable. I knew he hated me for trying to take these villains on but I was sure he would thank me when he could live the rest of his life without worrying about them.

'Alright everyone, playtime is over,' I told them. 'Laricko, get up in the crow's nest, keep an eye out for any nearing ships. Felima, help me draw up a work schedule. The rest of you, I want this deck spotless before sundown.'

'Aye captain,' they grumbled, but still got straight to work.

225

Evening descended and I retired to my quarters, entrusting the wheel to Hadivik. No other ships had been seen sighted since we left the Western Point but I knew the route between Sashak Island and the mainland (which sailors named *The Golden* Passage) was one often travelled by merchant ships and one we were quickly approaching.

When morning came I walked out to the main deck, the crew already lined up with the ship sailing head on. The wood beneath my feet shone, almost clean enough to see my own reflection.

'Good morning captain,' they called in unison, weapons at everyone's hip aside Laricko's.

'Good morning crew,' I replied. 'Today we start the real work. I want you to split up into pairs and do some hand-to-hand combat for several hours. No blades, no gauntlets, just bare fists. After that I want you to change partners and try your weapon skills for another few hours. Once that's done I want the rigging tightened and the deck swabbed as well as it was last night.'

'Captain?'

'Aye Laricko, I know, you still don't have a weapon,' I said, knowing what he was about to get at. 'I'm going to need someone helping me with steering and keeping lookout today, so come to me once your hand-to-hand is over.'

'Yes captain.'

And with that they were off, all energetic and ready to work hard. Seeing that they were more than capable of handling themselves, I got to my other duties.

And so it went like that, at least for next few days. They trained and got into a routine, getting a taste of what real hard work was like. I rarely interacted with the team other than Laricko but still had meals with them down below deck to make sure they were all still working at their best.

As we reached the end of the passage and my hopes of finding a target were plummeting, Laricko called from the crow's nest that there was a ship in sight. The others who had been sparring all halted, looking to me for direction. It occurred to me we had no cannons, no grappling hooks, nor any gear meant for raiding. What we did have however was a lot of alcohol and some deception tactics. I formulated our plan, called out some orders and awaited the incoming vessel.

'Help!' I cried over and over again at the top of my lungs.

The shouting alone was not enough to draw them near but the smoke would be. At the bow of the ship and at both sides we had set some old clothes alight. Adding rum really made it blaze and a thick cloud of smoke truly gave us the image of a ship in distress. The merchant vessel sailed closer, hoisting out hooks to pull the two boats together.

'What seems to be the issue?' the first man to board asked.

Only I stood in plain view, the others hiding and ready to attack.

'My ship has caught fire and I can't get it out!' I sobbed, playing up the role.

I had swapped to slightly less conspicuous garbs, though Wargal's dagger still rested at my hip. The merchant ordered some of his men across to the Hawk who moved quickly towards the closest flames. As they began to suspect something to be amiss, Deline, Hadivik and Thalkrin leapt out, holding them all at blade point as

Laricko came with rope to tie them. The merchant leapt back but was not as quick as Arkin who blocked the man's way back to his own ship.

'Please, don't hurt us,' the fat man sobbed, his eyes widening at the sight of Arkin's rapier.

'Then call for your men to stand down,' I grunted, catching glimpse of the dozen archers on the other ship with their arrows pointed towards us.

'I can't,' he said. 'I told the crew that if we're ever under attack, I'm expendable. They won't listen to me while I'm your prisoner.'

I sighed and lowered my head. 'So be it,' I said. 'Now!'

Dirk and Felima jumped out, bottles of booze in hand. They swiftly lit the fabric at the top and hoisted them towards the enemy ship. They exploded in a blaze of flame, burning our opponents. Some archers escaped the barrage and fired down on us. Arkin took the brunt of the arrows with three burying themselves into his legs and one into his shoulder. More arrows were knocked but the next flaming cocktails were already on target and wiped out the others. Most were jumping into the water, trying to escape the flames; a few others simply retreated from the edge of the ship. The merchant was quickly tied, and Laricko, Dirk and the injured Arkin stayed back to watch them all while the rest of us boarded the ship.

The fire was beginning to spread but we had some time. A few sailors came at us with swords but we made quick work of them and knocked them overboard. Dirk made for a good interrogator back on the Hawk as he called over information about where the valuables were. A chest half-filled with silver took two of us to lift, a score finer than most pirates dared to dream. They had little in the way of weapons but a few bows and daggers and a fine broadsword made for easy looting. We finished by taking the wine from their cellar – there was more for the taking but the fire was spreading rapidly now.

We boarded the Golden Hawk and removed the grappling hooks, cutting them free from the ropes for later use. Those who had fled overboard had now cleared the burning ship, but it seemed cruel to dump our prisoners when the smoke alone could suffocate a man. We kept them on board for a time, sa ling away from the carnage we had left behind. No matter how far away we got, the smoke could still be seen behind us for a good few hours after.

'Good idea using those bottles as explosives,' I heard Deline congratulate Arkin.

'Thanks,' he replied cockily, a hint of seduction in his tone. 'A stroke of genius if I do say so myself.'

'I wouldn't go that far,' she scoffed. 'And for the record, I'm not interested in guards.'

She gave a cunning smirk and strode away.

'Good thing I'm not a guard then,' he called after her.'

I could not help but to chuckle at their chemistry, or rather lack thereof. After a moment I noticed I was not the only one laughing. One of the tied up men had a smile on his face, the only of half a dozen without a mournful scowl. I met his gaze and the chuckle came to a halt, though the smile remained. I moved to where he sat, unable to move. He flinched with a small squeak as I reached out, startled when I grabbed at his hair and pulled.

Confirming my suspicions, the dark, shaggy hair came off in my hand and a river of blond fell loose down past his shoulders. I had been a fool to miss it before, as in front of me was clearly the face of a beautiful woman. She gasped as I smirked triumphantly.

'Your laugh betrayed you,' I told her. 'That and this shoddy wig.'

'Please,' she begged. 'Don't hurt me. I know what pirates do to women and...'

'Stop,' I snapped, clenching my fist. 'We're not those kind of pirates and the worst you'll get from us is being pushed overboard. But a question does come to mind. Why are you pretending to be a man?'

Felima had seen and heard the exchange and was over quickly, eager to hear the answer.

A tear trickled down the woman's face. 'It was the only way I could get a job,' she sobbed.

'Why did you need a job?' Felima asked her. 'Could your parents not provide for you?'

'No,' she answered, still teary. 'My mother died in childbirth and my father passed away a year ago.'

'What about a husband?' Felima pressed, more harshly than I would have.

I had to remember Felima was from an upper class upbringing, where women often went from their father directly to their husband. Even though the redhead herself had broken that mould, the ideals were clearly still with her.

'I refuse to take a husband,' the woman spat back.

'How come?' I asked before my crewmate could upset her anymore.

'I don't like men.'

An annoyance came over me as I was about to lecture her on how there were good men in the world but her eyes quickly portrayed her meaning.

'Oh,' was all I could manage.

'So what do you suppose we do with her?' Arkin asked over a tankard of mead.

'There's only one thing we *can* do,' Dirk groaned. 'We dump her with the others.'

'The others can find work,' I argued. 'They can still get jobs and live good lives. She can't.'

'Well why can't she?' Thalkrin scoffed. 'I've seen plenty of women pouring pints and running stalls.'

'Most of them are wives or daughters of the men who actually own the business,' I countered. 'And apparently you *have* to be one or the other where she's from to get work. If we just dump her she might never get work again.'

'I still don't understand why she can't marry a man,' Felima tutted.

'Darkskull already went over this,' Arkin chimed in. 'She likes women.'

'All the more reason for us to dump her,' the redhead spat. 'After all, it's illegal to be...*like her* in Issehai.'

'Girl, you're talking of what's legal and illegal in a room full of pirates,' Arkin reminded her and she piped down after that.

After a few more arguments I managed to convince the others it was only right to make the offer. I consulted with the others who had been managing the ship and the prisoners – Hadivik and Laricko said they would follow any decisions I made and Deline seemed intrigued by the woman.

That evening we led the prisoners to edge of the ship, one by one cutting their binds and throwing them into the murky water below. When we finally cut the woman's binds she closed her eyes and braced herself, opening them again when she did not feel the waves surrounding her.

'Rather than swimming back to shore, how would you like to join this crew of ours?' I offered.

She smiled for a moment but shook her head. 'I can't, I don't know the first thing about fighting and I could never take another's life.'

'You wouldn't have to,' I assured her. 'We have plenty of fighters. What we need is more people to work the ship – to steer or keep lookout while the rest of us are training. Do you think you could do that?'

Her answer showed through the embrace she gave me, strong and firm.

'Thank you,' she muttered, pulling away and sending a smile towards the rest of the crew, most of whom were less keen by the development.

'What's your name?' I asked her.

'Ellya,' she answered softly.

'Well Ellya,' I chimed, 'Welcome to the Golden Hawk.'

Chapter 20

Family Ties

We were pretty well set after the raid. We had bows and plenty of arrows for Laricko to get back to weapon training and Ellya made for a fine addition to the Hawk. Having been on merchant vessels for the last year, she was the best navigator amongst us and had no problem with steering the ship and helping the others with chores. Felima still gave her the cold shoulder but the rest of the crew took kindly to her after a while, even Dirk and Thalkrin who had been sceptical. Deline seemed to be welcoming her most of all and the two quickly came to be firm friends.

We stopped at half a dozen coast towns along our route from Veshul to Alliket, buying supplies with our endless flow of silver and drinking ourselves merry. Word was starting to spread about us and more than a couple of brawls along the way only re-established that fact. The names *Golden Hawk* and *Darkskull* seemed to be on everyone's lips, and I liked it that way – hopefully it would draw Daxon out.

During it all I made sure everyone was training their hardest. I made them fight until they dropped, I had them wielding weapons until they were not only competent but a force to be reckoned with and through it all I remained their friend and ally. It had been more than three weeks since we had left Blakereath together and a different group of people now stood before me. All were hardened pirates and they now looked the part.

I had splashed out on a new uniform and now all (including Ellya) wore a brown leather coat trimmed in gold atop a black waistcoat and white shirt. Brown trousers and fine black boots covered their bottom halves and a golden bandana was wrapped around each head bar mine. I wore a black tricorn hat, trimmed in gold and bearing the insignia of a hawk. It was the same insignia which was sewn onto each coat and represented on our new flag.

Not an hour into our departure from Alliket, a call came from Ellya in the crow's nest;

'Captain Darkskull, there's a ship tailing us!'

I ordered her to come and take the wheel, climbing the ropes to witness it for myself. True to her word we were being followed, but more disturbingly it was the flag of our chasers.

Three snakes...no...not snakes...cobras.

We had had no run-ins with them since The Western Point and I had hoped they had turned back, but no, they had found us.

'Everyone, battle positions,' I called to the rest of the crew, clambering back down and taking hold of my new sword.

The weapon was the finest money could buy, it was just a shame not a single blacksmith in any of the towns we had passed possessed an axe I was happy with.

'What is it captain?' Arkin panted, rushing over to me.

'Cobras,' I growled. 'Spread the word and get the fire power.'

We had set aside some bottles of rum specifically for moments like this, so we had no shortage of flaming projectiles to throw. However, much to my dismay, the enemy ship appeared to have canons and a lot of them. I knew our only option was to stop and try to negotiate. If enough of them boarded the Hawk, they surely would not blow us up. Still, fighting positions were a must.

'Laricko,' I called, grabbing the boy as he ran past. 'The Cobras probably think you're dead, so if anything goes wrong you're our secret weapon. Get up to the crow's nest and ready your bow. On my order, kill the woman who commands them.'

'Understood captain,' the lad said, though he was shaking. 'Wh...what if they get to you before you give the order?'

'Strike her down all the same.'

He nodded and scrambled up to his hiding spot. I ordered Ellya to turn the Hawk around and get below deck and for the others to drop anchor – Hadivik approached me.

'Captain, why are we stopping?' he cried.

'There's no way we'll out-sail them and to be honest I don't want to. I said this day would eventually come and while I wish we had more time it looks like it's here.'

'This is madness,' he accused. 'We're all going to die.'

I rested my hands on his shoulders. 'I know you're afraid, but I trust all of you are capable to take them on. We are pirates after all, we face danger head on rather than fleeing like cowards.'

The fear was still in his eyes but we both knew my decision was final. He grabbed his hammer and together we awaited the oncoming vessel.

The Cobras' ship was at least thrice the size of our own and larger than the Stallion by my estimate. Its mast portrayed a demonic snake which currently appeared to be flying towards us as they drew closer. We stood there, hoping that if we posed no threat they would not open fire.

I breathed a sigh of relief when their ship pulled up alongside our own. With grappling hooks and wooden walkways over a dozen figures boarded, the *mistress* herself leading the charge. Our crew stood at the centre of the main deck, weapons readied. I strode forward and so did the snakelike woman, both of us leaving behind our allies to meet once more face to face.

'I am glad to see you are not resisting,' the woman hissed.

'As am I to see that you didn't use those canons,' I countered.

'I have come to take what is mine,' she spat, infuriated.

During our first meeting she had seemed so calm and reserved, whereas now there was something more desperate behind her eyes.

'Then tell me what favour you wish of me and let us go on our way.'

'Oh forget that!' she snapped, much to my surprise. 'I'm not here to play games, so if you truly want to end this then hand him over!'

I flinched and took a step back. '*Him?*' I echoed, confused.

She clenched her fist as if she might strike me but when her gaze met mine she seemed to acknowledge the genuine confusion.

'Oh,' she said simply. 'He never told you.'

Before I could ask what in Issehai she was talking about, Hadivik was at my side.

'Forget it,' he yelled. 'There's no way you're taking me.'

He was on the floor in a second, his blood dripping from her outstretched fist. I unsheathed my blade and the rest of the crew stepped forward, mirrored by theirs.

'You must forgive me Darkskull,' she tutted. 'It seems I have not taught my son proper manners.'

Son?

Hadivik was recovering from the blow. By his lack of shock at the word I knew it must be true. I remembered what he had told me back in Blakereath, that all of his family were killed by the Cobras.

'Explain yourself,' I commanded the boy.

'It's true,' he grunted, getting to his feet. 'But I did not lie to you. This woman may have given birth to me but she is not my mother – everything inside of her that once was died the day that she killed my father.'

'Your father was weak Hadivik,' she told him. 'He had to die. He would not lead the Cobras with me.'

'Because he was not a killer,' the boy countered. 'And neither were your parents, nor his. They had nothing to do with it but you killed them anyway.'

'Yes,' the woman said. 'I did. They tried to rat me out to the guards, they wanted White Sky completely eliminated from their streets and I *would not* let that happen.'

'What about my sister?' he yelled. 'What was *her* crime? Your own daughter, why did *she* deserve death?'

At this a tear trickled down the woman's face but she still maintained her steely gaze. The Cobras were behind her, all watching us with readied blades. I could order the team to attack right now. Whoever was back on their ship would not fire on us with their mistress aboard. No, too risky. I had to let this play out.

'What happened with your sister was…unfortunate,' she sighed. 'But she stole drugs from the organisation and I could not appear weak to the others. It was after her death that I decided to leave you be but I never gave you permission to leave Blakereath.'

Hadivik was red with rage, his hand trembling as it gripped his hammer.

'You're a monster,' I interjected, taking another step towards the woman.

Her troops all aimed their weapons at me but she waved a hand and they lowered them.

'How dare you,' she hissed, unsheathing a knife. 'You know nothing of being a parent.'

Before I could reply Arkin stepped to my side.

'If *I* were a parent, I wouldn't kill my own daughter,' he scoffed.

'You're just a filthy serpent,' Deline added. 'Completely incapable of human emotion.'

'You killed my brother,' Felima said, calmly stepping up. 'You'll pay for that.'

'Everyone, this woman killed Perkyn. In the name of the Golden Hawk, I command you to avenge his death. No mercy!'

All at once our two forces collided. Hadivik charged for his mother with hammer aloft but another Cobra stepped in the way as she fell back. My own attention was diverted as one came for me; he was joined by another as more flocked onto the ship. The second collapsed immediately to the ground with an arrow in his neck – Laricko was improving as an archer. I managed to cut my opponent down but it was a slow process. These were not your everyday opponents, they were skilled and ruthless.

'Don't let their leader get away!' I ordered, spotting her rushing towards her ship.

Even as I sprinted after her I knew I could not get there in time. Laricko's arrow struck her leg and she collapsed to the ground. I leapt on top, knocking the dagger from her grasp. She reached to retrieve it but Dirk's foot sent it flying away. I pulled her to her feet, my blade at her throat, and glanced around – all who had boarded were dead, though archers from their ship pointed arrows at us.

'Drop your weapons or I kill her,' I threatened.

I knew my captive would likely tell them to open fire, so I held my free hand over her mouth. As soon as they made the decision to lower their bows, I commanded several of the crew to board their vessel and tie them up. When that was taken care of I released my hold on the woman and threw over my sword.

'What *is* this?' she questioned, taking hold of the blade.

I called up Hadivik and he came to my side, looking equally confused.

'It is not proper to kill an unarmed enemy,' I declared, putting my own spin on one of the Stallion's sayings. 'Hadivik, this is *your* fight. You are the reason they have attacked us and several of us have been wounded fighting your battle. It is time for you to redeem yourself and finally stop running.'

He seemed as if he may argue, that fear still more than noticeable on his face. But before he could, Arkin stepped up.

'Do it for your family lad, and for Perkyn,' the blond said.

He nodded and turned to face his mother.

'Oh son, you're going to kill the woman who raised you?' our foe taunted.

'Yes,' he growled. 'Yes I am.'

With those words he charged at her, swinging his hammer aloft. Quick as a serpent she ducked his blow and struck him hard in the stomach. He faltered and she sliced at him, holding no hesitation. He took a cut to the arm but was otherwise unscathed. The others were preparing to attack but I halted them.

'This is *his* fight,' I told them. 'Hadivik must overcome his demon.'

The boy swung again and then again, each time harder and faster than the last. She dodged every one, marking each with a retaliating cut. In fury he charged in recklessly, letting her sweep to the side and slice deep into his thigh. As he cried out in pain she drew behind him and struck him in the spine with the hilt. He collapsed to the ground writhing. His mother turned back to me and laughed.

'It looks like I am the victor,' she said cockily, but even as she gloated I noticed her fatigue. 'So if you don't mind I'll take my son and be on my way.'

'Not so fast,' I told her.

'Oh?' she said. 'Isn't it part of your code to spare the better fighter?'

'Indeed it is,' I affirmed. 'But your son is not the only one here who you've wronged.'

I turned to Felima who met my gaze with one of steel, stronger than I had ever seen her. She understood. I gave her the nod and she stepped up, readying her rapier and meeting her foe.

'Nice to see you again,' the serpent cackled. 'Come to join your brother? Send him my...'

Before she could finish Felima sliced at her. The woman raised a shaking hand to her cheek which was dripping with blood. She attempted to strike but

Felima knocked aside the blow with ease, slashing again. Her next attack sent the broadsword sliding across the deck and the next knocked our enemy to her knees.

'Everyone, get over here,' Felima called and we all obeyed. 'For Perkyn.'

With those words she stabbed the woman through with her rapier.

Dirk stepped us next. 'For Perkyn,' he said, stabbing her also.

Everyone got their turn, straight through the stomach to keep her alive as she watched us in pain and fear. I even handed Laricko my dagger so he could exact his own revenge. I chose to strike her across the face instead, taking great joy in watching her nose burst as tears ran down her cheeks. We helped the injured Hadivik to his knees so he was eye to eye with her. We gave him his hammer and despite his agony he clutched it with determination.

'Hadivik,' a feeble cry came from the once feared figure before him. 'Please.'

'For Perkyn,' the boy echoed. 'And for my family.'

With a single mighty blow he smashed her skull and the serpent was no more.

Chapter 21

Deal with the Devil

None of the Cobras accepted my offer of surrendering and joining the crew and I was far too afraid to simply dump them at sea and let them swim to shore. So instead I gave them each the chance to fight one of us and the crew proved themselves by killing each of their opponents. There were however crew below deck on their ship (almost a dozen of them) who simply worked out of fear of the gang and happily accepted the position. My own crew were sceptical, at least until I told them my intentions.

'We're taking this ship,' I said.

'Are you mad?' Thalkrin tutted. 'There's no way we can sail that thing.'

'No,' I admitted, 'But *they* can.'

Realisation seemed to dawn on them all. It was perfect. We would use them to sail and navigate and look after the ship under Ellya's command so the rest of us could maintain our training better than ever.

'Sounds almost too good to be true,' Dirk interjected.

'Well you best get used to things going our way,' I told him. 'We just singlehandedly took down one of the most dangerous gangs in Issehai.'

We took the time to welcome the new crewmates to the Golden Hawk as we transferred all of our supplies to the larger ship. I personally traversed the vessel from top to bottom, removing all evidence of the Cobras and getting to know my new home. I retired to my new quarters for a few hours, pleased by how spacious it was. While I lay back in my bed I thought of one extremely important thing.

It was time

I had assembled a crew of strong fighters with a wide range of talents who, despite many flaws, were all loyal beyond question. And now I had a heavily armed ship with people to sail it and only one thing left in my mind.

It was time for Daxon to die. Of that I had no doubt.

We cut the ropes to the old dishevelled vessel and threw our flaming bottles at it as we sailed away.

'It's a shame,' Ellya told me. 'I was just starting to get used to that ship.'

The rest of us also shared a sense of sorrow but for a much different reason. We had come to think of that boat as home, it was a piece of junk but it had been ours. For now, however, we would bask in the flames of the past as we set sail towards a brighter future.

We ate together that night as our new recruits sailed the ship under Ellya's orders. All of the original crew were there aside from Hadivik who was resting. One of the eleven men who had agreed to join us was a semi-descent medic named Jesko who reckoned the young blacksmith would never walk again. He had no feeling in the injured leg and his spine was irreversibly damaged. I left dinner early to make sure he was okay but the boy was already asleep.

We docked the new ship for the first time in Elikdale, a small town where the biggest issues were to do with snowy weather. It was known for being one of the most peaceful places in Issehai, but I was sure somebody here could help me.

My first stop was the local blacksmith which I rushed to eagerly, though was disappointed yet again by the lack of a well-made axe. Next was the carpenter to whom I offered a generous some of money to re-work the mast of the ship and more still to paint it top to bottom in a rich golden colour.

From there, a handful of us checked into an inn which was also home to the local tavern. The patrons were nothing special, your typical drunkards and townspeople – all of whom eyed us with eerie suspicion. With me were Dirk, Arkin and Deline; the four of us sat around a small table sipping at our pints as they gave us sceptical looks, clearly unsure why we were here. I did not speak, though my eyes regularly surveyed the room as I hoped for a figure worth speaking too.

'So, Darkskull,' Arkin said, breaking the silence. 'Now that we're starting to look like a real crew, who's your first mate?'

The smile on the blonde's face clearly indicated he thought it should be him but my gaze moved to the other two sat before me. Dirk was a good fighter, perhaps even stronger than Arkin after his relentless training, and despite our rocky start I knew he could lead well if given the chance. However, his arrogance would not let him back down from a challenge; I knew because we shared that trait. I needed somebody who would challenge my judgement and stop my recklessness and I feared Dirk would only reinforce it.

Arkin had challenged me on more than one occasion, always weighing in with the voice of reason – he was too sure of himself though. He had the knowledge and the experience, though at times he came across more childish than the younger crewmates. I considered him my best friend but that did not make him the best leader. That left Deline who was strong-willed and determined. She had made my life a living hell back in Blakereath and yet now I felt myself trusting her judgement more than anyone else's. Her approval meant a lot to me and she was fair with her decisions. That settled it.

'Deline,' I declared.

The woman's smile at Arkin's disappointed expression amused me; she sat back with that light sneer and did not speak a word. The ex-guard kept grasping at straws and finally (if for no other reason than to silence him) I agreed he could have the title of second mate. His ramblings were only a distraction however, for my eyes were now more focused on a cloaked figure sitting in the corner. Had he been there before? I could not recall.

'You three, please finish your drinks and head back upstairs to the room. I'll be up there later,' I instructed.

Without waiting for their response I stood and walked over to him, taking the empty seat and looking upon his bearded face. He was thin and rat like, in some ways resembling Wes. His hair was long however, and scraggly.

'What yer want?' he grunted, showing his seven teeth.

'Information,' I told him. 'You heard anything about the Stallion?'

'I don't know nothin',' he told me but something behind his tired eyes gave him away.

I pulled out a purse and threw it casually onto the table, silver spilling out. 'Let's not play this game,' I asked of him. 'You're an information broker and I want information.'

His eyes gleamed at the coins, a subtle smirk crossing his lips. It lasted but a second before he shook his head and grunted illegibly.

'Not 'ere,' he said. 'Elikdale might be quiet but walls 'ave ears.'

245

'Where then?' I asked, scooping back up the coins.

He ran a palm across his sweating brow and mumbled to himself.

'Tomorrow,' he said at last, 'By the old town cemetery. At dawn.'

I agreed to his terms, quietly moving away from him and retreating to our room. Informants could be spotted a mile off if you knew what to look for, it was a skill I had picked up in Cranwell. The other three were waiting for me, stopping their conversation abruptly as I entered.

'What was all that about?' Dirk enquired.

'Private matters,' I answered simply.

All of them eyed me sceptically. I thought maybe I should come out and tell them what I had planned but to do that I would have to explain everything that happened aboard the Stallion which I was not yet ready to do.

'Come on lad, don't be so mysterious,' Arkin chuckled, but I fixed him with an agitated glare.

'I said it was private,' I spat. 'So that's the end of it. And it's *captain*, not *lad*.'

They seemed shocked to hear me speak that way but Arkin could get under my skin sometimes.

'As you command...captain,' the blond mumbled and that was the last of the conversation for the rest of the night.

When dawn came I silently fled the room and headed straight for the cemetery. True to his word the broker awaited me, hooded and lurking in the shadows.

'So,' he grunted. 'What yer doin' lookin' for the Stallion?'

'My reasons are my own,' I told him.

I caught glimpse of the knife at his belt, not that I was worried, my broadsword was strapped to my hip and I had Wargal's knife too in case I needed it.

'They're dangerous people to be lookin' for is all,' he told me, eyes wide and bloodshot.

'I'm plenty dangerous myself,' I responded. 'Now are you going to give me information or not?'

'I don't know where the Stallion is,' he admitted. 'But I do know someone who could help yer, an expert on Daxon's crew shall we say. I can take yer to him, long as I get my payment.'

I reached for the purse in my pocket but paused. 'After you take me to him,' I pressed.

He shook his head. 'Now or I walk,' he demanded.

'How do I know you're not gonna just take my money and run off?' I accused.

Without a word he guided me over to an unmarked gravestone. He swept away the grass and dirt with his foot, revealing a wooden hatch beneath. One more quick glance around to make sure there were no onlookers and he pulled out a key to unlock the hidden doorway.

An underground tunnel, hidden right where nobody would dare to look. It was clever for sure but even as I threw over the coin purse and began to descend I was reminded of a similar situation back in Blakereath. He came down after me, closing and locking the hatch before sliding the key back into his pocket. If this was a trap, that key would be my only way out.

The man struck a match and lit a nearby torch, lifting it from its holder and lighting the way. I tailed him in silence, hand firmly on the hilt of my blade. The tunnel seemed to stretch on forever into total darkness in a single direction, with no turns nor hidden pathways. After what felt like an hour of continuous walking we finally came to a single wooden door.

'Hold this,' the man said before thrusting the torch into my grip.

He pulled out a chain this time with seven individual keys upon it. One by one he inserted each into a different lock – whoever I was about to meet was security conscious. We entered into a small circular room with nothing but another door opposite us.

'This is as far as I take yer,' the man told me. 'Knock twice on that door and my contact will come out to meet yer.'

'Hold on a second,' I went to say to him but he was already out of the room with the dreaded sound of the door being relocked behind me.

I was worried – I had come here all alone with no backup and without telling anyone where I was going or who I was meeting. I thought maybe I could hack my way back out, but no, I had come this far. There was only one thing left to do.

I knocked twice and stood back from the door, hand hovering above my hilt. There was nothing for a few moments, followed by the sound of it slowly creaking open. A figure came forward into the room and I froze.

I had seen him before.

There he was.

He looked the same as he had that day; tall with ebony skin and dark features, robes flowing even without a breeze. When he saw me he grinned, toothy and demonic – that frightful look of recognition in his eyes. I wanted to pull out my blade but I could not move. Was this his magic again? No, it was my fear.

248

'When my informant told me I would have a visitor today, I certainly did not expect it to be you,' he mused, low and powerful.

'Sursaroh,' I managed to whisper.

He laughed. 'It's nice to see you remember me boy. Yodrick, was iit?'

I managed a deep breath to calm my nerves. If he was going to kill me he would have done it already. Then again from what I gathered this man liked to play games.

'It's Darkskull now,' I told him.

'Oh, so you've accepted your father's mantel,' he said; my body tensed up once more. 'Oh don't look so surprised, I'd recognise those eyes anywhere. Tell me, why are you not with Daxon?'

'Why should I tell you anything, monstrous sorcerer?' I spat, my confidence building as I gripped the hilt of my blade.

He laughed again. 'Because it seems you're looking for your friend, and I can help you find him.'

'He's not my friend,' I retorted at once.

I pulled forth my blade but the sorcerer sighed.

'Boy, you know you are no match for me. With a wave of my hand I can bring forth creatures more monstrous than you could ever imagine.'

I paused for a moment before groaning and sheathing the sword.

'Good lad,' he said. 'Now, if you say Daxon is not your friend I imagine you learned the truth about what he did to your father?'

I nodded. 'That's right, and I swore I would kill him for what he has done.'

The sorcerer's gaze met my own and I knew he could sense the fire there.

'In that case I will help you find the Iron Stallion,' he promised.

I took a step back. 'Why should I trust you? What could possibly possess you to help me?'

'Think about it boy,' he said. 'If you kill Daxon it benefits us. We want him dead just as much as you do and this way I won't have to get my hands dirty.'

His demonic figure towered over me, human in appearance but clearly something much more evil. Farrow and anyone associated with him were bad people – even Wes had said as much. Still, why did their plans mean anything to me? I only had one goal, I only knew one thing for certain.

'Daxon has to die.'

'I'm glad we agree,' Sursaroh chimed with a light cackle. 'I will help you find the Stallion but first I need something from you.'

At once I tensed but managed to make out a confident sounding, 'What is it?'

'Do you have anything of Daxon's? A weapon he gave you or perhaps a keepsake?'

'No,' I spat. 'I cut every tie to him when I left the Stallion.'

'Perhaps something that belonged to another member then?' he suggested. 'As long as they're still aboard the Stallion.'

I touched at my dagger but Wargal was in Merrywood – his body anyway. I reached into my pocket and found the arrowhead, the last thing which linked Brongrim and I. Reluctantly I handed it over, feeling an icy touch as the sorcerer took it from me. He turned it over in his hands, observing it. He muttered a few strange words and the item began to glow.

'This will work,' he told me, handing it back. 'I've enchanted this arrowhead to find its former owner. See how it seems to pointing somewhere? Follow its direction and you will be led to the Stallion, provided your friend is still aboard.'

I moved the arrowhead in my hand and as he said no matter which way I tried to turn it the item kept pointing in the same direction.

'And so our business is done?' I asked him, expecting to have to pay a price.

'Indeed it is,' Sursaroh said. 'Now killing Daxon is all up to you. My informant will show you out.'

I turned and the broker was already stood at the doorway with torch in hand. I followed him back through the tunnel and up to the cemetery where he left me. Finally, with this arrowhead I would have revenge on the man who killed my father.

'Daxon, I'm coming for you!'

Chapter 22

Onwards

The rest of our stay in Elikdale was pleasant enough, though the three I had brought into town gave me several unsure looks. They knew I was hiding something, though they could not understand the gravity of what it was.

The arrowhead pointed eastwards. I checked it every day and still it directed me east. We would have to sail northwards of Saransa to get to the other side of Issehai and that would take weeks, by which point the Stallion may have moved on. Still, I had nothing left to go on so this was what we would do.

We checked back on the ship several times during our stay, making sure the crew were content and to survey the progress on the ship. The carpenter had all of his men working on it day and night which I expected for how much I was paying them. The rest of the crew always seemed to be whispering about me – I knew they were suspicious like the others. I remembered the hushed meeting about Daxon back on the Stallion and I feared the same was happening here. I had to tell them at some point.

In total, we spent a full week in Elikdale. By the end of it we departed in a ship fit for the king himself. The mast was a perched hawk with its wings spread wide and the entire ship glistened a rich golden colour. It did at one-point dawn on me most men would be content with what I had. I had grown up on the streets on Cranwell, a thief in trade. Now I was the captain of a luxurious pirate ship with a powerful crew and enough silver to last someone a lifetime. Most would stop here, accept this new life and be content to simply make a name for themselves. However, my vision was not lost. After all, I had amassed all of this to fulfil one goal – revenge.

Ellya had the wheel with the rest of her sailors manning the ship. My crew were sparring on the main deck. All of which left me to my own devices. I rested in my quarters, running my necklace through my fingers. I had not thought about the piece of jewellery for some time, and often disregarded it as a trinket. It was not much to look at, a leather chain with a metal hoop at its end – it was my father's.

Cold was the sea which I swam in, as was the gaze of the man before me. He stood on a raft, not much bigger than his stance yet it stayed afloat It was Daxon and, despite his harsh stare, he held out his hand to me. I ignored it and kept swimming.

'You'll freeze,' he told me, in his usual blunt manner. 'That or drown.'

'I don't care,' I spat back. 'I don't want your help.'

I kept swimming but the figure on the raft spoke again – this time it was my father. I saw him the way I remembered him, with sandy blond hair and eyes like reflections of my own.

'You should listen to him son,' he told me. 'After all, Daxon was my friend.'

'He killed you,' I sobbed. 'What kind of friend would do that?'

There was no answer and I kept swimming as I slowly froze. Then a wave hit me and I found myself being thrown around rapidly. I tried to breathe but was met with lungs full of water. I tried to scream, but nobody could hear.

We had been sailing for a week and were passing through the cold northern sea. Snow fell over the ship, turning gold to white. I voyaged down to the food hall in hopes of a warm meal and was surprised to be met by the rest of the crew, all there – bar Hadivik who spent most days in the armoury below forging and repairing weapons.

Their eyes darted up when they saw me, a few giving a polite, 'Good morning captain!'

'What are you all doing down here?' I questioned, clear from my expression that I was not impressed. 'If I'm correct you should all be in the midst of training by now.'

'It's too cold to train,' Laricko dared.

I scoffed. 'Too cold? I think that's for me to decide.'

'With all due respect captain, you're not the one who has to stand out there,' Arkin said.

'Fine,' I said. 'I'll join you.'

None seemed pleased as I led them to the main deck and had them take up their weapons. The sailors had swept most of the snow away, though it was still coming down on top of us.

'First and second mate with me,' I commanded, Arkin and Deline moving to my side.

Felima, Laricko, Dirk and Thalkrin faced us, weapons in hand. I took out my broadsword and prepared.

'State the rules,' Dirk said, taking lead of the opposition.

'If someone submits, takes a potentially killing blow or is unable to fight then they are defeated. First team to be fully defeated loses. Now, let's fight.'

Everyone jumped into action, Dirk coming straight for me with his cutlass. He slashed for my neck but I parried and spun to his side. I aimed for his ribs but he was too quick. We squared up again, and I heard a curse from Arkin. An arrow was in his shoulder but as I turned back to my own fight a booted foot struck my chest and I was knocked to the floor.

'You shouldn't take your eye off of the fight captain,' he sneered, approaching me.

I jumped back to my feet and blocked his incoming attack, twisting my grip to get the leverage and pushing him back. He ducked down and his blade slashed into my chest. I faltered, giving him an opening to strike me again. I grabbed his wrist with my free hand and twisted it back on itself. Dirk muffled a cry and pulled away from my grasp before I could break something.

Arkin retreated to the side-lines, more than a couple of arrows in him but nowhere critical. A moment later Thalkrin joined him. I stepped up and kicked Dirk, though he dropped his blade to catch my foot at the last second and swept the other leg. I went down, but he did not have a weapon to follow through. Catching glimpse of his cutlass, half buried in the fresh snow where he had dropped it, I made a reach for it but he got there first.

I jumped up and backed off, taking a moment for a quick glance around. Felima was out now and I watched as Laricko loosed an arrow at Deline's knee which took her down. The archer rushed to her and held a dagger to her throat; she was out too. Now it was Dirk and Laricko against me. I turned back towards Dirk in time to block an incoming attack but, as I did so, I felt an arrow in my back. My vision blurred slightly but I pressed on.

I turned and ran for Laricko who was still knocking another arrow, striking the bow from his hands and about to jab him when hands from behind pulled me away. Dirk threw me down into the snow and pointed his cutlass to me, Laricko over me in a second with another arrow pointed at my head. I dropped my blade.

'I submit,' I panted.

I could not believe it, we had lost. It seemed everyone was evenly matched and putting four on their team had sealed our fate. I had underestimated the likes of Felima and Laricko, for when the fight with Daxon arrived I would need them at my side. We retreated to the food hall where I made the decision. I invited Hadivik to join us, and cleared my throat.

'Everyone, listen up,' I called.

The eating, drinking and overall merriment died down in a second – I had trained them well.

'What is it Darkskull?' Deline enquired.

'I am not a fool,' I told them. 'I know you have all been talking about me, curious that I might have some hidden intentions which I have not told you.'

'Nobody thinks that captain,' Thalkrin insisted, though I shook my head.

'It is true,' I admitted. 'I have not been entirely honest with you and that was wrong of me. All of you have proved your loyalty to me and to the Golden Hawk but now it is time for *me* to prove myself. The first thing you need to know...is that my name is Yodrick Alton.'

And having started my story, I went on to tell them everything. I recounted my tale with Daxon and the Iron Stallion, how he killed my father and I hoped to one day return the favour. I mentioned Farrow but only in passing and purposely withheld my encounters with Sursaroh – they would only think me crazy unless they experienced his power for themselves. With everything else on the table, I told them I had a rough idea of where Daxon was and that that was where we were headed.

With all said and done and my story over, all I was met with was silence. They were processing, some perhaps even doubting what I had told them.

'I never signed up for this,' a voice said finally.

Deline was holding her head in her hands with a sombre expression, one that filled the faces of everyone there.

'If anyone wishes to leave the Hawk...'

'Don't be stupid,' Felima cut me off. 'Each of us joined the Hawk because we had nowhere else to go. Look at us; we're a bunch of misfits and rejects – the people who the world forgets about. Outside of this crew, we are nothing. That has not changed. And I hope everyone else agrees with me.'

They were nodding and I was moved by the girl's words.

Arkin turned to me. 'Serial killing pirate or not, I'll stand by you...captain.'

One by one, the others echoed their own versions of his words, with the general consensus that we would go forward with my plan. Together we were the Golden Hawk and we would seize the day.

For the next few days everybody was riled up, all training harder than ever despite our cold conditions. I joined them, seizing every moment of free time I had to push myself to the limit. Daxon was close, I could sense it.

On the third day Hadivik came to me – he had gotten good at using his hands to drag himself around the ship, though I still felt a sense of guilt whenever I laid eyes upon him.

'Captain, I have something for you. It's below deck if you would be so kind,' he said.

I nodded and followed him as he slowly led us down to the armoury where his makeshift forge was set up. He had been working with sub-optimal equipment ever since we left Blakereath. Following his injury, I had purchased all of the necessary equipment back in Elikdale, so he had everything he needed to craft weapons – that being said I did not expect the calibre of weapon he presented me with.

I pulled the cloth from his gift and smiled. The wood was strong and wrapped in iron like the one from Merrywood and its head was finely sharpened steel. Chiselled into the head was the image of a hawk with wings spread wide, so finely crafted I knew it must have taken many hours. I held the axe in both hands and gave the air a swing, amazed at how right it felt in my grasp. When Hadivik had started forging new blades he tested us for grip size and balance – this weapon was made specifically for me and I could tell in an instant.

'Hadivik, it's perfect,' I told, tearing slightly. 'How can I ever thank you?'

'Consider it *my* thanks captain. You all helped to defeat the Cobras and I finally received justice for my family.'

I smiled and nodded, though my weapon was not the only one he had been working on. The others all received custom-made items, none as breath-taking as mine but all crafted with care. Each bore the insignia of the hawk and Arkin joked we were all covered in more birds than the Blakereath Statue was in bird shit.

We spent a day getting used to our new toys, finally feeling ready for what was to come. One by one the others turned in for the night, though I stayed out there under the night sky and the snow that came with it, preparing. Soon only Ellya and a few of the sailors were above deck, navigating by the light of the moon under direction of my enchanted arrowhead.

'Captain,' the blonde called to me.

I approached the gorgeous woman at the wheel, a little disappointed that she had no interest in men.

'Yes Ellya?'

'You work yourself too hard, why not rest by the wheel for a while and have a drink with me?' she suggested.

Gone was the timid girl I had first met, for even in her voice I could feel confidence. She had changed. I had changed too. Gone was the boy from Cranwell who picked pockets, for now I was a man. I looked the part too. A thin stubble now covered my jawline and my hair was almost at my shoulders. My frame was broader, more muscular and I was perhaps even a few inches taller than when I had left Cranwell.

'That would be nice,' I agreed.

'Rillak,' she called to a nearby sailor. 'Fetch the captain and I some mead.'

'Yes ma'am,' he replied, scurrying away below deck without hesitation.

'You've certainly whipped them into shape,' I complimented.

She gave a shy smile and laughed. 'It just feels right, like I've always been meant to do this, you know?'

I nodded, though in truth I had felt out of place since the start. I enjoyed being captain and knowing I had the trust and respect of my crew, though a part of me felt like it was misplaced. All I could do was hope that once Daxon was dead I could get on with my life.

The drinks were brought quickly, each of us taking hold of a tankard.

'Onwards,' she toasted, smashing our drinks together and taking a long swig.

We stayed there for a long time, chatting. Apparently she had her eye on Deline, thinking her a potential future lover. I was not one to judge, though I knew not whether I should discourage her. I had always simply assumed Deline liked men, though the flirtatious way I had seen her act around Ellya would suggest otherwise. Regardless, the mention of it sent a strange pang to my chest – the origin of which I could not determine. We spoke of things like this and of duties and even of back home. It was nice to take my mind away from the mission, if only for a short while.

I was shocked when the sky began to lighten with the first rays of dawn – we had been here all night.

'Ship spotted,' a sailor (Torgl) from the crow's nest called.

I was so relaxed it took me a moment to realise what he had said. Adrenaline now beating in my chest I rushed to the bow of the ship and there it was. Practically invisible under nothing but the moon but in sunlight I saw it clearly.

It seemed larger than in my memory, though we still outsized it. Even from here the iron horse at its bow was clear, seemingly galloping across the waves. It had worked, Sursaroh's magic had finally led me to it.

The Iron Stallion.

Chapter 23

Unexpected Guests

E verything was a rush of emotions. Within minutes I had the entire crew on deck, all armed and ready to fight. People who I considered friends were on that opposing ship but also some who I considered enemies. If it came down to it, I hoped I would not have to kill Brongrim or Wes in the crossfire but that did not mean I would not do it if I had to.

'Is it...*him* captain?' Felima asked.

I noticed her trembling as I gave a slow nod.

'Aye, it's him alright.'

I had wanted to do this on a good night's sleep but I would take what I got. It almost seemed too good to be true, they were sailing right for us.

'Another ship sighted!' the same voice from before called from the crow's nest.

I rushed to the side of the Hawk. Slightly to the north (and closer to the Stallion than us) another vessel seemed to be appearing out of thin air. The snow had lightened and there was no fog to cover it, so how had we not spotted it before?

I saw the flag – a bloodied shield over a dark background. The mast was haunting, a headless woman leading the charge, it was as frightening as the first time I laid eyes upon it.

'What in Issehai is that?' Laricko belted. 'Another pirate ship?'

'The Headless Maiden,' I muttered. 'Sursaroh is here.'

It all made sense to me. It explained why Sursaroh had agreed to help me, he had enchanted the arrowhead knowing I would lead him directly to Daxon. Yet somehow he had overtaken us, not by much but the Maiden would reach the Stallion before we could. Magic, perhaps. It seemed he could use it to hide the ship, so it was likely he was speeding it up also.

'Who's Sursaroh?' Thalkrin asked and I felt a pang of guilt for not telling them of Farrow's sorcerers.

'A very dangerous man,' I told him.

Who I brought here, I added in my head.

Still, we sailed at full speed towards the action, watching as the other two ships collided. When we finally reached them it seemed that it was Stallion that had been boarded. We threw out our grappling hooks and latched on to the ship; I spared no time in being the first one to cross over. I paused for less than a minute, waiting for the rest of the crew to join me – against the entire crew of the Iron Stallion and, with the threat of Sursaroh, I did not want to rush in alone despite the adrenaline pumping through me.

'Captain,' Arkin called as I was about to lead them towards the centre. 'What's our plan?'

'The plan is still the same,' I told them. 'We go after Daxon. If anyone tries to stop us we will fight and do what is necessary but do not underestimate any of them, attempting capture will surely lead to our demise. Kill them if you have to but Daxon is mine.'

Without further reasoning I marched to the middle of the ship where two opposing forces were already waging war. All of the crew were there, all except

Varen, fighting against armoured grunts. By the screams they made when they died I determined these were not Sursaroh's conjurations but real people. The sorcerer himself stepped forward.

'Daxon,' he bellowed in his low, booming voice.

Finally, amongst the flashing of blades, the captain of the Stallion step forward. If possible he looked even fiercer than before, his hair and beard longer and wilder.

'Sursaroh!' he cried, running the nearest grunt through with that crystal blade.

The Elder Blade. The one he had killed my father for. I would take it from his corpse and smash it into a million pieces.

'Surrender now Daxon and I might let your crew live,' the robed man offered.

'You think I'd ever submit to likes of you?' Daxon hollered. 'You wretched scum, I'll kill you where you stand!'

'Not yet you won't,' another voice called.

It took me a moment to realise that the voice was mine. All eyes were on the crew and I in an instant. Daxon was staring at me and I swear he was quivering.

'Yodrick?' Akaya's voice sounded. 'Is that truly you?'

'I've come to follow up on my words,' I growled at Daxon, ignoring Akaya as I strode forward.

Those that remained of the Maiden's grunts slowly backed away as I approached.

'Oh Darkskull, how nice of you to join us,' Sursaroh chimed. 'And may I say a fine thank you for leading us here.'

There was muttering from both crews but my attention was entirely fixated on the pirate before me.

'Darkskull?' he questioned. 'You're going by Darkskull now?'

'Captain Darkskull to be precise,' I spat back at him.

The others were moving, blocking the path between him and I. Akaya, Gurdgrin and Korhal stood with their weapons raised – Akaya with spiked, steel gauntlets. I raised my axe in defiance.

'Move aside,' I ordered them.

'Yodrick lad, you don't know what you're doing,' Korhal reasoned.

'Yes I do,' I yelled at him. 'And I'm not your *lad*, nor any friend of yours, and like I said it's Darkskull now. Darkskull, like the name of the man you all helped kill!'

'I did no such thing,' Gurdgrin argued, the vicious man looking even more scarred than before. 'And nor did Brongrim or Wes or Mamorhah.'

Out of them only Brongrim had his weapon raised and it was pointed at me. An arrow was knocked and the string was pulled back. I felt betrayed by my friend but in the light of dawn a tear sparkled on his cheek.

'If you choose to defend this villain you're as guilty as he is,' I told them. 'Now for the last time, move aside or my crew will have no option but to attack.'

I glanced back to them, all within a dozen paces and weapons at the ready. Laricko had an arrow pointed for Brongrim and I wanted nothing more than to tell the lad not to shoot him but I could not.

'While this is all good fun and all, I'd like to interject,' Sursaroh chuckled. 'I'm under orders to kill Daxon and retrieve the Elder Blade.'

'It's yours once I kill him,' I told the sorcerer.

'No Yodrick,' Daxon called from behind his bodyguards. 'Whatever happens and whatever grievance you have with me; we cannot let the blade fall into Farrow's hands.'

'I'm sick of all this talking,' I scoffed. 'Hawks, attack!'

As soon as I made the first lunge for Korhal an arrow hit my shoulder. Brongrim took an arrow to the arm as well. Soon all three were on me but not for long. Korhal made a one-armed slash with his machete which I fended off, knocking aside the attack as I turned to parry one of Gurdgrin's hatchets. I turned away from it too slow and Akaya's punch caught my elbow, the spikes smashing into the bone. Dirk and Felima came in with their own attacks as I held back a groan.

Off to our flank Arkin and Deline were dealing with Brongrim and with Mamorhah who had decided to join the fight. Felima's rapier slashed against Gurdgrin, cutting yet more flesh from the already mutilated man. Dirk's cutlass caught him again as he was retreating to get into throwing range. With my attention on my comrades, the machete sliced at my torso; I took a nasty cut before stepping up and kicking the green-haired man backwards.

From amongst them Daxon rushed forward with his mighty blade aimed at me. I leapt out of the way but was not quick enough as he turned to strike again. Thalkrin appeared, charging Daxon from the side and knocking him off balance but the dark youth was swept away by Gurdgrin.

'I don't want to do this,' Daxon grunted through gritted teeth as he struck at me again.

'Then give up and accept your fate,' I retorted as I parried his blow and swung around with my own.

266

I turned the axe in time to block a flanking attack from Korhal with my hilt and sliced across his side, spinning back towards Daxon.

'You can't let Farrow get a hold of this blade,' he pleaded, standing his ground and blocking my incoming attacks.

He seemed afraid but in that moment I did not see the man I had known; he was not the one who had taken me away from a rundown city and trained me to be stronger – only a killer who had ruined my life. Gnashing my teeth   swung again and again, finally ripping into his flesh. He faltered, pressing his free hand against the open wound at his thigh.

'Please,' he cried.

I paused. He was begging. I had never seen Daxon beg before.

'Why is it so important to you?' I pressed, marking my question with a strong kick to the stomach.

He stumbled back, finding his footing and raising his guard but making no move to attack.

'The Elder Blades,' he panted. 'They have power. Power beyond your imagining. They can make the wielder unstoppable.'

'Then explain why I'm beating you,' I growled, kicking him again.

His face was reddening, his eyes becoming darker.

'Fine!' he spat, brushing off my next kick. 'I didn't want to do this but it looks like I'm going to have to show you.'

With those words he lunged at me, the blade glowing with a soft blue light becoming brighter and brighter. It was faster than his previous attacks and I narrowly dodged it. He came in again, stronger, stronger than I thought possible. I held my guard with both hands, though as his weapon hit my own I went flying back – landing on the ground at least five feet away.

He approached, slowly, a monstrous glint in his eye. In that moment he looked like a demon, his face contorted like something inhuman. The blade's glow faded and the expression was gone as quickly as it had appeared.

'Please understand,' he said, barely audible over the clashing of steel. 'This is more important than you or I.'

A flicker of doubt ran through my mind. I had striven for this moment, the chance to face the man who destroyed my family and ruined my life. However, Daxon seemed sincere. Could it be true?

No.

He was a liar and a monster and I would destroy him.

'You're wrong,' I groaned, getting to my feet. 'This is all about *you*. What *you* did. I swore by the maker you would burn, so let me live up to that promise.'

I lunged at him again, fury in my heart. He was off guard and my blade was about to tear into him – finally, my revenge!

I did not understand how he could have pushed me but I felt the force of it. I was on the ground, dazed. We were all on the ground, even Daxon. Scrambling to my feet I turned to the figures at the tiller. Sursaroh had his hand joined with a stranger, a woman I had never seen before. She also wore robes but her skin was pale and sickly where his was dark and rich. I knew from her appearance she must be Farrow's other sorcerer.

'Sorry for the light push,' Sursaroh laughed. 'But I was getting a little bored.'

'That force,' I heard Felima stammer. 'What was that?'

'That my dear was magic,' the woman cackled. 'And strong magic too. Then again, did you expect any less when facing the most powerful beings in all of Issehai?'

'Greskel,' Daxon growled, getting to his feet. 'So Farrow would rather send both of his lackeys than face me himself?'

'On the contrary,' another voice said.

The sorcerers parted and from between them a red-haired man came force. His hair was spiked and the grin on his face practically split his cheeks. And those eyes, even from here I could tell they were as black as a starless night.

I heard Daxon murmur a single word; 'Farrow.'

Laricko was hurt from his archer battle with Brongrim, the latter looking as if he might lose the other leg. Dirk was bleeding heavily, as were Korhal and Mamorhah. The others had smaller injuries but nobody appeared particularly fit and healthy. My eyes turned to Daxon and his gaze resembled my own. He was staring at Farrow the way I had stared at him when I found out about my father. It was an expression of complete hatred.

I clenched my fist around the haft of the axe and gritted my teeth. Farrow unsheathed a blade, similar to Daxon's but longer and more jagged. His gaze washed over us all and he began to chuckle.

It seemed like my fight with Daxon would have to wait.

Chapter 24

Joining Forces

'How nice to see you again Daxon,' Farrow laughed. 'How long has it been?'

'You wretched scum!' Daxon spat back, his knuckles turning white around the hilt of his blade.

'And who is *this* we have here?' the red-haired man asked, pointing a long finger towards me.

'My name is Darkskull,' I said, stepping up proudly. 'Captain of the Golden Hawk.'

'I recognise that name,' Farrow chuckled. 'The last man who bore it was a laughing stock, no drive in him.'

I gritted my teeth and raised my axe. Step by step I approached the three figures with anger in my heart. They met my challenge, likewise walking forward until we were only a few paces apart.

'Out of our way foolish boy,' Greskel tutted and, with a measly hand gesture, I was flying back.

I landed near the others who were still recovering from the first blast of magic.

'Are you okay captain?' Laricko called, moving to my side.

'I'm fine,' I groaned. 'But be careful of those two, you saw what they're capable of.'

'What even are they?' Dirk bellowed.

'Sorcerers,' Arkin confirmed. 'My mother told me the old legends when I was a lad but I never thought any of it could be true. It...it just can't be.'

'Open your eyes, moron,' Deline scolded him. 'It *is* true; you saw what they can do.'

As they were bickering the trio were still approaching, with Daxon at the front of us ready to take the fight. The crew of the Stallion were flocking to him, injured but still as ready to fight as ever. One was missing though – I had not seen Wes since the fight had started and was pretty sure he had never joined in. *That sneaky bastard,* I thought to myself, *I wonder what he's up to.*

We all got to our feet, eagerly watching on as Farrow came ever closer. The lackeys from before were flocking to him, though in the blink of an eye his sword sliced through his own men, glowing mysteriously as they fell lifelessly to the ground. Daxon's blade was glowing too and he seemed surprised by it.

'Confused?' Sursaroh asked him tauntingly. 'It's not often two Elder Blades come this close together but when they do they both receive the same level of...*charge.*'

The word *charge* seemed to mean something to Daxon and the others, like something only the crew of the Stallion understood. Greskel and Sursaroh linked hands again and as they threw them up figures manifested around the Stallions, eleven in all. I recognised similar magic to what Sursaroh had used on the Maiden but this was different. These figures were fully armoured and each an impressive eight feet tall. The gaps in their armour and helmets blazed with black flames, proving there was no flesh beneath.

'By the maker,' Felima gasped. 'What *are* those things?'

'The sorcerers' magic, at its most terrifying,' I muttered.

'What do we do?' she asked, clearly petrified.

Even as the question was being asked, the colossal figures closed in on Daxon's crew. I could barely see what was happening other than flashes of steel and cries of fury.

'Eleven against six hardly seems fair,' I told them. 'Let's even the score.'

On my order Laricko moved to the side and began firing arrows at the giants as we charged in with a hefty battle cry. I lunged and gave a strong two-handed swing to the legs of the closest abomination. It fell to its knees and dropped its sword, now closer to my height, and Akaya came in from its front with an armoured punch to the helmet. The metal flew off and the source of the black flames billowed from inside the armour.

She gave a short smile to me but our foe was not done. Even headless, it leapt back to its feet and backhanded the female pirate with its enormous gauntlet. She went flying back, knocking Mamorhah to the ground also.

'Now you see the true extent of our power,' the male sorcerer was crying with glee. 'My soldiers have no flesh for you to cut and no heads for you to decapitate. They're invincible!'

The others were also quickly realising what he said was true, with at least three of the metal demons fighting headless. I rapidly swung into the back of my opponent but the blows were mainly glancing off. It slowly turned around and swung for me. I leapt out of the way and raised a guard as it retrieved the humongous bastard sword and approached me, abandoning the circle formation.

Laricko's arrows rained down on the creature, distracting it for a moment as I ran in and cut at its legs once more. I roared as my axe came down on it with a flurry of unrelenting blows but it was no use. No matter how many pieces of armour I knocked away from the thing it still got back up. Before I could back away, its sword came for me. I tried to retreat, but the tip of the blade still caught me. My knees ached as I fell to them, blood splattering across the floor. Wooziness consumed me, unable to go on as I thought for a moment that I might die.

But Mamorhah gave the creature a swift stab to its back, drawing it away from me, giving my archer a chance to let loose some arrows and take hold of its attention. I shakily got to my feet, ripping off a sleeve and tying it around my wound, pressing on through the pain. The others were not in much better shape than I, all coming to the conclusion that we were fighting a losing battle. Everyone was in the midst of combat with the metal giants, all except Daxon who was engaged in a relentless fight with Farrow. I watched them for a moment, their sword skills seemingly matching one another. The sorcerers were now nowhere to be seen, likely protecting themselves from attack. I remembered back on the Maiden how Wes had hurt Sursaroh and thus stopped his conjurations – that was the key.

I wanted so badly to go off and search for them but a cry for help drew my attention. It was Laricko, the thing had backed him against the side of the ship with no chance for escape. I rushed for them, hoping my legs could get me there quick enough. The thing was raising its blade, ready to kill the archer.

'Laricko, duck down!' I commanded as I reached them.

The boy did what I said, crouching as I rammed into the soldier with all of my strength. It staggered forward at my push, tripping over Laricko's hunched over frame and toppling into the sea. I watched as the black flames extinguished and the armour evaporated into nothing.

'Are you okay?' I asked the boy.

He nodded but his chest was heaving.

'If only we could do that with all of them,' he muttered, but we both acknowledged it simply would not work like that.

The conjurations were slow and dumb but even if we all rushed for the edge of the ship, they would not be stupid enough to let themselves fall in. We staggered back towards the battle where everything was going badly. Daxon and Farrow were both torn to shreds but still pressing on, their blades now glowing and a wild expression on each of their faces. The crews were faltering, all practically ready to drop.

I charged for a foe, striking it in the back. Mamorhah was the one facing it from the front, his dual blades keeping him in the fight. My attack had the monster pause for a moment, giving my ally the chance to flurry attack with great power. Pieces of armour fell away but the majority of it remained. With one remaining arm the things swung its sword at the large pirate who jumped back at the last second, but the swing kept coming as its entire body spun around and it caught me in the arm. The axe fell from my grasp as the enemy locked onto me and lifted its sword for another blow.

'No!' Mamorhah cried, leaping onto its back with his arms clasped around the metal neck and his swords discarded.

The thing struggled to and fro, eventually throwing him to the ground. I retrieved my axe and came to help but it was too late. With one mighty swing the beast collapsed the pirate's chest and he cried out in utter agony. Hands trembling, I took a revenge swing and knocked off the helmet as Arkin rushed to us. He jumped up onto the creature and thrust his rapier down into the black flame. With a jolt Arkin leapt off and the giant fell to its knees and died, the armour and black flame fading.

Arkin's hand was badly burned but he seemed as energetic as ever.

'It's hidden deep, but each of them has some kind of heart down beneath that black flame, they're not invincible.'

There were several less than before – this could be our chance to turn the tide. But before I could get too relieved about this new revelation, Mamorhah let out another pained cry. We rushed to him, ribs sticking out of his chest and crimson flowing through his shirt.

'You saved me,' was all I could say, seeing the man helpless for the first time.

'Yeah,' he said, coughing up blood with the word.

Tears began to stream down my face but he still had a grin on his.

'Twice today I've had to protect you,' he groaned through the pain, echoing the words from the first night we met. 'I guess I am a babysitter after all.'

He gave a small chuckle, blood running from his smiling mouth. His head fell back and his eyes dimmed as he let out his last breath. I sobbed over the body, grateful to my old crewmate for giving his life to save mine.

'He was a good man,' I told Arkin. 'A good man who did not deserve to die.'

The blonde's hand found my shoulder as he tried to console me but there was only one thing that could make me feel better. I leapt up and charged and the nearest foe, taking its helmet clean off with a single swing and plung ng the haft of my weapon into its chest. The iron around the wood protected it from the black flame and the creature fell down dead. I turned my attention to the next one.

With both crews at my side we quickly took the giants, until there was no visible sign they had ever existed. When the last one was done I turned my gaze to Daxon and Farrow, still going at it without fail. I knew the sorcerers would be back any second to bombard us with attacks once more, so I had a small window to end all of this. I rushed for the two pirates, axe ready. But even as I came within a few feet of the red-haired villain I felt my body freeze.

I could not move, knowing instantly it must be magic but it was different than on the Maiden, it was cold; I could feel it in my blood. It clasped like a vice around every inch of me until I could hardly breathe. Colder and colder my body was getting, until my eyes failed me and the magic hit my heart. I was down, on the floor, gasping for breath. The magic was gone but I was still shaking. In my frail state I glanced to Wes whose jagged blade was buried deep in Greskel's side. She cried out and jerked herself from the sword, raising her palm and clutching him with her magic.

'Laricko, take her out,' I called.

The boy launched an arrow but she turned with her other palm outstretched and the projectile froze in the air. An instant later she was struck with another and Brongrim smirked to me. She fell and we rushed to them, restraining the sorceress's hands and covering her mouth as Wes got back to his feet.

'Where the fuck have you been?' Akaya questioned him.

'It's a long story but you won't have to worry about Sursaroh for a while,' he said.

We fetched rope and tied Greskel to the tiller with Arkin, Korhal, Brongrim and Deline keeping watch over her.

'So you've decided to join up with us birdie?' Wes asked as he embraced me.

I was not expecting the hug but did not protest. Those who were not watching the sorceress began running back towards the two pirates who were still engaged in combat but beginning to tire.

'Just until this is all over,' I told him. 'My view on Daxon is still the same.'

'Well if you try to kill him I'm gonna have to stop you,' Gurdgrin muttered as we approached the flurry of blades.

'This is for Ekrin!' Daxon was screaming as he gave all he had trying to kill the redhead.

'Still sobbing over that Daxon?' Farrow was taunting him with baited breath. 'It's pathetic that you can't get over something that happened almost twenty years ago.'

I had no idea what they were talking about but rushed in all the same with the others at my side. Farrow saw the flank a mile off and turned to parry my incoming blow. He grinned like a maniac, laughing as his blade shined and he pressed me back. Daxon charged in again but was swept off his feet by a well-placed kick. Wes leapt at the villain but a heavy blow to the arm knocked his blade from his grasp. Farrow seized the opportunity and punched him to the floor with inhuman strength.

Felima charged next with a clumsy jab, though the pirate captain was quick. With minimal effort he pulled her towards him, spinning her around and latched his free arm around her neck. His sword stayed pointed at the rest of us as he backed off with his new hostage.

'Let her go!' Laricko screamed, aiming an arrow at him.

'Now now,' he said. 'Back off or the girl dies.'

'Kill him,' Daxon begged as he struggled back to his feet.

'No,' I ordered. 'It's too dangerous.'

'Take the shot Laricko,' Felima instructed. 'Take the...'

She was cut off as Farrow moved his hand and pressed it against her mouth. He pointed his blade to her neck to prove he was not joking.

'You heard her,' Daxon yelled to the archer. 'Take the shot.'

'No,' Thalkrin argued. 'We don't fire upon our own crew.'

'We have to take him out,' Dirk objected.

Every eye was on Laricko, the rest of us too far away to do anything. The boy looked ahead, his hands shaking.

'I can't,' he said at last, lowering the bow.

I breathed a sigh of relief but was instantly tense again when I heard the low, rumbling laughter. Sursaroh appeared at Farrow's side, battered and bruised but still standing.

'I thought you took care of him,' I scolded Wes.

'I thought I did,' he admitted.

'Nice to have you back Sursaroh,' Farrow said, smiling. 'You think you can take them out for me?'

'I'm weakened master,' he groaned. 'But I should be able to get most of them.'

278

'Great,' Farrow said, a different kind of smile crossing his face.

His eyes were blacker than black, dark with the cruellest of intentions. Without warning nor hesitation he raised the blade at cut Felima's throat.

'No!' I cried as he dropped her to the ground, my shout exceeded by that of Laricko who took no delay in firing an arrow.

The sorcerer raised a hand and it disintegrated. I froze, not from his magic nor from fear; I froze as my eyes met those of the redhead girl, looking blankly at the sky.

Felima was dead.

Chapter 25

A Change of Heart

managed to snap myself out of it as a barrage of flames came at us. I rolled to avoid the sorcerer's magic but heard screams from the others and could smell burning flesh. I did not look back, instead charging straight for the man who had killed my crewmate.

Sursaroh went to lift his palm but Farrow stopped him, squaring up to me with blade held high. I rushed him but the man batted away my axe like it was nothing. I spun around for another attack but his strike got there first. His blade had stopped glowing but his expression was as fierce as ever. He sliced at my arm, cutting deep as I gritted my teeth and pressed forward. I caught his leg but he brushed off the injury and struck me in the face with his free hand.

'You're just like your father,' he cackled as I steadied my stance. 'Weak.'

I roared and charged for him again, swinging and hacking with all of my force.

'Don't you dare say anything about my father,' I cried. 'You're not half the man he was.'

'How could you ever know?' he taunted. 'After all, your friend Daxon slaughtered him before you could even get to know him.'

'Shut up! Shut up! Shut up!' I yelled, striking harder and harder, faster and faster.

'He says Daxon is no longer his friend,' I heard the sorcerer's voice. 'In fact, he wanted to kill him only a few hours ago.'

'Then why are you fighting me boy?' Farrow directed to me. 'Side with me and we can kill him together.'

He was trying to get into my head and I was not about to let him. He had killed Felima, Sursaroh's creatures had killed Mamorhah and they would both pay for their deeds.

'I'd never side with a monster like you,' I retorted, catching his side with the blade of the axe and hacking it further into him.

He suppressed a groan and backhanded me with all his strength. My axe went sliding across the deck and I fell to my knees.

'Sursaroh, how about you change his mind?' the villain said, grabbing my shirt and hoisting me back up as ebony hands took hold of me.

The moment they touched my skin, everything faded. The image began to clear, though it was not the same as before.

I was still on the Stallion in the midst of a battle. I could not move, for I was not even sure I had a body – I could only observe. The battle was not against Farrow but between different pirates. No, I recognised some.

Wes was there but a decade younger. He was fighting a dark-featured woman with green eyes; I realised it was Akaya. He was winning but an older man came to her aid – it was Varen, still with one good eye. My gaze shifted to some people who I did not recognise but they were fighting against a green-haired man with a machete which I knew instantly was Korhal. Finally, right in the centre of the battle, I saw them.

Daxon and my father.

My father looked the same as I had remembered but wearing the tricorn of a captain. Daxon had a simple bandana around his head and his hair beneath it was much shorter. His beard was thin and his jaw not as strong. From the look of him I would guess he was about thirty years old.

They were in the midst of combat, going at it with everything they had. In my father's grasp was the Elder Blade, the sword I had always known as Daxon's. Daxon was wielding an axe, as expertly as he had while teaching me. I floated closer to them without willing it, seeing every action and hearing every word closely.

'You don't have to do this,' my father was saying.

'I'm sorry Jarthal,' Daxon replied. 'But it's the only way.'

My father struck with a weak overarm attack and Daxon's parry disarmed him. My father stood, defenceless, simply staring at the bearded pirate.

'Daxon,' he muttered.

Without hesitation Daxon sliced the axe through his neck. I tried to look away but I was physically unable to. I was forced to watch as his head came tumbling from his shoulders. Daxon dropped the axe and picked up the blade. His eyes went wide and for a moment they turned completely black. He held the crystal-like steel to the sky and let out a roar of victory.

The scene faded away and I was back in front of Sursaroh.

'Wh...what just happened?' I stammered.

'I showed you what happened between Daxon and your father to prove to you the man has no remorse. He is a monster and must be eliminated,' the sorcerer's words rang out.

A fury built in my stomach at seeing my father die in persor and I could feel myself nodding to his words. As I turned around I locked my gaze on the pirate who had ruined my life. He had managed to extinguish his burning clothes and was now rushing for Farrow. The red-haired man handed me my axe and I accepted it.

'Die, traitor!' I screamed, intercepting the captain's attack and knocking him back.

'Yodrick, what are you doing?' he asked, trying to get past me.

All I felt was anger, all I saw was red. He had to die.

'What I came here to do!' I answered, marking the words with a vicious slash to the side.

He was bleeding, I grinned. It was not enough though, I needed to live up to my promise and make him burn, make him burn down below with the demons. May the maker have no pity on him and let him rot. I lunged again, this t me batting the blade from his grasp and back towards the others who were approaching rapidly. He backed away, hands held up in defence.

'Yodrick, you're not thinking clearly,' he begged. 'Sursaroh must have used his magic to twist your thoughts.'

'No,' I spat back. 'This is *all* me. You ruined my life, killed my father and therefore also killed my mother. I grew up on the streets of Cranwell begging for scraps of food. I joined with thieves to make it in this world and was beaten time and time again. I killed my friend, fighting him for this ring on my finger – for years I blamed myself for it but it never would have happened if you hadn't started it all.'

'Please Yodrick,' he begged once more. 'You can go ahead and kill me for everything I've done but allow me one final moment of relief. Move aside and let me kill the vile monster behind you, so I can finally die in peace.'

'Shut up,' I growled, smashing the haft of my axe into his face.

He staggered back with a bloody nose but maintained his footing.

'You're the only monster here,' I told him, raising my weapon for the killing blow.

'Yodrick, behind you!' he cried.

How pathetic of him, I thought, *like I'd ever believe that.* But even as my axe was coming down I heard the others yelling it too. I spun around and parried the incoming blow from Farrow's jagged Elder Blade. The attacker scowled and recoiled for another blow. I held up my guard but he laughed.

'Foolish boy,' he told me. 'You think you can take on someone like me? You see, unlike Daxon I'm not afraid to use the power of the Elder Blade on someone like you!'

The blade glowed and his eyes shone with the appearance of a demon. He sliced down and the haft of my axe split in two. I scurried away slowly, half-frozen with fear.

'Now, Darkskull junior, say hello to your father for me!'

I held my hands up in reflex as he launched his final attack but it was not necessary. A dark figure leapt out and blocked the attack. As it fell to the ground before me I realised it was Daxon, an extremely deep cut across his stomach.

'Yodrick,' Gurdgrin called, rushing to my side with the others.

Farrow chuckled, looking down on the man who had taken the blow.

'You're a fool Daxon,' he said, but the others were beginning to surround him.

'Go on Darkskull,' the familiar low voice said from beside me, soft enough that the others did not notice him. 'Avenge your father.'

I wanted to strike the sorcerer down, to go and help the others who were now fighting Farrow, but his words echoed like a thousand voices in my head. Rage, unrelenting rage. Daxon met my gaze.

'Yodrick,' he muttered softly, like my father had before he killed him.

I reached for my dagger, pulling free the short blade and pointing it for Daxon's throat. He was on his back, unable to do anything to stop me.

Time to kill him.

But even before I went to strike him, a scream ran out more terrible than anything I had ever heard. There alongside Sursaroh was Wes, Daxon's Elder Blade in hand and the tip of it through the sorcerer's stomach. Sursaroh's scream got even louder, louder and higher until I was forced to drop my weapon to cover my ears. Everyone else was doing the same, all except from Farrow who used the opportunity to rush away from them before they could stop him.

The sorcerer's scream finally relented as his skin burned and cracked until he fell to the ground in a blaze of black flames. All that was left were his robes and a pile of ashes within. Sursaroh was dead.

My attention flashed back to Daxon but only for a moment. The rage had gone and I was no longer so desperate to end his life here and now. It seemed he had been right; the sorcerer had somehow been using his magic to manipulate my emotions – an impressive power but now he was no more.

Everyone rushed for the fleeing Farrow. Greskel was at his side instantly and those who had been guarding her were rushing towards the two of them.

'Well it's been fun but I think it's time for us to go,' Farrow called out, taking hold of the sorceress as they both disappeared in a cloud of black smoke.

All of a sudden the Headless Maiden was moving, sailing at breakneck pace away from us.

'Those demons!' Korhal spat.

'Let them go,' I said, glancing around at everyone. 'We're in no position to take them in a fight.

'They have canons!' Dirk argued. 'What if they destroy us?'

'No need to worry about that,' Wes interjected. 'When the fight started I snuck away to their ship and disabled them.'

'I like you,' Arkin told him, approaching with the others.

'Don't get too happy,' I insisted. 'I'm sure we'll run into them again.'

'Wes, what else did you do while you were gone?' Akaya enquired.

'Well once their canons were taken care of I came back to the Stallion and noticed Sursaroh was gone so I went looking for him,' he told us, letting out a mournful sigh. 'Which brings us to the next piece of bad news. I found him in Varen's room, Sursaroh killed him.'

'The bastards!' Gurdgrin growled.

I felt myself tearing up again. Mamorhah, Felima and now Varen. Sure I had left the Stallion with little regard for the old man, but he had still been my friend. It was all getting a bit too much for me.

'That's not all,' Wes said. 'It looks like he and Greskel used their powers to do something to the ship, there's no way the Stallion will sail.'

'You can come aboard our ship,' I offered.

'Truly?' Akaya asked with wide eyes.

I still felt a pang of betrayal but knew helping them was the right thing to do.

'Of course,' I told them.

'What about Daxon?' Korhal asked. 'Do we have permission to take him aboard too?'

He was still on the ground and bleeding heavily. I felt my teeth grinding and my fists clenching, for I knew I owed him that much for saving me.

'Yes, bring him aboard,' I said. 'And take him to my quarters.'

It was time for Daxon and I to have a little chat.

Chapter 26

Grallwick

I had everyone bandaged up and fed by the sailors. When Ellya asked what had happened, I told her I would explain it all another time. At my orders Daxon was brought to my room, bloody and unconscious but still alive. They all brought their things from the Stallion; alcohol and food to last months, chests filled with treasure and valuables, weapons from the armoury.

We also brought the three corpses aboard, laying down Felima in her room with her face covered and finding spare rooms for Mamorhah and Varen. Laricko stayed by Felima, crying for hours on end. It was not healthy to leave him there but I did not have it in me to pull him away. Gurdgrin stayed by Varen and I watched over Mamorhah for a while before Korhal came to pay his respects.

I made sure the ship was sailing south towards land but after that I felt lost. It was strange having even the Stallions looking to me for guidance but it made it much harder when I knew I had none to give. We had lost, well and truly. Wes may have been able to take out Sursaroh but three of ours were dead and all of us were mourning. I managed to find Daxon's second in command up in the crow's nest, drowning his sorrows in a bottle of rum. The raised platform was wide enough for both of us and I sat behind him.

'Mind if I join you?' I asked.

'It's *your* ship,' he replied. 'Gave some silver to one of your sailors to leave this post for an hour, you ought to train them not to be bribed.'

I chuckled and Wes handed me the rum. I took a long swig and handed it back, letting out a deep sigh.

'So how come you're up here?' I enquired.

'It relaxes me,' he answered. 'Always has, being this high up and away from everyone down there, it's just calmer, you know?'

I had never seen the man behaving so serious, with perhaps the exception of Wargal's funeral. The permanent smirk and cocky attitude had been wiped from him, leaving him sombre.

'Yeah, I know,' I told him. 'Everyone keeps asking me what to do next but I'm as lost as the rest of them.'

'Are you going to kill Daxon?' he asked me.

I gave a nod, unwilling to risk my words betraying me. I grabbed the bottle and took another swig for confidence.

'I have to.'

'I understand,' he said, nodding along. 'Like I said to you once before, I've only been sticking by him because I thought he was the best person to take down Farrow. But today, he missed his chance. The sorcerers were out of the way so they weren't using their magic to help him, and Daxon has far more experience with the Elder Blade, but even with such an opportunity he couldn't pull it off.'

'So you've lost your faith in him?' I asked.

'I don't know if I ever had faith in him to begin with, not truly – at least not in a long time. And he's dying now, with a good chance he won't recover anyway. I say go for it, make yourself feel better and get vengeance for your dad.'

I was a little taken back by his bluntness, knowing that Wes was not happy with Daxon but never expecting him to condone the man's death.

'Why do you hate him so much?' I asked.

'Same reason as you,' he chimed. 'Because he killed your dad. Jarthal meant a lot to me, I cared for him deeply. I hope you never have to face it, having someone who you've known for years being suddenly taken from you – it's hard.'

'Yeah,' was all I could say.

We sat in silence for a while, watching the sun in the sky and drinking until the bottle was empty.

'Captain,' one of the sailors called up.

I glanced down to the man who I recognised as Jesko the medic.

'What is it?' I asked.

'He's awake.'

I nodded, though unsure if he could even see the gesture from here. I began to pull myself from the crow's nest and climb down.

'Avenge him,' Wes said solemnly. 'For both of us.'

As I descended I pondered what Wes had meant but the thought was quickly shifted by the eagerness to visit Daxon. I entered my quarters alone, seeing the pirate captain in his weakest state yet. He had bandages around his torso where Farrow's blade had cut him but they were already soaked through with blood. I closed the door behind me.

He struggled to a sitting position, the Elder Blade across his lap. I wondered for a moment whether he was going to try to defend himself but knew he was smarter than that.

'Come to kill me?' he groaned, with a light cough which splattered more blood across the sheets.

I stopped for a moment. 'How did you…'

'Please Yodrick,' he cut me off. 'Let's not play these games.'

'Fine,' I said. 'Yes, I've come to kill you for your crimes against my father.'

'And the Stallion,' he added, much to my surprise. 'I've committed crimes against the Stallion too.'

'I don't care about that,' I tutted.

'Well you should,' he reasoned. 'After all, you're still technically part of the crew. You drank the horse's blood and said the sacred vows – only the captain of the Iron Stallion can release you from them and I never did.'

'You sent me away!' I spat back at him.

'That I did,' he said. 'But I knew in my heart one day you would return to us. You are the blood of the Stallion, more so than anyone here. After all, you are your father's son.'

'Don't talk about my father,' I yelled, taking hold of the sword at his lap and pointing it to him.

'Hold on,' he begged. 'I know you're angry and I accept that this will be the day I die, but I must ask of you a favour first.'

'Why would I grant you any favours?' I scoffed.

'Because I saved your life.'

Despite my anger I could not argue with that. He was surrendering to my blade anyway; I could at least listen to his request.

'Go ahead, what's this favour?'

'Simply to hear me out,' he told me. 'Let me tell you *my* story with no interruptions, so I can at least try to explain to you why I did what I did. I'm not trying to justify my actions, but I do want you to know the truth.'

'And then you'll face your punishment?' I enquired.

'That I will,' he accepted. 'The medic said I have a few days ahead of me at best, so I'll die either way. I'd rather it be by your hand than Farrow's.'

'Fine, I'll listen,' I relented.

He smiled and thanked me, beckoning me to sit saying it might take a while. I pulled a chair to the bedside and sat beside him.

'Now I hope you're comfy, for this is a long story,' he began. 'I'll start at the beginning. I was born Daxon Grallwick, the son of a common blacksmith in Sialstone. I had a happy childhood, despite us not having much money. My father worked many hours and had me helping in his forge as soon as I was old enough to walk.'

I wanted to ask him where this story was going and why any of this mattered but I had agreed to listen with no interruptions so I kept my mouth shut.

'By the time I was ten years old I was forging blades,' he continued. 'I helped in every way I could and became a good smith doing it. When I reached manhood my father told me I needed to follow my own path, so I moved to Cyndor where I worked as a blacksmith's apprentice and eventually took ownership of the forge and got an apprentice myself. I met a woman during this time – Aggis. She was beautiful and I fell deeply in love with her. We were married within a couple of months and she gave birth to our son – Ekrin.'

I at once recalled the name, both from his diary and what he had said to Farrow back on the Stallion.

'When I was twenty years of age, I received a letter from my mother saying my father had died. I went back to Sialstone for his funeral and ended up staying there to care for my mother who had fallen sick and to keep my father's business going. A year passed and life was good. Aggis helped with the forge and looked after my mother; Ekrin was coming up to his fourth birthday. It was then that a gang of unknown pirates docked on Sialstone's shores, their captain coming straight to the forge with a few men. His hair was crimson and he had a wild look in his eyes.'

'Farrow,' I muttered.

'Yes,' he affirmed. 'He demanded I make the most powerful weapon the world had ever seen, promising to pay me handsomely for it. I was a little put off my him – he kept speaking of power as if it were the only thing that had meaning to him. Still, we needed the money so I took the job. I spent an entire week on it, working every hour I could muster and was exhausted by the end of it but I had crafted a blade better than I, my father or the old smith in Cyndor had ever made before.

'I presented the blade to Farrow with pride but he took one glance at it and threw it into the fire, deeming it terrible. When I demanded he pay me for my work he got angry. His men restrained me and Farrow tried to grab Aggis. When she struggled against his grip he took out a dagger and killed her right in front of me. He said it was a lesson, to never disrespect him. He killed the love of my life...'

The pirate clenched his fists and began to cough up blood again, a tear coming to his eye. His obsession with Farrow now made sense to me, he was trying to avenge the death of his wife.

'Then my son walked in,' he continued through the pain. 'Ekrin saw him mother on the ground and ran to her. The pirates all drew their swords but I begged them to spare him. Farrow agreed to let my boy live but instead took his anger out on me. He beat me within an inch of my life with his own bare fists. He kept yelling over and over, "You'll regret the day you ever insulted Farrow Bloodneck!" That was how I learned his name. He went to leave but my son – brave lad that we was – rushed to Farrow and began hitting him. In anger, Farrow punched Ekrin, knocking him back into the table where he hit his head. I like to think it was quick – my son's death. With how hard Farrow hit him it probably was, at least that's something to be thankful for.

'After that I couldn't bear to keep living my life. I stayed in bed a lot – the pain was not so unbearable when I was asleep. But my mother still needed looking after and since I was unable to take care of her she died soon after. I had no one. But the death of my mother was a wakeup call. I swore vengeance on the pirate who called himself Farrow Bloodneck and decided to seek him out.

'Unfortunately this was before Farrow was known to every pirate in the world, there were only a few who had ever heard the name and none of them knew where he was. I travelled from town to town and eventually found a man who told me about a pirate crew who could find anyone, given the right price. I sought out their captain, a large man named Borthip who had a cruel attitude and a mean temper. I offered him the little money I had left but he laughed at the amount and turned me away.

'Luckily, the captain's first mate took pity on me and convinced old Borthip to agree so long as I work aboard his ship as payment. That man was called Jarthal and that was the first time I met your father.'

'So he's the reason you joined the Stallion?' I pressed.

Daxon nodded. 'Yes, and because of it Jarthal and I quickly became good friends. After the loss of my family I needed someone like him. He taught me to fight, focusing on his signature weapon – a battle-axe. The crew was extremely different back then, with Korhal and Varen as the only people you'll know. They were good men but never particularly close with us, none of the crew were.

'Anyways, a few years past and it became clear to me Borthip wasn't even looking for Farrow. During this time, we got a new recruit; Tork Wessor, who you'll of course know as Wes. He became good friends with both of us but was always closer to your father. Wes hung off his every word and would always get envious when your father and I spent time together without him. Eventually we learned not to leave him out of things and that was that.

'After three long years aboard the Stallion, old Borthip died of a heart attack from eating too much. That left the ship to your father and he spared no time in beginning the hunt for Farrow. We still did not have much to go on but fortune smiled on me once again. While docked in Tindrad, we heard a rumour about a legendary weapon said to be deep within a sea-bound cavern near the coast of Sashak Island. Remembering Farrow had been after a powerful weapon, we set out to find it.'

'And that's how you found the Elder Blade?' I enquired, feeling bad for interrupting again.

'Well, yes and no,' he answered. 'The weapon was indeed the Elder Blade, but that was not how we found it. It took a long time to find the cavern in question and during this time your father and I began to drift apart – he had all of these new responsibilities as captain and we never had much time with one another. He made me first mate but that did not fix the problem. When we eventually found the cavern, we were met with a surprise.

'Where the sword had once lay, there were only skeletons and a lone diary. The book explained observations of the weapon, how it seemingly had the ability to fuse with its wielder and grant them power. Apparently, this power came from the souls of the dead –whenever someone was to die near the Elder Blade, the weapon would store their energy to be called on at any time by its master.'

I took a moment to think about this. I remembered seeing Daxon's sword glow for the first time during that fight back in Cranwell, it was after people had died. And again, that same glow as I was passing out back in Merrywood. Both Daxon's and Farrow's Elder Blades had glowed when Farrow slaughtered his own men this morning. And the part about calling on the power at any time, I was sure that that was what I had witnessed from both Farrow and Daxon when their expressions became demonic and the blades glowed once more.

'The book speculated there were ten other weapons like this sword, scattered around Issehai, Akrul and Zarensha,' Daxon carried on. 'Knowing this was either a load of shit or that we were dealing with dark magic from the old tales, your father wanted to forget all about it. I was stubborn however and insisted it must be in Farrow's possession. Jarthal would have none of it and decided to disband the crew and retire to Cranwell. In retrospect that was probably when he met your mother, but I knew nothing of this at the time.

'I was determined to find the blade though, so I reassembled the rest of the crew under my own command and sought out the blade. It did not take us long to find it but it was not Farrow who had it. Instead it was a lowly scavenger from Bleakmarsh who admitted to killing the man from the cavern and intended to sell it to a rich lord. We captured the man and I sought out your father to prove everything to him. Jarthal took hold of the blade but found its power did not work for him. Dismissing it as rumour he killed the scavenger but as he did he felt its power flooding into him. It was through this we realised that one could on y come into true possession of an Elder Blade by killing its former owner.'

'And that's why you killed my father,' I interjected, still angry despite his saddening story.

'Yes it is,' he admitted. 'Though I did not do it then and there. I allowed him to take back captaincy of the Stallion and he went by the name of Darkskull from then on. Again, knowing what I do now, it was probably to protect you and your mother. By this point Farrow was becoming a legend to other pirates, known for never losing a battle and for killing every man who crossed blades with him. It was around this time your father welcomed a young girl named Akaya to the crew, it was a bold move since she wasn't a man but we all respected Darkskull too much to argue. He also kept disappearing back to Cranwell but never told anyone why.

'Finally we found Farrow but even with the Elder Blade on our side it was not enough to defeat him, for he had gained the help of Sursaroh and Greskel whose magic powered his attacks. Several of the crew died and Varen lost an eye but we managed to get away. After that I tried to convince your father the only way to defeat Farrow was to kill more people with the blade to charge its magical power. Your father was a good man at heart however and would not kill so freely.

'That would have been the end of it but having just faced Farrow for the first time in years I was set on my revenge. Knowing he could not do what was necessary to defeat Farrow, I challenged Jarthal for captaincy. Akaya, Varen, Korhal and some others sided with me, while Wes and the rest of them sided with him. Several died in the battle and I killed your father. Mad with power I killed all of those who had fought with him who would not submit to me, thus leaving only Wes alive. Some of those who had fought with me left the Stallion afterwards, ashamed of what they had done. I was ashamed too, but the blade's power had its hold on me.

'It made me paranoid and we all feared your father had been assembling his own crew back in Cranwell since he visited so often. That fear led to the events of ten years ago and solidified my name as Daxon, the pirate captain who would kill anyone who crossed his path. After that we recruited Brongrim, Gurdgrin, Mamorhah and Wargal, and we've been sailing ever since in search of Farrow, with the memory of your father haunting me every day. And that Yodrick is my story.'

It dawned on me once he had finished how long he had been talking. Sitting here listening to this side of it had given me time to calm down. I still hated him for doing what he did but at least now I understood it. The revelations about the Elder Blade were unbelievable but I had thought the same about magic and sorcerers. Now, looking at this weak man before me, I felt only pity. I remembered his words as I attacked him on the Stallion, stopping him from getting to Farrow: *You can go ahead and kill me for everything I've done but allow me one final moment of relief.*

Move aside and let me kill the vile monster behind you, so I can finally die in peace.

Now he would never get to fulfil his wish and avenge his family and he was relenting to my blade entirely aware of this. If he could let go of his anger after almost twenty years, I could let go of mine.

'I'm not going to kill you.'

Chapter 27

Urohthral

H is eyes widened as I said the words, as if beckoning me to clarify.

'I'm not going to kill you,' I said again. 'I hate you for what you did, but I understand it. I would've killed Korhal or Akaya or any of them today to get to you, so I can understand why you killed my father to get to Farrow.'

Daxon smiled.

'I'm glad,' he said. 'But I'm afraid you *do* have to kill me.'

I was taken aback, confused by what he meant. I had offered to spare his life and he was rejecting it with a smile on his face.

'I know I've done a lot of talking but let me explain,' he said. 'Like I said before, the Elder Blade's true owner is whoever killed the last one. If I die from this wound, Farrow takes ownership of this blade. Not only will its power not work for anyone but him but he'll be able to sense it and track you all down. I'm asking you to kill me first, to be the one who lands the final blow. That way that sword in your hand will be yours and you will be able to control its power.'

'But why me?' I asked. 'Wouldn't you rather Korhal or Akaya take the blade?'

'No,' he said simply. 'You're the only one who I believe is strong enough to kill Farrow. You might not be as good with a sword yet but you will be. I've underestimated an Alton's ability before, and I'm not going to make that mistake twice. No, you're the true leader of the Stallion, a captain by name and by birth-right.'

'But how do I proceed? What do I do once it's over?' I asked of him.

'When Farrow and I were fighting aboard the Stallion, he let me in on a secret. I'm not sure why he told me – maybe because he thought he would win or perhaps just to gloat, but it's information which changes everything.'

'What did he say?' I enquired, eyes wide with curiosity.

'He confirmed the existence of eleven Elder Blades,' Daxon said. 'Apparently Sursaroh and Greskel have lived for millennia and they told him about an ancient being named Urohthral who existed during the dawn of humanity. According to the them, it was Urohthral who gave the sorcerers their powers, to help him enslave the human race, and only his blade could kill them. Farrow told me the Elder Blades are in fact all fragments of the same weapon – the weapon which he used to reign with an iron fist. That is why an Elder Blade can kill a sorcerer.

'But despite the dozens of sorcerers under his control, the humans rose up against him. They took Urohthral's weapon while he slept and used it to kill him. Like the Elder Blades themselves, the weapon could absorb the power of souls and it took his. Afraid one day his soul would break free and allow him to rise again, the humans shattered the weapon into eleven pieces and scattered them across the world.'

'Even if what he says is true, why did Farrow decide to tell you this?' I asked.

Daxon gave me a sombre glance, as if the world itself was about to end.

'Because Farrow plans to reunite the pieces,' he told me and I felt myself shiver. 'Apparently there is a ritual and once the fragments are all in the same place he can bring the ancient entity back into this world to rule over humanity once more.'

'But why would he do that?' I bellowed. 'He would be enslaved too!'

'Apparently the sorcerers told him the one who brings Urohthral back will be rewarded with the power of a sorcerer and will rule by his side. To a power hungry madman like Farrow, that's the ultimate dream.'

'So...' I muttered, 'If this is all true...then it's my job to keep this blade away from him.'

'Not just that,' Daxon told me. 'You must also seek out the other Elder Blades to stop Farrow from seizing them.'

'That sounds like a challenge since nobody knows where they are,' I admitted.

'A challenge which I truly believe only you can do,' he told me. 'I have left strict instructions with Korhal that the Stallions are to follow you as their new leader, with them I'm confident you can stop Farrow and potentially save the world from a doomed fate.'

I was terrified and a large part of me did not believe any of this stuff about Urohthral and the Elder Blades but it was too much of a risk for me not to act on it. I stood and raised the blade again, looking to the dying captain whose eyes were on me.

'I guess...I should probably...'

'Go ahead,' he told me.

'Are you ready for it?' I asked, sobbing now, for I did not want to kill the man in front of me.

'I am,' he said. 'I have passed everything I know and everything I own onto you. You are the blood of the Stallion and I believe in you. If I have to die, I am glad it is by your hand.'

I lowered the blade.

'I can't do it,' I sobbed. 'Daxon...captain...I can't kill you.'

'You have to,' he reasoned. 'It's for the greater good of humanity.'

I leaned down and embraced him, feeling the warm blood as it flowed from his chest even now.

'I am the man I am today because of you...captain,' I cried, holding him there.

I felt his weak hands on my back, hugging me in return. I stayed there for a few moments until his hands receded and I knew it was time. I stood upright and raised the blade again.

'Goodbye, Captain Daxon of the Iron Stallion.'

He nodded and closed his eyes. 'I doubt it but I hope wherever I'm going I'll see your father again and finally be reunited with my wife and son.'

Tears trickled from the corners of his eyes but he still had a smile on his face. I aimed the blade and, fighting every instinct in me telling me to stop, I stabbed it into his heart. He let out a final gasp and his body relaxed into the bed.

The man who had trained me. The man who had taken me from a life of common thievery and brought me into his world. The man who had been like a father to me. The man who I had hated and despised. The man who I had forgiven. This man was dead.

I dropped the glowing blade and fell to my knees, sobbing. It was so much that I barely noticed the feeling of power flowing into me. I do not know how long I stayed there but it was the most pain I had ever felt. In one day I had lost four good people, for that was what they all were, even Daxon. He was a good man at heart and I knew if the maker was also good he would see his wife and son in the next life.

I eventually picked myself from the floor, tying Daxon's sheath around my waist and putting away the blade. It was all over. I left my quarters and closed the door behind me, turning to Korhal who was waiting for me.

'Is he dead?' the man asked with tears in his own eyes.

Daxon must have told him about everything. I nodded and he also cried.

'I know you hated him but he was good man,' the green haired pirate wept.

'I know,' I said, surprising him, now apparent that I had also been crying. 'In the end I forgave him. He died not for me but for the greater good.'

Korhal explained what he could to the rest of the crew and they welcomed me as their new captain. Normally that would call for a celebration but none of us were in the mood for merriment. That night we docked in the northern land of Saransa, beyond the mountains. There we buried three of our four fallen allies, respecting the Stallion tradition. Laricko pressed that Felima's body should be returned to her family's crypt, so I respected his wishes.

We all said a few words in remembrance of our friends and many tears were shed. When it was all over I wanted nothing but to throw myself in the sea and float away. But Daxon had believed in me and I knew my work was far from done.

'Thank you for this, Darkskull,' Korhal said as we walked back to the ship. 'A Stallion should always return to land and you respected the tradition well.'

'Call me Yodrick,' I told him. 'I'm no longer afraid of embracing my past. Plus, Captain Yodrick has a nice ring to it. Cry it out for all the world to hear, Captain Yodrick Alton, the man who will kill Farrow.'

Back on the ship I had a few drinks with the others, who – as per their tradition – were telling stories about the newly dead and celebrating their lives. I stayed for a while, sitting beside Brongrim (who had been told by Jesko his one remaining leg would heal) and drinking every time somebody made a toast, which was often. I left early though, unable to force myself to be happy when all I felt was despair. On the main deck Ellya was at the wheel and a few sailors were busy manning the ship as we sailed into the night.

Wes was once more up in the crow's nest and once more I joined him.

'How come you're not with the others, drinking and having a good time?' he asked.

'I could ask the same of you,' I said, sitting down beside him.

'Well, I'm drinking,' he answered, handing me the rum with I gulped down gratefully. 'So what do we do now?'

'I've had Ellya plot a course for the nearest town,' I told him. 'I doubt we'll find much information there but we need to make a start. We'll seek out libraries, try to find anything relating to the blades. Hopefully we can get to them before Farrow does.'

'Sounds like you have it all figured out,' he told me.

'I wish,' I admitted. 'Truth is that planning is all I can do to stop myself from breaking down.'

'I've found drinking helps,' he joked, taking another swig. 'But I'm sure you can do it Yodrick, you're a good man and you'll be a fine captain of the Stallion.'

'And you'll be a great first mate,' I told him, taking him off guard.

He nodded and smiled, showing me he would do it. I did not enjoy the idea of breaking it to Deline that she had been demoted.

Together Wes and I sat up there, talking a little but mainly looking at the night sky and the open sea.

'So, onwards?' he asked finally with a chuckle.

I looked to the stars and to our journey ahead and nodded.

'Onwards.'

The Elder Blade Chronicles Will Continue with Book 2

18814886R00178

Printed in Great Britain
by Amazon